The Payback

Items should be returned on or before the last date shown below. Items not already requested by other borrowers may be renewed in person, in writing or by telephone. To renew, please quote the ~~KT-470-632~~ barcode label. To renew online ~~...~~ This can be requested at ~~your...~~ Renew online @ **www.dublincitypubliclibraries.ie** Fines charged for overdue items will include postage incurred in recovery. Damage to or loss of items will be charged to the borrower.

Leabharlanna Poiblí Chathair Bhaile Átha Cliath
Dublin City Public Libraries

Dublin City
Baile Átha Cliath   Drumcondra Branch Tel. 8377206

Date Due	Date Due	Date Due
02 JUN 2011	23 JAN 2013	17 JUL 2015
27 JUN 2011	13 JUL 2013	
09 AUG 2011	29 AUG 2013	
21 MAR 2012	24 OCT 2013	18 AUG 2018
	07 MAR 2014	

The Payback

Simon Kernick

W F HOWES LTD

This large print edition published in 2011 by
W F Howes Ltd
Unit 4, Rearsby Business Park, Gaddesby Lane,
Rearsby, Leicester LE7 4YH

1 3 5 7 9 10 8 6 4 2

First published in the United Kingdom in 2011
by Bantam Press

A CIP catalogue record for this book is available
from the British Library

ISBN 978 1 40747 319 2

Typeset by Palimpsest Book Production Limited,
Falkirk, Stirlingshire
Printed and bound in Great Britain
by MPG Books Ltd, Bodmin, Cornwall

MIX
Paper from
responsible sources
FSC
www.fsc.org   FSC® C018575

This book is dedicated to the occupant of room 927, Victory Executive Residences, Soi Rangnam, Bangkok, November 2006 to August 2008. You, and only you, know who you are, and thank you so much for finding me when you did.

PROLOGUE

As soon as the man in black walked into the cluttered little office, a briefcase in one gloved hand, a large, lethal-looking pistol in the other, Nick Penny realized that in an occasionally distinguished career of stepping on the toes of those with something to hide, he'd finally planted his size nines squarely on the wrong ones.

'You've been a bad boy,' said the man in heavily accented yet perfect English, coming towards Penny's desk and raising the pistol so it was pointed at the centre of his chest – a cold, knowing expression on a face that was otherwise perfectly ordinary.

Penny was frozen to his seat. 'Please,' he whispered, conscious of his heart hammering in his chest. 'I don't want to die.'

'No one wants to die, Mr Penny,' said the gunman evenly. 'Unfortunately, in this matter you have no choice.'

Instinctively, Penny shut his eyes and gritted his teeth, waiting for the impact of the bullet.

But the gunman didn't pull the trigger. Instead, he took a seat opposite him. 'Where you do have

1

a choice, however,' he continued, waiting until Penny opened his eyes again, 'is the manner in which you depart.' He motioned towards Penny's open notebook. 'I want you to write three short letters. The first will be to your wife, asking for her forgiveness, and apologizing both for your deception and for what you are about to do. You will address her as Nat and sign it Nick. The second will be to your former lover, saying that you can't take the pressure any more. You will address her as T, and sign it P. The third will be to your daughters, Ella and Amelie. Again, you will ask for their forgiveness. You will also add that you hope one day they will understand your actions. You will, of course, sign this letter "Love Daddy".'

Penny flinched at the mention of his two daughters. He stared at the gunman, wondering how on earth this man knew so much about him. Not only the names of his family, but also that of the woman he'd been seeing secretly for the past three months. He'd worked incredibly hard to cover his tracks there, having no desire to cause Natalie undue upset, but even so, he'd been found out by a complete stranger, and one who even knew the pet name his lover had used right up until the end of their affair, two weeks earlier. Mr P. He'd loved the way she'd purred it when they were in bed.

The man must have bugged her house, as well as his own, which meant he was a professional –

something that was obvious by his calm, un-flappable manner, and the blankness of his expression. But to Penny, it also meant that he could be reasoned with.

'Look, there must be some way we can sort this out,' he said, trying hard to keep the fear out of his voice.

'I'm afraid there isn't,' said the man, his expression unchanging. 'You are to write those letters. Then you are to hang yourself from the overhead beam with rope that I will provide you with.'

Penny instinctively looked up at the RSJ that ran from one end of the office to the other, knowing it would easily hold his weight, then back at the man sitting opposite him. He was finding it difficult to believe that this was happening. He'd always known that some of the work he did carried with it an element of danger, but never in his worst nightmares had he expected to be staring down the barrel of a gun and pleading for his life.

'Please . . .' he whispered.

'Start writing, Mr Penny, and don't worry if you've forgotten what to say. I can dictate.'

Penny frowned. 'You can't make me do it,' he said with a lot more confidence than he felt. 'That gun's a nine-millimetre. It'll make a hell of a noise if it goes off in here, and you don't have a silencer.' He knew that the downstairs office was empty, and that the guy who worked next door was hardly ever there, but it was still possible that he could spook the man enough to make him think twice.

3

But it didn't work. The man gave him a thin, bloodless smile. 'That's true. But I'm not going to need to fire it. I have something far better.' Still keeping the gun trained on Penny, he leaned down, unclipped the briefcase, and produced a small black netbook. He opened it up one-handed and placed it in the middle of the desk, with the screen facing Penny. 'Press Enter and tell me what you see.'

With a growing sense of dread, Penny did as he was told.

And froze.

His face crumpled. 'Oh Jesus.'

On the screen was a view of the rear of the cottage he shared with Natalie and his two children, taken from the woods at the end of the garden. By the way the screen was shaking slightly, it was clear that someone was filming the cottage with a hand-held camera. In the foreground, he could make out the trampoline, as well as the plastic Wendy house that the girls had all but grown out of now. Because of the time of year, it was already dark and there were lights on inside. As he watched, terrified that something might have happened to them already, he saw the unmistakable figure of Natalie, her auburn hair in a tight ponytail, moving about in the kitchen, looking as if she was getting the girls' tea ready. The camera panned in on her, so that her top half took up much of the screen as she poured water into a saucepan, blissfully unaware that she was being watched.

Looking up from the laptop, Penny watched as the gunman put a mobile phone to his ear and barked a command into it in Russian. A second later, the camera panned away from the cottage and the man holding it set it down, turning it round so that it was facing him. The cameraman took a couple of steps backwards so that the whole of his top half was visible. He wore dark clothing and a balaclava, and Penny felt his heart lurch as he saw the huge hunting knife in his hand, the metal glinting in the moonlight.

'The man you see there is an associate of mine,' explained the gunman matter-of-factly. 'He's awaiting my orders. If I tell him to, he will go inside your house and round up your family, and then he will cut your wife's throat in front of your children, before cutting their throats one after the other.'

Penny swallowed. He felt physically sick. 'You can't do this,' he groaned, his voice shaking.

'We can, and make no mistake, Mr Penny, we will – unless you do what you are told.'

'But they're just bloody kids,' he said desperately, rubbing his hand across his forehead, wanting to launch himself at the man opposite and tear him apart limb from limb, but knowing, in reality, that he was utterly impotent.

The gunman shrugged. 'That's not my concern. And in case you think I'm bluffing, I have to tell you that my associate is both psychotic and sadistic. Luckily for me, he's also reliable. He has killed on my behalf on three separate occasions, and neither the age nor sex of the victims means anything to him.'

'Oh God . . .'

'But if you do what I say, no harm will befall them.'

'How do I know you're not lying? How do I know you won't kill them anyway?'

'Because my client wants only you to die. And he wants your death to look . . .' He paused a moment. 'Unsuspicious. Can you say that?'

Penny found himself nodding.

'If you write suicide notes and hang yourself, then it will look unsuspicious, but if we are forced to kill your family, then obviously it won't, which would cause my client problems. Therefore we would prefer to avoid such an outcome. Of course, your death will be unfortunate for your wife and children – they will no doubt be very upset – but it will be considerably better for them than the alternative.'

'I know who your client is,' said Penny, his mind, like his pulse, racing. Like any human being in his situation, he couldn't accept that he was going to die. Instead, he was hunting for a survival strategy. Any strategy. 'Look, I know now I'm out of my depth, so I'll stop everything to do with the investigation right now. I'll never write another bloody word about it. You have my word on that.' He slapped a hand on his heart to signify that he meant what he said, hoping above all hope that it was enough.

But it wasn't. The gunman simply smiled again. 'I don't believe you, Mr Penny. Nor does my client. I'm afraid either you write those notes, and do what I say, or I will give my associate the order to butcher your family. Take a good look at his knife and imagine it slicing across the throats of your wife and daughters while they scream for mercy, knowing that no one will hear them, because your nearest neighbours are more than a hundred metres away. That's the problem with living somewhere isolated, isn't it?'

Penny shook his head from side to side. 'Oh Jesus,' he sobbed as it finally hit him that his life was almost certainly about to end. 'Oh God.'

'You have ten seconds to make up your mind.'

Before he'd become a father, Penny had always scoffed when his friends who were parents had told him that they wouldn't hesitate to die for their children. He'd always been unable to understand the enormity of such a concept. But now that he had two beautiful daughters of his own, he knew with absolute certainty that they were right. In all honesty, he wouldn't have died for Natalie. Their marriage had long since degenerated into a meandering, loveless routine. He wouldn't have died for his lover, either. He was infatuated with her, maybe even loved her; but, in the end, he'd always known it wasn't going to last for ever. But Ella and Amelie . . . there was no question. And he knew the man seated opposite him was deadly serious, because he knew exactly who the gunman's client was, and what that monster was capable of.

Penny cursed himself for ever getting involved, for making himself so easy to follow and to trap, for buying an isolated cottage where the massacre of his family could take place without a soul knowing about it. He cursed himself for everything, even though it was far too late to change a thing.

Then he stared into the pale face of the gunman, trying to locate a chink of humanity in the cold, professional demeanour, but finding none.

'How can you live with yourself?' he asked with a final, instinctive show of defiance.

The gunman allowed himself a small, knowing smile. 'Far more easily than you could understand,' he answered, removing a length of rope from the briefcase as Penny opened his notebook and began writing.

PART I

THE AXE RISES

CHAPTER 1

Hong Kong. It's the king of modern, twenty-first-century cities, an architectural marvel that grabs you the moment you leave the airport and travel along the smooth, almost traffic-free road, over immense bridges stretched like steel skeletons across a blue-grey sea that brims with junks and cargo ships heading in and out of one of the great natural harbours of the world. Seven million people live on this scattering of tiny mountainous islands, parts of which are still swathed in the same sub-tropical greenery that was there a thousand, probably even a million, years ago. Yet they're also home to a forest of glass and concrete skyscrapers that charge upwards, as if in competition, into the swirling white mist that so often clings to the mountain-tops. Whether you like big cities or not, you can't help but be drawn to it.

Personally, I don't much like them. I spent almost twenty years in London and that was easily enough urban living for several life-times. These days home is the hot, sleepy town of Luang Prabang in the forests of northern Laos, only a

11

few hundred miles from Hong Kong as the crow flies but a million miles away in every other sense, and infinitely more preferable for a man like me. But even so, I still felt a small sense of awe as I stared out of the window of the taxi taking me to Hong Kong Island and my destination.

I'd only been here once before, about eighteen months ago, and that time it had been to kill a man – a brash, corrupt British ex-pat who thought he was invincible but wasn't. But that's another story. The reason for this visit was to see the man who was my occasional employer. His name was Bertie Schagel and he was Dutch.

Now normally I like the Dutch. They're a genial bunch and they always speak excellent English, which makes communication easy. Bertie Schagel spoke excellent English, but he was not a nice man. In fact, he was one of the most repellent people I've ever met – and I've been unfortunate enough to meet quite a few of them in my life. But I owed him big-time and he'd spent the last three years calling in the debt. It was Schagel who'd sent me here the last time to kill the ex-pat, because that seemed to be one of his primary businesses, liquidating people on behalf of other people, and in the dog-eat-dog world of modern globalized capitalism, there seemed to be no shortage of work.

In truth, I knew very little about Bertie Schagel. For security reasons, we always met in different locations around South East Asia whenever he had a job for me to do, and I had no idea where he actually resided. I didn't even have a phone number for him. He did all his communication via email from different hotmail addresses, always keeping details to a minimum. When he wanted me for a job, he wrote a message in the drafts section of an email account that only he and I had access to, giving me instructions about where we were to meet. I would read and delete it, then write another message in the drafts section in response, usually confirming my attendance. That way, no actual correspondence was ever sent across the net, which meant our conversation couldn't be monitored by any interested parties. Schagel was extremely careful in the way he did business. To be honest, I couldn't even have told you if Bertie Schagel was his real name, although I suspected strongly that it wasn't. All I knew for sure was that he was utterly ruthless, and if I could have stopped working for him, I can promise you that I would have done.

But for the moment at least I was tied to him, so that when he called I came running, just like he knew I would.

I got the taxi driver to drop me off in front of L'Hotel, a gleaming forty-storey structure in the Causeway Bay area of the city. Then, when he'd pulled away, I picked up the bag I'd been told to bring containing enough clothes for three days, and doubled back along the Causeway Bay Road, with its monolithic buildings looming up on either side of me, until I came to the green oasis of Victoria Park.

It was late afternoon and unseasonably warm and humid for February, with the sun managing to poke its head through the clouds as it began its descent over Kowloon. A t'ai chi class for senior citizens was in progress on one of the greens, while couples of all ages sat on the benches lining the pathways, some holding hands as they enjoyed both the warmth and each other's company.

I kept my head down as I walked. I didn't want to meet anyone's eye. These people might have been Chinese locals who would probably never in a million years have recognized me as a fugitive ex-police officer from England, a man wanted on murder charges by Interpol for almost the whole of the previous decade, but I'd learned through bitter experience that there's no such thing as being too careful. Looking round furtively, I felt a pang of jealousy. Having been on the run for so long, I was in a state of perpetual loneliness, and it pained me to see the settled, shared lives of other people, because to do so served as a constant reminder of what I hadn't got.

At the end of the park, I crossed the footbridge over the six-lane Victoria Highway and, remembering my instructions, walked along the modern waterfront of Causeway Bay harbour, amazed at how quiet it was, until I came to a flight of stone steps that led down to the water. A motorized white dinghy containing a muscular western man

I didn't recognize, in T-shirt and sunglasses, bobbed up and down below me. The man gave me a cursory nod as I walked down the steps and clambered aboard, then, without a word, he started the engine and pulled back.

The harbour was lined with a varied cluster of boats, with the most expensive nearest the shore-line, while the local junks were relegated to a far corner, next to the outer harbour wall. It was therefore no surprise that our journey lasted all of fifty yards until we came to the back end of one of the sleekest, most expensive-looking yachts in the place. Bertie Schagel was not the kind of man to scrimp when it came to his own comfort.

A second westerner in T-shirt and sunglasses appeared on deck and took hold of the proffered rope as I came up the back steps. I slipped on the fibreglass and almost tumbled backwards, and he had to grab my arm to steady me. I nodded in thanks, recognizing him from my last meeting with Schagel in a Singapore hotel, slightly embarrassed to have lost the cool demeanour I like to portray in situations like this.

The guy pointed towards the lower deck, and taking a last look at the setting sun, I went through an open door and into the air-conditioned cool-ness of a dimly lit room where a very large man with a very large head sat in a huge leather tub chair that still looked tight around his rolling, multi-layered midriff. Bertie Schagel's thinning grey hair was slicked back, and he was wearing a black suit with a black open-necked shirt beneath it, from which sprouted a thick, wiry wodge of chest hair. He had an outsized glass of something alcoholic in one hand and a Cuban cigar, already half-smoked, in the other, making him look uncannily like Meatloaf in a Gordon Gekko fancy-dress costume.

'Ah, Dennis, good you could make it,' he said with a loud smile, not bothering to attempt to extricate himself from the chair, which would have taken far too long. 'Take a seat. Would you like a drink of something?'

Normally I would have baulked at the prospect, as I never liked to mix business with pleasure, or spend any more time with Schagel than I absolutely had to, but the flight from Bangkok had taken it out of me. I told him I'd have a beer. 'Singha, if you've got it.'

'We've got everything,' said Schagel, before leaning over his shoulder and calling out to someone to bring it through.

A few seconds later, a dark-skinned Thai girl with dyed-blonde hair came through the door behind him, carrying the beer. She couldn't have been more than eighteen at most, which made her at least thirty years short of Schagel, and she was wearing tight denim hotpants and an even tighter, garish pink halter-top that clung like a second skin to her boyish body. As she set the bottle and a coaster down on the teak coffee table, Schagel leaned forward and, with an unpleasant leer,

16

slapped her behind with a painful-sounding thwack. The girl flinched with shock but otherwise made no move to acknowledge what had happened, and retreated from the room without meeting my eyes.

It was clear that Schagel was humiliating her for my benefit. He seemed to like doing that. Once, at another of our meetings, I'd been made to wait while he'd yelled abuse at someone in an adjoining room (I never knew if it was a man or a woman because whoever it was didn't speak once), ending his tirade with an audible slap before lumbering back into the room and greeting me with one of his sly, knowing smiles. I think it was his way of reminding me that he was the boss, the one in control; that he could do exactly what he liked, and there was not a thing that I, or anyone else, could do about it.

Only once had I ever defied his orders. He'd wanted me to kill a middle-aged Russian housewife based in Kuala Lumpur on behalf of her businessman husband, who it seemed didn't want to have the hassle of a divorce. The husband must also have been mightily pissed off with her about something because his instructions were that she was to be kidnapped, taken to an isolated location, and then beheaded live on film, a copy of the footage to be delivered to him afterwards.

It never ceases to amaze, or sadden, me how twisted human beings can be. As Schagel had told me about the job, I was thinking about how low

I'd fallen to be having such a conversation. He'd offered me a hundred and fifty thousand US dollars to do it – triple what I would normally expect – and it was clear he was getting paid a hell of a lot more than that. But I'd turned him down flat.

I'm not a good man. I've killed people in my life who've probably not deserved it. In fact, scotch that, I know I have. I've acted as judge, jury and executioner when I've had absolutely no right to do so. But I've also lost a lot of sleep over what I've done. Woken up in the middle of the night, sweating and terrified, as the ghosts of the past haunt my dreams, knowing that they'll always be there with me right up until the end of my life, and possibly even beyond. I've got morals. I like to think the hits I carry out are on people who've done some kind of wrong. That they're not innocent. This woman was guilty of nothing, and I drew the line immediately, knowing that ultimately my sanity depended on it.

Schagel hadn't taken it well. He'd threatened and cajoled me, claiming that he could have me arrested at any time and then I'd be spending the rest of my life in jail. He could have done too. He knew far more about me than I knew about him, having set me up with the fake identity I now lived under. And, unlike me, he had some very powerful friends. But I'd stood my ground and eventually he'd given up. He didn't betray me to the authorities, either. I guess, in the end, I was too useful to him for that. Unfortunately, I still read in the newspapers a few weeks later that the headless corpse of a fifty-six-year-old Russian woman had been found floating in the Klang River just outside KL. My stand might have served to make me feel a little better, but it hadn't done her much good.

I picked up the beer and took a long slug, relishing the coldness and the hoppy taste. Sometimes in life there are few things better than a cold beer.

'So, to what do I owe the pleasure of your company, Mr Schagel?'

'Ah, straight to the point, Dennis. That's what I like about you.' He smiled, lizard-like, and crossed his hands on his lap, loudly cracking the knuckles. 'So, I shall be straight to the point also. It's a job in the Philippines – a country I understand you're familiar with.'

I nodded. The Philippines. I hadn't been there in over six years, and I immediately wondered how exactly Schagel knew I was familiar with it. I certainly hadn't told him, and as far as I was aware no one knew about the three years I'd spent there after I'd first gone on the run from the UK. But for the moment I let it go. 'Who's the target?'

'An Irish ex-pat and long-term resident of Manila. His name's Patrick O'Riordan.' Schagel reached down behind his chair and grabbed a plain brown envelope, which he handed to me.

I opened it and pulled out an A4-sized black-and-white headshot of a fit-looking western man in his early fifties with a shock of bouffant-style curly white hair and high, well-defined cheekbones. He was looking straight at the camera, a confident half-smile on his face, as if all was well in his world. Which it probably was.

'It should be a straightforward assignment,' continued Schagel. 'As far as the client has led me to believe, Mr O'Riordan will not be expecting anything.'

Sometimes the people you target are suspicious of what's coming and take measures to protect themselves, or check for surveillance, which makes tracking them slightly harder. The good thing from my point of view is that this usually means they're guilty of something. But if Patrick O'Riordan – whoever he was – wasn't expecting anything, it was possible he was an innocent man. That, or a foolish one. Either way, it unnerved me a little that right now he was going about his daily business unaware that two people were discussing the mechanics of his murder a thousand miles away.

'What's his background?' I asked.

'He's a journalist for the *Manila Post*.'

'Someone must really dislike his work.'

Schagel smiled. 'Someone does. Did you know that more journalists are murdered in the Philippines than in any other country in the world?'

'I didn't,' I said, although it didn't surprise me. In my experience, the Philippines was a lawless, corrupt place where people from all backgrounds tended to use the gun as a first rather than a last resort.

'Mr O'Riordan lives with his wife in the city. The client only wants him targeted, but if the wife gets in the way . . .' Schagel shrugged his shoulders, and his outsized head seemed to sink into them. 'Then you will need to get rid of her too.'

My face showed no reaction to his casually callous tone, but by the way he was looking at me I could tell he was watching for one. Testing whether or not I could be relied upon to put a bullet into the woman if she got in the way.

I asked him what the pay was.

'The remuneration for this particular job is seventy-five thousand US dollars, payable at the end of the task in the usual manner.'

The usual manner was in the form of a deposit paid by a Hong Kong-registered shell company into the numbered Panama-based bank account that Schagel had set up for me three years earlier. I would then move it to an account that I held with the Bangkok Bank (also set up by Schagel), and from there I could send money transfers as and when I needed them to a local Laotian bank. The sizes of the payments made were never enough to bother the authorities, and although it was plenty of hassle, it was a hell of a lot less suspicious than carrying large amounts of cash around between countries.

Schagel puffed lordly on his cigar. 'In Manila, you'll be supplied with an unused gun with a suppressor attached. Use that. The client would prefer O'Riordan to be targeted in his own home, and that when you have dealt with him, you set fire to the place.'

I nodded to signify that this was OK, even though it meant that I was almost certainly going to have to kill his wife too – a task that filled me with a hypocritical distaste.

'The only stipulation with this job is that it has to be done fast. Very fast. I have already booked you on the Cathay Pacific flight tonight at ten p.m. Your flight home is open-ended, but the client wants him dead by two p.m. local time tomorrow. That's why the pay is higher than usual.'

'There's no way I can guarantee that, Mr Schagel. I don't like hurrying these kinds of jobs. You know that. Too many things can go wrong.'

'And that's why the client came to me. Because he wants a professional to do it. Someone who can act swiftly and decisively.' He waved the stub of his cigar at me. 'You have proved many times that you are this kind of professional, Dennis. So do this task for me. O'Riordan has to die by two p.m. tomorrow, otherwise the job is off and I am left looking bad.'

I started to say something but he put up a hand, signifying that it wasn't up for discussion, and I knew better than to try. He motioned towards the envelope in my hand. 'There's also a phone in there. In the notes section, you will

22

find Mr O'Riordan's home and work addresses, and several of the establishments he frequents in the area.'

'What if he isn't in the city?' I asked, rummaging inside and pulling out a new iPhone.

'I am reliably informed he will be.'

It seemed Schagel's client knew a lot about the man he wanted killed, but that suited me fine. It made things a lot easier.

'There's also a pre-programmed telephone number on there for use in emergencies if you need to get hold of me day or night. Call it, leave a message, and I will be back to you within the hour. When you've given me confirmation that the job's done, delete everything from the phone and get rid of it in a way it can't be found. Now, have you memorized the target?'

I nodded, putting the phone in my jeans pocket, and handed him back the envelope with the photo inside.

I've carried out four hits on behalf of Bertie Schagel in the past three years, and he's always operated in the same way. Methodically, and with every angle covered. Always in a position to deal with any unforeseen problems but leaving behind absolutely nothing to link him to the actual crime itself. But at least he was reliable, and in my line of business, that's something that's priceless.

I also knew not to ask too many questions. I never did any more. Not since the Russian woman. I still liked to think my targets were all bad guys (and they had all been guys) who'd deserved to meet a sticky end, but I couldn't put my hand on my heart and swear it with total confidence, especially now that I'd found out O'Riordan was a journalist. But because I'd turned down that one job, I knew that Schagel no longer trusted me entirely. He liked his operatives to be like him, utterly devoid of human compassion. Thankfully I had yet to stoop that low, although occasionally in the dark, solitary moments when I contemplated my place in the world, I wondered if it was only a matter of time before I finally did.

He downed the remainder of his drink, then gave me a look that told me our meeting was over. 'I can organize a taxi to the airport for you if you wish?'

'No, it's OK. But there is something I've been wanting to talk to you about.'

He looked suspicious. 'Really? What's that?'

I hadn't been looking forward to this part of the conversation, but I also knew that it had been coming for a while. 'My retirement. I've done quite a lot of work for you now, but I'm making a living running my other business, and I want to make a go of it. I'll do this job for you, but afterwards, I'd like to bring our relationship to a close.'

Schagel looked at me through the cigar smoke with an air of vague amusement, as if I'd told him an inconsequential joke and he was humouring me. 'You haven't forgotten, I hope, Dennis, what I did for you?'

I hadn't. It was why I owed him. If Bertie Schagel hadn't come to my rescue, I would have been facing the prospect of the rest of my life behind bars. He hadn't done it for altruistic reasons, but even so, he'd still done it. 'No,' I said, 'but I reckon when I've done this job, number five, that I'll have paid my debt to you.'

'It cost me a great deal of money and effort to remove you from custody. You are wanted for mass murder by the British authorities, and they have notoriously long memories. Yet I still managed to secure your freedom.' He paused. 'There will come a time when your debt to me is repaid. I've always told you that. But right now, I need you and the services you provide, and I pay you well for your troubles, do I not? Even though, on occasion, you haven't, as the Americans would say, played ball.' He cleared his throat. 'But if you do this job for me within the timescales you've been set, then maybe we talk again. OK? But make sure you do it.'

You had to hand it to Schagel. He was a good salesman and the way he put it almost made me feel guilty that I'd brought the subject up. And the truth was, I had to do what he said, because that was my problem these days: I was in hock to the wrong sort of person.

'OK,' I said, and got to my feet, knowing I was about to embark on a journey that would leave another stain on an already blood-splattered conscience.

25

But if I'd had the remotest clue about the terrible darkness I was about to head into, I would have caught the first plane home and taken my chances, even if it did mean spending the rest of my days in jail.

CHAPTER 2

Their faces were cold and defiant, even though she knew they must have been terrified. They were, after all, little more than kids – the oldest only just turned eighteen, the other two, seventeen apiece – and their guilt had already been confirmed twenty-four hours earlier by the foreman of the jury. According to the rules of the English legal system, there is only one sentence for murder: life imprisonment. It was now simply a matter of the judge announcing the minimum term each of them would serve, and everyone in the crowded courtroom knew that she was not going to be lenient. The circumstances of the crime were too extreme for that. Their victim, Michael Fremi, only sixteen years old, had been a promising student who should have been celebrating receiving nine GCSEs, five of them As or A stars. Sadly, Michael would never know what he'd achieved, because early one Friday evening the previous August, the three defendants, who'd been lying in wait at the end of his street, had ambushed him as he walked home from a friend's house. Apparently, he'd stood up to one of them,

27

Karl Brayer, the previous week when Brayer had tried to steal a friend's mobile phone, forcing him to back down in the process, and this was his gang's revenge. In a short but extremely violent attack, which witnesses later claimed had lasted barely seconds, they'd stabbed him a total of sixteen times, using three different knives. One of the blows had pierced his heart; another had severed his carotid artery. It was never really in any doubt that they'd meant to kill him.

DI Tina Boyd of Camden's Murder Investigation Team, or CMIT as it was better known, had been on duty that night and was one of the first to the scene of the killing. One of the things she remembered most was Michael's distraught mother cradling his dead body in her arms, unable to let him go. He'd had his eyes closed, a peaceful, almost angelic look on his young, unblemished face. And the blood. She couldn't forget that either. There'd been so much of it that it had still been running into the gutter when she'd arrived.

They'd caught the killers quickly. They always did in cases like this, which always made Tina wonder why on earth these kids did it. Surely they realized that the end result – arrest, custody, conviction – was inevitable? Were their lives really that empty? Sadly, she knew the answer was yes, and as she stood there watching the defendants now, knowing that the guilty verdicts meant another good result for the team, she couldn't feel much in the way of satisfaction.

Then the judge, a middle-aged woman with a naturally haughty face who looked frankly ridiculous in her wig and robes, began speaking and a stony hush fell over the courtroom.

Tina zoned out as the judge described the gratuitousness of the crime, and the sheer wickedness of the perpetrators. She'd heard it all before, and the words always sounded artificial, mainly because everything the judge said depended entirely on the jury's verdict. If they'd decided it was self-defence, she would have now been apologizing to the three defendants and telling them they were free to go. One of Tina's biggest gripes about the British legal system was that, however good the case she and her colleagues brought against the people they arrested, the outcome still rested on the whims of twelve members of the public who, far more often than not, had no prior knowledge of the law.

There was a loud cheer from behind Tina in the public gallery as Karl Brayer received his minimum term. He'd got seventeen years, making him thirty-five before he'd be considered for release, his youth by then no more than a fading memory. Brayer turned slowly and deliberately in the direction of the cheering and sneered with as much contempt as he could muster.

It was then that he caught Tina's eye. It had been she who'd charged him with murder in the interview room, and seeing her now, he drew a forefinger slowly across his throat, mouthing the words 'pig bitch'.

29

Tina smiled at him, putting just about the right amount of pity into her expression, feeling good about the world for the first time that day. It would take more than a jumped-up kid like Brayer to scare her, not after all that she'd been through over the years. 'I could show you people who'd make your hair stand on end,' she thought as she held his gaze, pleased that he was the first to turn away as the judge sentenced the other two defendants to sixteen years each.

And then it was over, and the security guards were man-handling the three of them away from the dock as they all struggled angrily, macho to the end, enduring a welter of abuse from one section of the public gallery, and cries of support from their families in the other.

Tina shook hands with two of her colleagues who'd come with her to watch the sentencing, then leaned back across the seats and hugged Constanta Fremi, Michael's mother, who was weeping and smiling at the same time as the various emotions brought on by the tragedy she'd suffered got the better of her.

As soon as she was out on the street in front of the court building, Tina switched on her phone and lit a cigarette. She told the two colleagues – her new boss, DCI Bob Levine, and her sometime partner, DC Dan Grier – that she'd catch up with them back at the station. She had an appointment in Finchley with a witness to another street stabbing that had also ended in murder. The witness was a twenty-year-old single mother, Gemma Hanson, who was allegedly being intimidated by the families of those involved and was thinking of withdrawing her statement in advance of the April trial. Tina needed to shore up her resolve, because without her evidence their case against the suspect would almost certainly collapse. Witness intimidation was far more common than most people knew, and the police simply didn't have the resources to protect everyone complaining of it. Realistically, all Tina could offer were encouraging words and the vague promise of extra police patrols in the neighbourhood. They'd already installed a panic button, but the last time Gemma had pressed it, after a brick had come sailing through her front window, narrowly missing the baby's cot, the local uniforms had taken more than fifteen minutes to turn up. Tina knew her task was not going to be easy.

She sheltered in a shop doorway from the worst of the biting February wind and took a long, almost desperate drag on her cigarette, enjoying the harsh hit from the nicotine as it surged through her system. She only had one voicemail message, from a DS Rob Weale of Essex CID, asking her to call him when she had a moment. Although she didn't recognize the name, she was intrigued enough to hit the call-back button.

He answered after three rings, announcing his name and rank in a strong Essex accent that was only half a degree away from 'cor blimey' cockney.

'It's Tina Boyd,' she said, taking a last drag on her cigarette and stubbing it underfoot. 'You called me.'

'I did, yeah. Thanks for calling back. I understand you've been having some contact with a journalist by the name of Nick Penny. Is that right?'

Tina tensed. 'He's an acquaintance of mine, yes,' she answered defensively.

'Then I've got some bad news for you.'

She knew straight away what it was but she asked the question anyway, feeling a wrenching tightness in her gut. 'What?'

'He died last night. It looks like suicide.'

'It isn't,' she said firmly. 'It's murder.'

DS Weale cleared his throat. 'I had a feeling you might say that. I'm at the scene now. I think we need to talk.'

CHAPTER 3

For a number of years, Nick Penny had been a successful investigative reporter for the *Guardian* newspaper. He'd exposed the shady dealings of corporations and governments, leading to the resignations of a number of senior figures for corruption. Then, the summer before last, Tina had approached him with a tape recording she'd made of a senior politician directly incriminating a shadowy gangland figure called Paul Wise in a plot to cover up a murder. Wise, a man with suspected links to drug smuggling, prostitution, terrorism and, most sickening of all, paedophilia, had long been Tina's nemesis, and with this tape she'd seen an opportunity to bring him to justice.

The politician had been killed before he had a chance to repeat the allegations in court, and Tina had feared that if she gave the tape to the Crown Prosecution Service then it was possible it would disappear, given the number of friends Wise seemed to have within the establishment. Tina might not have agreed with his politics, but she trusted Penny completely, and he'd repaid her trust by getting the *Guardian* to print the transcript of the tape in full, even though it had been made illegally.

At first it had looked like Wise was finally going to be brought to justice. The British government had formally asked for his extradition, even though an extradition treaty didn't exist with northern Cyprus. But Wise had not survived as long as he had by giving up easily, and using the financial resources at his disposal, he'd fought back hard. Appointing a team of top lawyers, he'd sued for libel the *Guardian*, Nick Penny himself and, most controversially, the estate of the government minister who'd made the allegations in the first place.

It was a clever move. Britain has some of the most draconian libel laws in the developed world, and within weeks the minister's son had announced publicly that he didn't believe the voice on the tape was that of his father. The writ against the estate for libel was dropped soon afterwards. Then a court in northern Cyprus had thrown out the British extradition case, citing lack of evidence. Finally, the British government began to backtrack as it became clear that the taped confession alone (even if it was proved genuine) wouldn't be enough to convict Wise, and that there was nothing else connecting him to the plot, or any of the other criminal activities he was suspected of.

Penny had been sacked from the paper as its owners tried to distance themselves from the affair, and by the time Tina had returned from an extended holiday in central America the story had long since disappeared from the front pages. Wise had not only remained free, he was actually in a stronger position than he'd ever been, since there were now very few people willing to take him on.

It was just after one p.m., almost two hours after the phone call from DS Weale, when Tina parked her car outside the two-storey prefab unit in the far corner of a half-empty industrial estate where Nick Penny had kept his office. Since his sacking, it had been the base for what freelance journalism work he could get (which hadn't been a great deal). It was also the place from where he was undertaking his unofficial investigation into Paul Wise's activities, trying to find some chink in his armour – an investigation which Tina had been helping with, as much as she was able.

Penny had claimed that he couldn't work properly in the idyllic little cottage a few miles away near Great Dunmow that he shared with his wife and two young children, because of the noise, but Tina had always thought he'd been mad setting up somewhere like this. It was an ugly, lonely place, and worse than that, it wasn't safe for a man doing what he'd been doing, as had now been proved. There was no security at the gate, and the majority of the office lots were vacant – a hangover from the recession – so it wouldn't have been difficult to take him out without any witnesses. She'd warned him about this but he'd told her he was being extremely careful. 'And anyway,' he'd said, in one of their last conversations, 'it'd be way too risky taking me out. I'm too high profile.'

But now they had.

Tina was surprised to see that there was only a single squad car, as well as a possible unmarked, in the parking spaces outside. There was no scene-of-crime tape sealing off the premises, nor any signs of SOCO. Only a very cold-looking uniformed copper in a fluorescent jacket standing guard outside the front door. With Penny dead less than twenty-four hours, it could only mean that they weren't treating the death as suspicious, and Tina felt an immediate flash of anger.

She showed the uniform on the door her warrant card and went up the narrow formica steps to the cramped first-floor room where she'd come only once before to see Penny. They'd met regularly over the past months, but whenever he'd thought he might have a lead worth talking about she'd always insisted they have their discussion in a place where it was less likely they'd be overheard. Penny had thought her paranoid – she knew that – particularly as none of the leads he was turning up were high quality, but Tina had had enough experience of their adversary to know that his ruthlessness and his desire to clear up loose ends could never be underestimated.

A young man in a suit and protective gloves – the only occupant of the room – stood up from the laptop he was examining and turned to greet her as she knocked on the door and stepped inside. He was tall and powerfully built, with short, cropped blond hair and a round, cheery face which had still not quite lost its puppy fat. Tina put him at about twenty-seven, though she reckoned he could probably pass for three or four years younger.

The man gave her a small, sympathetic smile and put out a hand. 'DI Boyd, thanks for coming. I'm DS Rob Weale. Mr Penny's wife told me that you'd met up with him a number of times recently.'

'That's right,' Tina answered as they shook.

She slowly looked round the room. It was cluttered, as it had been the last time she'd been here. Files, newspapers and books were piled up on the windowsill, and much of the available floor space was taken up with unopened cardboard boxes. Nothing looked particularly out of place, except Penny's chair, which had been moved out from behind the desk. Tina felt her jaw tighten as she scanned the contents of his desk: the photo of his two smiling girls; another one of his wife, Natalie; his stained West Ham United coffee mug sitting forlornly between the laptop and an overflowing Heineken ashtray. He'd been warned twice by the building's owners not to smoke in the office but, like Tina, he liked to cock his nose at authority. She sighed. She'd liked Nick Penny.

There was no sign of his body now, and only the vague, almost imperceptible smell of decay in the frigid air, mixed with stale smoke, confirmed what had happened here.

'Would you like to talk somewhere else, ma'am? I can imagine it's not that easy for you doing it here.'

'I'm fine,' she answered, keen to get things moving. She forced herself to say the words: 'How did he die?'

'He hanged himself from there,' answered Weale, motioning towards the steel girder that bisected the room a foot and a half above his head. 'He stood on his chair. He'd swallowed a load of Bombay Sapphire before he did it. When he didn't come home last night, and his wife couldn't get hold of him, she called the police. A local patrol car found him when they came by here just before ten p.m. The bottle was by the chair, and the initial toxicology results show he was more than four times over the drink-drive limit when he died. We haven't got an exact time of death, but the pathologist thinks it was between five and seven p.m.'

Tina put a hand on the desk as the full enormity of what had happened suddenly hit her. 'Did he leave a note?'

'He left three. One to his wife. One to his children. And one to someone he only addresses as T, and which he's signed with a pet name, suggesting that it's possibly a lover. Would you have any idea who that might be?'

Tina felt her jaw tighten as she met his gaze. 'Yes,' she said. 'It's me.'

CHAPTER 4

Keeping her demeanour as cool and professional as possible, even though she was churning up inside as different emotions – grief, embarrassment, and most of all guilt – swirled about her system, Tina asked if she could see the notes.

'They're definitely genuine,' said Weale. 'His wife recognizes the handwriting.' He too looked embarrassed at Tina's admission, having clearly not expected it. It made him look even younger somehow.

'Did she see the one he wrote to me?'

'No.' Weale rubbed his head a little self-consciously. 'We didn't feel there was anything to be gained at the moment by letting her know he was having an affair.'

Tina sighed, feeling relieved. 'I know you don't have to show me the letters, but I'd still appreciate it if I could take a look.'

Weale seemed to think about this for a moment, then nodded and produced three transparent evidence bags from a tattered leather briefcase propped on a box in the corner of the room. 'I can't let you touch them, I'm afraid, but you should be able to read them through the plastic.'

Each note was laid out flat inside the bag and he held them up one by one for her to read. They were all very short and apologetic, as he said sorry to those he was closest to for what he was about to do, and Weale was right, they'd definitely been written by Nick. She recognized his distinctive, very messy handwriting, as well as the doodle of a smiling face that he'd put at the end of the note to his daughters. He'd drawn a similar one on the birthday card he'd sent her a few months back. He'd also addressed her as 'T', the name he'd always called her by, and signed it 'Mr P', the name she'd sometimes used for him. It was also clear that Nick had made a real effort to make the words legible, which they just about were. No mean feat for him at the best of times. Damn near a miracle after he'd necked half a bottle of gin.

She swallowed hard, desperate not to look weak in front of DS Weale, and just about managing it.

'Look, I'm not here to judge what happened between you two,' said Weale, putting the bags back in the briefcase. 'And I'm going to do everything I can to make sure it doesn't get made public.'

'Thanks.'

'How long were you seeing him for?'

She sighed. 'I worked with him on and off for about a year, and we'd been seeing each other for the last three months. But it finished two weeks ago.'

'Who finished it? You or Mr Penny?'

'I did.' She paused, then looked Weale squarely in the eye. 'I know how bad this looks, but it wasn't suicide. How much of Nick's background do you know?'

'I know about his run-in with Paul Wise. And' – he looked uncomfortable – 'I know about Wise's connection to you.'

Just the mention of Paul Wise's name filled Tina with a cold, intense rage. 'Nick and I were looking for any evidence that could be used to reopen the case against him,' she told Weale, seeing no point in keeping the subject of their meetings secret. She'd been warned by her superiors in the Met not to say anything publicly about Wise, nor to get involved in investigating him, on pain of dismissal, but it was going to come out soon enough anyway. 'Nick was doing most of the digging. I was helping him when I could.'

'How?'

'By giving him information where he didn't have the authority to get it himself. That kind of thing.' She hoped Weale wouldn't ask for details since what she'd been doing could easily cost her her job.

He nodded slowly, clearly having trouble taking this all in. 'And had you found anything that could be used?'

She didn't say anything for a moment. In truth,

she'd been hugely disappointed by Penny's progress. Realistically, finding evidence where organizations like the Serious Organized Crime Agency, with all its resources, couldn't was always going to be a long shot, and the fact was he'd turned up little of use over a long period of time. In the last few weeks she'd started to give up hope, suspecting that Penny was becoming more interested in her than he was in finding evidence against Wise. With Tina, of course, it was the other way round, which was one of the reasons she'd decided to end the relationship. 'No. We used to discuss his progress whenever we met, but it wasn't going well. At least I thought it wasn't.'

'And had you spoken since the end of the affair?'

'Yes. We spoke on the phone just over a week ago. Last Thursday.'

'And how did he seem then?'

'He was still upset about the fact that I'd finished things, but he'd accepted that it was over. He asked me during the call if we could get back together. I said no, and we talked about the case, and agreed to speak later this week. I'm thinking he must have found out something between times. I saw you were looking on his laptop. Is there anything on there?'

'There's a file entitled "The Project" in the documents section. It details his investigations into Wise's business dealings, although it doesn't mention him by name. It just uses the soubriquet "W". Not exactly foolproof. It wasn't particularly well hidden, and there wasn't much on there that would be of any use in building a case against him.'

Tina stared down at the open laptop, wishing she was dealing with someone older, and more experienced. 'There must be something else. Are you sure you've looked everywhere?'

'I spent two years on CEOP going through the hard drives of child molesters, DI Boyd,' he replied testily, 'so I know what I'm looking for, and I've been picking apart this machine for the best part of the last hour. There's nothing.' He paused. 'You've got to see things from my position. I find a man hanging in his office. On closer investigation, it seems he's facing financial ruin, with a court case hanging over his head, no job, very little income, and huge debts. He owes twelve thousand pounds to various card companies and is three months behind on his mortgage payments.' Tina opened her mouth to interrupt, but he held up a hand. 'Added to this, the woman he'd been having an affair with had just finished it two weeks earlier, which would only have added to the pressure. And to top it all, he left three notes, all seemingly heartfelt, and all in his own handwriting. That, to me, spells suicide. And nothing you've said makes me change my view of that.'

'I understand what you're saying,' she said, and she could as well. In his position she'd have thought exactly the same thing. 'But Nick was

43

investigating a man who's not only been involved in a number of murders over the years, but who also has form in faking suicides. He had someone murder my previous boyfriend – a DI in the Met, John Gallan – six years ago and make it look like suicide, even going so far as to fake a note.'

'But this is very different, ma'am. Nick Penny wasn't a threat to Paul Wise. He was a disgraced journalist staring at financial and personal ruin.'

'I knew Nick. And I can promise you now, categorically, that he wasn't the type to commit suicide.' But even as she spoke the words, Tina realized how hollow they must have sounded.

To be fair to Weale, he didn't argue the point. Instead, he shrugged his broad shoulders. 'What do you want me to do?'

'Investigate more closely what Nick's been doing this past week. Scour that laptop. He'd found something, I'm sure.'

'Then, why didn't he tell you about it? I'm sorry, ma'am, but it'll be up to a coroner to decide whether or not this death was unlawful. Right now, I believe it was suicide, and I haven't got the resources or the time to try to prove otherwise.'

He started to turn away, a sign that for him the interview was over, and Tina felt a sudden overpowering anger at the thought of that bastard Wise getting away with murder again because no one was competent or far-sighted enough to work out what was happening.

'Bullshit,' she snapped, her voice louder than she'd been expecting.

Weale gave her a look that suggested she should be careful what she said, and she took a deep breath, knowing she had to calm down. There was no point pushing things. Weale had made up his mind and he didn't look like the sort who was going to budge. But she was convinced that Nick Penny had been murdered, and the most likely explanation was that it was over something he'd found out in the past week.

'I'm sorry,' she said, knowing she had to keep the big DS onside. 'It's not been an easy day.'

He gave her a sympathetic smile. 'Apology accepted.'

'Did you find his mobile phone?' she asked him.

'Yes. It was in his trouser pocket.'

'But only the one?'

Weale looked at her uncertainly. 'According to his wife, he only owned one mobile phone.'

Tina shook her head. 'He had two. The other was an unregistered pay-as-you-go. I bought it for him for when he was making calls to me, or calls relating to his investigation into Wise. I thought it would be a lot more secure that way, and safer for him if the calls couldn't be traced back to his phone. It was a Motorola K1 fliptop. He used to keep it with him all the time.'

'That wasn't the one in his pocket.'

'I didn't think it would be.' She took out her own mobile. 'Let me call it now.' But when she punched in the speed-dial code, an automated message told her it was switched off, and she guessed that it would remain that way for ever.

'It doesn't change anything,' said Weale as she put her mobile away. 'That phone could be anywhere.'

But as far as Tina was concerned, it changed a lot. 'Can you do me a favour? If I give you the number of the pay-as-you-go, and the operator, can you get hold of the records for the calls made and received in the past three months and email them to me?' There had been a time when Tina could have got that information herself but she'd bent the rules too many times in the past few years and now there was a much tighter rein on her activities. 'Please. As a favour.'

He gave another uncertain look. 'If anyone finds out—'

'They won't. I'll just take a look at them and if there's anything that really sticks out I'll get back to you, and you can take it from there. If not, then I'll shred them and that'll be that.'

He thought about it for a couple of seconds, then nodded. 'All right, but I'm trusting you.'

'I'm a woman of my word,' Tina said firmly, thinking about a promise she'd made herself a long time ago. That one day she'd sit in court watching as Paul Wise was sent down for the rest of his life. Right now, that moment felt as far away as ever. Yet she was certain that Nick Penny had stumbled on something, and that if she could find out what it was, then once again she'd be back on his tail.

CHAPTER 5

The day it all went wrong for me was 11 August 1989.

That was the day I killed a man for the first time. His name was Darren Reid and he was a drug-addicted thug with a list of criminal convictions as long as my arm. He'd been holding his common-law wife and their two young children hostage at the terraced house they'd shared in Haringey, armed with a gun and a carving knife. I was part of the armed response team sent there to try to bring the situation to a peaceful conclusion. But, unfortunately, things hadn't worked out like that. Reid had been off his head on a potent mix of speed, booze and high-strength dope and was waving the gun around erratically. I don't know if he ever had any intention of hurting his family, but as we crouched behind our squad cars in the hot sun waiting for him to make some kind of move, stymied by the hugely strict rules that govern all armed British police operations, it wasn't something anyone wanted to risk finding out.

And then, naked from the waist up, he'd

appeared at the front window, flinging it open and shouting something slurred and unintelligible at us. He'd raised the gun and pointed it out of the window. I'd already received instructions through my earpiece telling me not to fire, but that was before the gun had been aimed in my general direction. I was pretty sure he wouldn't hit me, his gun hand was too unsteady for that, but my nerves and my patience were frayed, and suddenly, in one epiphany-like moment, I'd had enough. There were further instructions coming through the earpiece but to this day I couldn't tell you what they were. I wasn't listening. I was already squeezing the trigger.

I shot him twice in the chest, killing him near enough instantly, and from that moment on, my fate was sealed. The gun turned out to be a replica; I was suspended for two months while a detailed investigation was carried out as to whether I'd been justified in my actions, with criminal charges hanging over me the whole time. Even after I was reinstated, when it was found that I had no case to answer, I was permanently removed from firearms duty, and my path up the career ladder ground to a resounding halt. Innocent I might have been of any crime, but as far as the brass were concerned there was an unpleasant aura of controversy about me that meant I was best avoided.

Before that August day I would have considered myself a good cop. No liberal idealist – I've never been one of them – but at least a man who cared passionately about his job and the people he was paid to protect, and who wanted to do it to the best of his ability until he was forced by age to retire.

After that, I never really recovered. Perhaps there was more self-pity in my actions than I ever would have admitted at the time, but I became progressively more cynical. The law became a subject of contempt for me, as I came to realize that it was designed to protect the rights of the criminals, not the victims. The job became a battle. Us against them. But 'them' wasn't just the criminals. It was the establishment who paid my wages and made the laws, which now began to seem totally unjust. It was the bosses more interested in kissing arses and meeting quotas than in protecting their people. It was the members of the public who didn't seem to care what was happening on the streets around them, who hurried on by when they saw crimes being committed, too cowardly to intervene. Sometimes it seemed like the 'them' was everyone, and the 'us' was simply me, a lone copper engaged in a one-man battle against the injustices of the world.

I was twice the subject of complaints by prisoners regarding my treatment of them. The first was made by a violent thug wanted for two counts of GBH who'd spat in my face during an arrest, and then made the mistake of laughing about it while wearing handcuffs. We were in his mum's house at the time, where he'd been hiding out, and in front of four other arresting officers I'd headbutted him and broken one of his teeth.

His complaint hadn't been upheld, but only because all five of us had stuck to the same story, that he'd injured himself trying to escape. But suspicion had still hung over me as a result, and when three years later another complaint was made against me, this one was taken very seriously by the Police Complaints Commission.

The complainant was a convicted paedophile who I'd arrested on suspicion of raping the five-year-old daughter of the woman he was living with. He'd looked so incredibly smug as I'd put him in the back of the car, claiming in smooth, educated tones that it was all a mistake and that the child was lying, that I'd got in after him, and while my colleague waited outside I'd put a hand over his mouth while simultaneously twisting his balls with such pent-up ferocity that I'd caused a rupture in one of them. He'd spent three days in hospital as a result, and although my colleague claimed to have heard and seen nothing, my story that he'd slipped while getting into the car was never going to hold up, especially as according to the doctor who treated him his injuries were entirely consistent with the type of assault he was accusing me of.

I would almost certainly have lost my job, and might even have ended up in the dock, if it hadn't been for a man called Raymond Keen – who, after

51

Bertie Schagel, was possibly the least likely knight in shining armour you were ever going to meet.

I'd met Raymond at a charity function some months earlier. He was a colourful, well-known and, frankly, crooked local businessman who ran a highly successful funeral parlour, but who was suspected of having his finger in a fair few less savoury pies. However, I'd found him good company, and we'd been out for a drink on a couple of occasions, even though (or perhaps because) I knew that associating with a man like him would be frowned upon. One night I told him about the complaint that had been made against me. He listened, asked me where the complainant was being held in custody, then said that he'd get it fixed.

At that time, I didn't know the kinds of crimes that Raymond Keen was capable of, or how far his reach extended, and assumed that he was just giving me an empty promise. But a few days later, the complaint was dropped. Just like that. No reason was ever given. The cloud of suspicion remained above me, but at least I was back in the job.

And that was how Raymond and I had entered into business together. After that, it was difficult to turn down his requests for favours. Most of the time he wanted information, either for his own use or on behalf of other criminals: a warning about an impending drug bust; tips on how to find someone in the witness protection scheme.

Small things, but as the years went by, they steadily grew bigger and more serious, like a slow-moving but ultimately fatal cancer, until finally one day he asked me to break the ultimate taboo and kill someone for him.

The someone in question was a particularly unpleasant businessman called Vincent Stanhope, one of whose sidelines was child pornography. Stanhope apparently owed Raymond a large sum of money, which he was refusing to pay, and Raymond had decided that to protect his under-world reputation, Stanhope was going to have to die. He was offering me ten grand cash to carry out the job.

I came very close to saying no, and I often wonder how things would have turned out if I had. I'm being honest when I say I truly never wanted to become a murderer. What made me say yes was a case we were dealing with at the time. It's one that haunts me still, mainly because of the complete lack of any proper motive.

Tim Atkins was a perfectly ordinary, law-abiding, thirty-three-year-old local government worker. One day, he and his wife were walking along Regent's Canal with their two young children when they came upon three young men smoking cannabis and blocking the path. Mr Atkins asked them politely to move so he could manoeuvre the youngest's pushchair through. In answer, the biggest of the three, a complete waster, well known to us, by the name of Kyle Morris, had punched him in the face with such force that Mr Atkins had fallen straight back and struck his head on the concrete, suffering catastrophic brain injuries in the process. He never regained consciousness and died in hospital several hours later. His children, both of whom witnessed the killing of their father, were two girls aged five and twenty months.

Morris hadn't given a shit. When we'd brought him in less than twenty-four hours later and told him what had happened, he'd shrugged, said that it was nothing to do with him, and had then answered 'no comment' to every question we'd asked, looking far too pleased with himself, knowing he had the protection of the attractive, public-school-educated lawyer sitting next to him, who as far as I could see didn't give a shit about what he'd done either. There was no fear of the consequences of his actions, no regret for the way he'd casually ruined so many lives, and I remember thinking then how desperate I was to kill him – to put a gun against his head, to make him beg forgiveness, and then pull the trigger – and if I couldn't do it to him, then I wanted to do it to some other bastard who deserved it.

I was only ten minutes out of that interview when I phoned Raymond and said I'd take the job. Three nights later, I waited for Vincent Stanhope by the lock-up he sometimes used, and when he emerged from it and went to his car, I walked up behind him and, without a moment's hesitation, put two bullets directly into the back of his head.

It felt easy at the time, but afterwards, when I got back to my poky little flat, I threw up repeatedly before going into shock as my conscience reacted to what I'd done. I didn't sleep that night. Instead I sat up smoking and drinking, playing the killing over and over again, paranoid thoughts of being arrested by my own colleagues and spending the rest of my days in prison filling my thoughts, until finally a grey, sickly dawn broke over central London, and I threw up all over again.

That was over ten years and perhaps twice as many bodies ago now, and I don't throw up any more when I kill someone. I've become hardened to it. I still like to think that the ones I take out are the bad guys, but now, whichever way I care to look at it, I am a professional killer. And as Bertie Schagel helpfully pointed out, a good one too.

And Kyle Morris? He got four years for manslaughter and was released after just two and a half.

As I boarded the Cathay Pacific flight to Manila that night, stuck in economy with all the guest workers returning home for their holidays, it struck me that there really was no justice in the world.

CHAPTER 6

When Tina Boyd shut the front door of her end-of-terrace cottage behind her and walked through to the kitchen, she felt more like a drink than at any time in the past six months. She had, however, resisted buying a bottle of something on the way home. There was no way she was going back to the booze now. Not after the damage it had done to her over the years. Thankfully, there wasn't a drop of it in the house. Instead she poured herself a pint of orange juice and sparkling water – her evening tipple these days – and took a couple of sizeable gulps before sitting down at the kitchen table, lighting a cigarette, and contemplating the latest developments in her turbulent life.

From the start, Tina had regretted getting involved with Nick Penny. She knew from bitter experience that affairs with married men never worked out, and caused pain for all concerned. It had happened one night several weeks before Christmas when he'd come round to her place for one of their update meetings. More and more, they were tending to meet at hers. It was easier to talk there without anyone listening in, and at the time she hadn't thought there was anything untoward about having a married man round, because their relationship had just been business, even though she found him vaguely attractive. But that night he'd poured his heart out to her about the strains of the libel case, the pressure on his marriage, everything. She'd listened and sympathized, feeling sorry for him, because she knew how hard things could get sometimes, knowing from the way he was looking into her eyes that he wanted something to happen.

She hadn't made any overt move, but at one point when he was talking, she put a hand on his arm and gave it a squeeze, and then when she'd got up to go to the kitchen to refill her water glass she'd brushed her hand against his – a small but knowing gesture.

He'd followed her into the kitchen, put his arms round her waist, and pulled her to him.

They'd kissed. Hard. The first kiss she'd experienced since a fumbled one-night stand in Costa Rica the previous summer. And though she'd pulled away and protested, the weakness in her tone was obvious, because he'd kissed her again, and this time she hadn't pulled away. They'd made love on her living-room floor, and it had been everything lovemaking should be: intense, passionate, noisy.

Afterwards, she'd felt horrendously guilty. She'd never met Penny's family but knew full well what damage she must be inflicting on his relationship with his wife, even if he had been the instigator. And the thing was, she couldn't even blame the booze. She'd done it all of her own accord.

She'd tried to draw a line under what had happened. Told him that it couldn't happen again. Yet it had. On far too many occasions. So many that it had soon become the reason for their meetings, and the ongoing investigation into Paul Wise had taken a back seat, something that nagged at her even more. She really liked Nick Penny, far more than she'd expected. Although he was in turmoil in his personal life, he wasn't needy, could still make her laugh, and remained driven by his convictions. But she knew it couldn't last and that one day, probably sooner rather than later, it would end in tears and recriminations. So she'd called it off. He'd begged her to reconsider, but she'd been adamant. It had to end. For the good of both of them, and the good of their case against Wise. Eventually he had accepted the inevitable, and promised to call her only when he had further information.

They'd spoken only once since then, the previous Thursday. He'd told her he missed her and asked if she'd reconsider her decision, but had seemed fine enough when she'd said no. There had been no sign of any deep depression that might have ended in suicide. As she'd told DS Weale, Nick just didn't seem to be that kind of guy. There had still been too much life in him, even given the knocks he'd taken, for him ever to have considered ending it all. It was one of the reasons she'd found him so attractive.

And now he was dead. Just another name in a growing list of dead people who'd become close to Tina. Her partner in CID, DI Simon Barron, stabbed to death more than six years ago now. Then her lover, John Gallan, an apparent suicide that she knew was the work of one of Paul Wise's henchmen. Back then, people at work had started calling her the Black Widow – a moniker that would probably have faded if it hadn't been for the death a few years after that of her boss in CMIT, DCI Dougie MacLeod. He'd been murdered during a case Tina had been heavily involved in, and once again she'd become the Black Widow, this time in the media. God knows what everyone would make of this latest death.

She knew it would take all her self-discipline not to fall off the wagon this time. Given that she had a high-profile history with the media, her relationship with Nick was almost certainly going to be made public, which would mean lurid headlines; the wrath of Nick's wife; embarrassment and wisecracks at work. The next few days were going to be tough.

To try to head things off as best she could, Tina had called the station as soon as she'd finished with Weale and spoken to her new DCI, Bob Levine. Levine was a solid enough copper, and was regarded fairly neutrally by those under him, but like a lot of the older male police officers he'd always been wary of her, and Tina knew that he'd have preferred it if she hadn't been part of his squad. She'd told him what had happened, not leaving out any details, knowing that they'd come to light anyway, and unsurprisingly, he'd been furious. Not so much with the fact that she'd had an affair with Nick, but more with the fact that she'd remained involved in an unofficial attempt to get Paul Wise.

'How do you think that would have looked in court if Penny had got done for libel?' Levine had demanded. 'That you'd been working with him? You might have ended up being sued yourself. You've got to learn when to let go.'

Tina had heard this plea plenty of times before. A year back, she would have told him in no uncertain terms that she would let go when Wise was finally convicted of the crimes he was responsible for, but this time she didn't bother. Instead, she wearily apologized before giving him the rest of the bad news from the day. Gemma Hanson, the single mother who was their witness in the upcoming murder case, had decided to withdraw her statement identifying their alleged killer, even after Tina had spent more than an hour trying to persuade her to relent, and promising to get her fast-tracked into the witness protection programme.

At this point, Levine had become sympathetic, knowing how much pressure she was under, and had told Tina to take the rest of the day off.

'Take next week off as well. Have a rest. You're due it.'

She wasn't quite sure if this was an order or not, but in any case, she'd accepted. At least it would give her an opportunity to look into Nick Penny's death.

But she knew she was going to have to be careful. Nick's killer had known about the affair, even though it had finished a fortnight earlier. Either Nick had volunteered the information or, more likely, the killer had been watching him and had seen the two of them together. Since their last few face-to-face meetings had been here in her new house that could only mean one thing: he'd been watching her too.

She stubbed out the cigarette and walked over to the window, looking out into the blackness of her small garden, unable to see anything, before yanking the curtain across, and repeating the process on every window on the ground floor. The thought of being watched made her feel both violated and uneasy. She loved this house. Located in a pretty Hertfordshire village just outside the M25, she'd bought it because she could no longer bear to live in the apartment that had been her home for the previous three years. There were too many bad memories there. This place represented a new start for her, away from the violence and temptations of the city – a small, friendly community where the air was fresh and where she didn't need the booze to prop her up. And now it felt like it too had been invaded.

She wondered then if her house had been bugged. It was fairly secure, with decent locks on the doors and windows, but she hadn't got round to getting an alarm system installed yet, and knew from experience that it wasn't that hard to break into somewhere without leaving a trace if you knew what you were doing. And she had little doubt that anyone hired by Paul Wise would know what he was doing.

Tina cursed herself. She of all people should have known that you could never underestimate someone like Wise. It wasn't as if she didn't have the capability to check that her house was protected from electronic eavesdropping. In her bedroom drawer she kept a shop-bought bug finder that could pick up almost all over-the-counter listening devices, but she hadn't bothered using it for months now. If she was honest with herself, she hadn't expected Wise or any of his associates to be checking up on her. She and Nick simply hadn't unearthed anything that would make it seem worthwhile.

There was only one way to find out whether or not her suspicions were justified, but as she started up the stairs to get the bug finder, her mobile rang.

It was DS Weale. He asked her how she was doing.

'I've been better. Any news?'

'Only that I've managed to get hold of those phone records you wanted. I've just emailed them through to your personal account.'

'Thanks,' she said, suddenly feeling worried that she was being listened to and taking care to choose her words. 'And there's nothing on there that stands out?'

'It's just the numbers, I'm afraid. No names attached. You'll have to check them yourself.'

'Thanks. I appreciate what you've done.'

She raced up the stairs, aware that she needed to access her account fast to intercept his mail. If there was someone bugging her place, he may well have planted spyware on her PC capable of picking up every keystroke, which meant he'd have access to all her email.

Which meant that . . .

'I don't want anyone to find out I've helped you, ma'am,' continued Weale, sounding a little unsure of himself now. 'So if you could delete the email and not tell anyone about it . . .'

Reassuring him she wouldn't, she rang off and strode into her bedroom, switching on the light.

Then froze as she heard movement behind her.

CHAPTER 7

Tina didn't even have time to turn round, her assailant was that fast. An arm encircled her neck, dragging her backwards into a choking headlock.

Out of the corner of her eye she saw a gloved hand come into view at waist height, holding a syringe. She was still wearing her thick winter coat, so her assailant pulled it back to expose the top of her jeans-clad thigh and turned the syringe round in his fingers, ready to jab it into her leg. At the same time he increased the pressure on her neck so that she could barely breathe as she was pulled into his chest.

But Tina had been on the wrong end of violent assault too many times before, and she reacted fast, using her forearm to knock the hand holding the syringe out of the way, buying herself a precious second and a half. She kicked her legs up in the air and reached back with her free hand, grabbing her assailant between the legs and yanking his balls with all the strength she could muster.

He grunted with pain and his grip on her throat

slackened, allowing her to wriggle free. She felt him instinctively stab her with the syringe, but this time the coat got in the way, and although it hurt, she knew it hadn't broken the skin.

He grabbed at her but she managed to dive across her brand-new double bed, rolling off the other side and landing on her back on the carpet.

Now she saw her attacker properly for the first time. He was a big guy, at least six three, with broad weightlifter's shoulders and powerful arms. He was dressed in a dark hooded top with the hood pulled up, and a scarf covered the bottom half of his face. Above it, his skin was pale and his eyes narrow and cold.

And then a second man, dressed similarly but a lot smaller, came into the room. Now Tina knew she was in real trouble, because he was holding a nine-millimetre pistol which was raised in her direction. Her assailant began to move round the bed towards her, still holding the syringe.

'Come quietly, Tina Boyd,' said the gunman calmly in a foreign accent that she recognized immediately as Russian.

She was trapped. There was pepper spray in her coat pocket but she knew it would do no good against people like this. Not when one of them had a gun.

The man with the syringe was smiling now. She could see the laughter lines forming round his eyes. He was enjoying this – the bastard – and she wondered if he was the one who'd killed Nick Penny.

A potent cocktail of fear and rage surged through her and she sat up suddenly, leaned back, and yanked out one of the drawers from her bedside table. She grabbed something out of it and threw the drawer at the man with the syringe.

He swatted it away easily, the contents spilling over the bed. Underneath the scarf she could hear him chuckling – a deep, rumbling sound – as he regarded the weapon she'd grabbed: a simple handheld torch.

'Inject her,' snapped the gunman. 'Quickly.'

The man with the syringe loomed above her, a wall of muscle, then leaned down in order to haul her up, speaking a steady flow of Russian to her in excited, breathless tones.

Which was when Tina yanked the lid from the top of the torch, flicked a switch on at its base, and rammed the bulb-end hard against her assailant's leg, just above the knee. There was a loud, angry crackle as eight hundred thousand volts of electricity surged out of the torch, which also doubled as a stun gun. She'd bought it the previous year in Panama, just to make her feel safer at night, and this was the first time she'd used it in anger.

Tina held the button down to keep the current flowing, but for a couple of seconds her assailant didn't move, and she thought with a sudden panic that it might not be working. But then he let out an audible yelp and stumbled backwards, falling to the floor and juddering wildly as the shock surged through him.

'Move and I'll kill you!' shouted the gunman, pointing the gun at her head.

But Tina knew that if they intended to kill her so soon after they'd murdered Nick they were going to have to make it look natural, which meant there was no way he was going to pull the trigger. So she grabbed her bedside lamp and chucked it at his head, before jumping over the bed and making straight for him, pressing the button on the torch as she did so.

Unlike his colleague, the gunman knew the damage she could do with it and he reacted decisively, grabbing her wrist and twisting it painfully as they fell together into the wall.

Her wrist felt like it was going to break, and instinctively Tina dropped the torch, but she still had the presence of mind to get hold of his gun arm so that he wasn't pointing the weapon at her. Then, recovering as best she could, she drove her head into his face, kicked out at him, and turned and ran out of the door.

He was after her like a flash, and before she could get to the stairs he'd got hold of her again and was pushing her bodily towards the bathroom.

She fought back furiously, lashing out with her legs and trying to kick him in the shins, but he was a lot stronger than she'd expected and the momentum was with him. Together, they crashed through the door opposite and into the unlit bathroom, Tina in front.

That was when she saw that the bath was full,

and she realized immediately that they'd run it in order to drown her.

Digging her heels into the newly tiled floor, she tried to turn round, but he had her in a surprisingly tight bear hug, the gun gripped firmly in his right hand, tantalizingly close but impossible to grab. He might have been a lot smaller than his colleague but it was becoming abundantly clear to Tina that this man was the more dangerous of her two assailants.

As if to prove this, he suddenly let her go, and before she had a chance to react he punched her once, very hard and very accurately, in the kidneys, before grabbing her coat by the collar and pushing her into the tub.

The cold water sprang up to meet her and she instinctively held her breath as her head went under. Knowing she only had one chance, she managed to flip herself round in the water so she was on her back and facing upright. Her attacker's expression was determined as he clambered in on top of her, pushing all his weight into her midriff. A gloved hand covered her face like an immense spider, and she was pushed under again.

She struggled wildly beneath him, making no noise as she worked to conserve the air inside her and hold down her rising panic. She'd always had a fear of drowning, ever since she'd fallen in the river at the age of four, at an outdoor birthday party. Now those terrifying cold moments came back to haunt her as she felt the pressure begin to grow in her lungs, knowing she only had a matter of seconds before the big attacker with the needle recovered from the electric shock she'd given him and rejoined his colleague. Then she'd be finished.

She managed to slide a hand out from under her and in one movement grabbed the oyster-shaped china soap dish from the top left corner of the bath where she always kept it and slammed it into the side of her assailant's head.

He cried out and slipped slightly in the water, and though he didn't release his grip on her, it loosened enough for her to strike him again in the same place, and with a little more momentum, an increasing desperation in her movements as the urge to breathe grew ever stronger.

Grunting, he grabbed at the offending arm, but in doing so he shifted his weight from her midriff and she managed to break free from the water, knocking him to one side as she slid round in the tub, sending waves of water splashing over the side. Behind her, from the hallway, she could hear staggering footsteps as the big man returned to the fray.

'Bitch!' hissed the gunman, losing his cool and striking her in the cheek with the barrel of the gun as they struggled together in the water.

She felt a cut open up but adrenalin overrode the pain of the blow and she forced herself upright, still gasping for breath, and jabbed her middle finger into his eye, feeling its softness as she tried to poke it out. He yelled out in pain and she scrambled over him, yanking at the handle on the bathroom window. She couldn't remember whether or not the bloody thing was locked, but knew that if it was, then she was finished, because the big man was already at the bathroom door, a low foreign curse rumbling from his lips.

The window flew open and she started to climb out of it.

'Get the bitch!' hissed the gunman, grabbing her by the leg. 'Put the needle in her!'

The big man ran across the bathroom, syringe outstretched, but Tina could sense freedom now and she used her free leg to stamp savagely on the gunman's face. As he let go and threw up his hands to protect himself, she rolled out the open window, grabbing on to the windowsill as she fell, so that a second later she was hanging by her fingertips.

The big man thrust out a hand to grab her arm, his eyes narrow with rage, but before he could get hold of her Tina let go and fell the final eight feet on to the patio. A pain surged up her legs as she landed feet first before rolling on to her side, exhausted, bleeding from the cut to her face, but otherwise unhurt.

For a long moment the big man stared down at her as if unsure what to do; then Tina made the decision for him by letting loose a blood-curdling scream for help. Getting to her feet, she stumbled towards the fence that separated her from her next-door neighbours, the Carters. They were on holiday, sunning themselves in the Caribbean, but her attackers weren't to know that because the Carters liked to keep some of the lights on to deter would-be burglars, and there were also plenty of other houses nearby whose occupants would hear her.

She screamed again as she reached the fence and clambered on to it, feeling a delirious sense of freedom. She took a quick glance back, saw that the big man was no longer in the window, and jumped down the other side and into the Carters' garden, pausing to catch her breath. Seconds later she heard a car pull away on the road out front.

Still dripping with water and shivering from the cold, she stayed where she was for a full minute, panting steadily as she listened to the sound of the engine fade into the distance.

Only when it disappeared completely did she finally realize she was safe.

CHAPTER 8

Manila is everything that Hong Kong isn't. Flattened in the Second World War by both Japanese and American forces as they fought over it, it was rebuilt as an immense featureless sprawl of low-rise concrete and breeze-block buildings, interspersed with dirt-poor, overcrowded shanty towns where extended families live in filthy one-room huts with corrugated-iron roofs that look like they've been cobbled together with the contents of a rubbish dump, which in many cases they have. It's one of the most densely populated cities in the world, with some twenty million inhabitants living on top of one another, and a few very wealthy ones sitting behind the high-security gates of their plush, freshly painted condominiums.

It had been a long time since I was last here. Just over six years. And it hadn't changed much. Still dirty, noisy and with appalling traffic, even given the time of night. A chaotic jumble of cars, rickshaws, motorbikes, tricycles with sidecars, and brightly coloured converted buses called jeepneys clogged up the roads as my taxi from Ninoy

Aquino Airport crawled its way into the city. It was almost one a.m. when we finally turned into a comparatively quiet backstreet in Manila's Ermita district, not far from the bay. The taxi pulled up outside a small guesthouse, set back behind a wrought-iron fence topped with coils of barbed wire. The room had been booked in advance for two nights in the name of Robert Mercer, which was the identity Bertie Schagel had set me up with three years ago, and the one I always used now.

A couple of shabbily dressed hawkers appeared out of the shadows as I got out and paid the driver. One tried to sell me a fake Rolex, the other cigarettes, but I pushed past them, my sympathy for their plight tempered by my tiredness, and rang the bell on the gate.

I think I woke the owner up. It took him several minutes to answer the intercom, during which time the hawkers kept hassling me and ramming their wares in my face, and when he finally did, I had to repeat my name three times before he came out and unlocked the gate, scowling at all three of us, which I thought was a bit off, before ushering me inside.

My room was a small box with a single bed and a view of the back of the building next door. The air-con unit on the wall hummed and rattled angrily and a cockroach the size of a small stag beetle marched confidently up one of the walls.

The owner – a short, miserable man with a

droopy moustache, who looked like Charles Bronson – stood in the doorway. 'OK?' he demanded, as if daring me to say no.

'Sure,' I said.

There followed an awkward silence; I think he was waiting for a tip. I didn't give him one, figuring that showing me to my room was an essential part of his job description, and after a few seconds he got the message and left. When he'd gone, I stuck the chain across the door and threw my overnight bag on the bed, before putting on a pair of plastic gloves and reaching under the mattress.

The gun was there, as I'd been told it would be, and I took it out and inspected it. It was an M-1911 .45 pistol, with a suppressor attached, manufactured by a company called Firestorm, which I remembered as a local, Philippines-based company. It was a cheap but reliable and easy-to-use weapon that I'd used once before some years back, and the one I was holding now looked clean and new. There were two eight-round magazines taped to the side of the handle and I unloaded them both and checked the bullets – semi-jacketed hollowpoints, better known by their colloquial name 'dum-dums', designed to cause as much tissue damage as possible by expanding as they hit the soft flesh of the victim. If I took my target out at close range, he wouldn't have a chance. However, with a .45, the noise was likely to be pretty loud, even with the suppressor attached, which increased the risk several times over. A .22

would have been a better option, but you have to work with the tools you've got.

I reloaded a magazine, inserted it in the barrel, and racked the slide, before pointing the gun two-handed at the door. It felt reassuringly heavy in my hands, and I cocked the hammer and glared down the sights, my thumb resting on the safety catch, feeling that rush of power and invincibility that comes from being a trigger-pull away from being able to kill any man in the world.

I stood like that for a good ten seconds, and as I did so, the rush steadily dissipated and was replaced by a much more profound sense of disgust.

With a sigh, I uncocked the hammer and put the gun back where I'd found it, then opened the window and stared out into the gloom, wondering if this was what my life had really come to. Striking macho poses with real guns in cheap, grimy hotel rooms in lonely far-off cities, en route to commit murder on behalf of other people. I had a sudden urge then to be back home in Luang Prabang, sat out on my balcony and watching the sun go down beyond the Mekong River. I'd lived there for nearly three years now – a sleeping partner in a small travel agency and money exchange, catering to the intrepid backpackers who came there to enjoy the sights of the city and the magnificent natural scenery surrounding it.

I wasn't happy. If truth be told, I haven't been happy for a long time now, but I was settled at least and, as I'd told Schagel, I could just about scrape a living from the business, even without the hefty subsidies provided by my other, un-official job.

But, of course, Bertie Schagel was the constant dark cloud on my horizon. If I could be rid of him and his hold on me, then I could finally leave this grim, savage life behind and live in peace.

For the moment, though, I was going to have to do what I was being paid to do, even though I didn't like the sound of this job. You can't just go blundering in as Schagel wanted me to do. When you're targeting a person, you have to get to know them from afar, and that takes time. You need to follow them, learn their routines, the places they frequent and when they frequent them, while always looking for your opening. It's not a pleasant task, watching a living, breathing person going about his daily business, knowing that you're the one who's going to end it all for him – in fact, it's deeply depressing – but if you want to survive, it's also absolutely essential.

It's a lot harder than people think to take someone out without being seen. It took me over a week to work out how I was going to do it with the ex-pat businessman in Hong Kong. The problem was, he lived in an apartment complex with round-the-clock security on the door, and worked in a similarly secure office environment in downtown Hong Kong Island. There was nowhere to park a car outside either place, making it hard to remain inconspicuous while I kept an eye on things. Also, he always drove between the two locations on busy, very public roads, making it impossible to take him out en route.

In the end, with Bertie Schagel breathing down my neck demanding results, I'd had to resort, quite literally, to radical tactics. Early one evening on the ninth day of the job, before my target had returned from work, I called the local office of the *South China Morning Post* from a backstreet call box and, putting on a particularly dodgy and very non-specific Asian accent, told the man on the other end of the line that I represented a group called the Uighar Islamic Mujahideen and that we'd planted a bomb in the target's apartment building in retaliation for the Chinese government's brutal treatment of our Uighar brothers in Xinyiang Province. The bomb, I explained loudly and angrily, would explode in exactly fifteen minutes. Then I hung up.

Ten minutes later, I joined the large crowd of more than a hundred evacuated residents on the pavement outside the walls that surrounded the target's building. I stood among them in the darkness, keeping myself to myself and avoiding conversation, until an hour later, with the crowd now double that number, the police and fire brigade finally gave the building the all clear. I'd gambled that the security guards on the gates wouldn't look too closely at the people milling back in, but would be glad to have them no longer causing an obstruction on the street, and I was right. I walked right on through, but instead of going into the building itself I headed into the underground car park, donning a cap and glasses as I did so, and found a spot out of sight behind a pillar in a corner by the rubbish bins. Then it was simply a matter of waiting.

He drove his black Porsche Boxster into the car park at just after nine p.m. – a little later than his usual time for arriving home. The place was empty, as I'd calculated, and as he manoeuvred into his spot I strode over to the Boxster's passenger side, my footsteps muffled by the deep rumble of its engine, pulled open the door and, leaning inside, shot him twice in the face before he'd had a chance to turn off the ignition.

I still remember the look of shock on his face – the sure knowledge carved all over it that he was about to die – and the flash of doubt that I'd felt as I pulled the trigger. When I walked away, I'd told myself – as I always do – that this man was an embezzler, a fraudster who'd defrauded the wrong people, and he was simply paying for his sins.

But the point is, I'd taken my time on the job and, harsh as it might sound, that was why I'd been successful. Now I had a maximum of twelve hours, and in a place like Manila it wasn't going to be easy.

I shut the window and sat down on the bed, suddenly feeling exhausted. At the very least I needed a couple of hours' shut-eye before I got to work. But as I started to strip off, a loud, shrill ring came from my trouser pocket. It was the iPhone Schagel had given to me.

'Have you arrived?' he asked curtly.

'I have,' I answered, just as curtly. 'I'm in the hotel room.'

'And the box?' he said, using our standard code word for a gun. 'Is that all to your satisfaction?'

I said it was.

'Then I have some good news. The address of our mutual friend is only six hundred metres from where you are. In the maps section of the phone, you will see how to get there. You might want to go there now.'

'I don't think it's going to be as easy as that,' I said, beginning to get tired of this conversation.

'On the contrary. I think it's going to be very easy. Have a look under the pillow on your bed.'

I did as he instructed and saw a key ring with three very new keys attached to it lying on the mattress. 'Are they what I think they're for?'

'Absolutely. One opens his main gate, the other two open his front door. See, we've made it very easy for you, my friend. All you have to do now is turn up. We want to make it look like a break-in, though. So do a bit of work on the front door when you've finished, and then call me.' And with that, he hung up.

I put the phone back in my pocket and sat still for a few minutes, thinking that this was going to be a lot easier than I thought. But, easy or not, I wasn't going to do it without some sleep first. Both Schagel and the target would simply have to wait.

I set the alarm for five a.m., stripped off and lay back on the bed, shutting my eyes and banishing all the evils of the world from my thoughts – a process that should have taken a man like me a lot longer than it did.

As it turned out, I was asleep in seconds.

CHAPTER 9

It was ten minutes before Tina finally plucked up the courage to go back inside her house. No one had responded to her screams, but then it was a wet, windy evening and people would have had their TVs on. In the end, it hadn't mattered. The men who'd been sent to kill her had failed, and she was thankful for that. But she also knew that she couldn't stay at home that night. It was too dangerous. Her would-be assassins weren't just going to give up. The knowledge that she was now a direct target scared her too. Without any witnesses to what had happened, it was going to be hard to secure any protection from her colleagues.

But she was also excited, because it had to mean that Nick Penny had discovered something significant.

Still wet and shivering, she double-locked the front door behind her and put the chain across it before hurrying through to the kitchen. She laid a long carving knife on the table beside her and switched on her laptop. Her assailants might well have bugged her home PC – something that was notoriously easy to do with spyware – but she didn't think they'd have had the chance to do anything to her laptop since she took it with her everywhere. But if they had access to her email addresses then she needed to move quickly before they had a chance to intercept the message from DS Weale.

Signing into her personal hotmail account, she was pleased to see that his message was still there, along with a single Word document attached. She immediately downloaded the attachment and saved it to the USB stick she always kept with her, before deleting the message so there'd be no trace of it. After that, she allowed herself the luxury of a two-minute hot shower to banish the worst of the cold. Finally, she hurried through the house, putting some essentials – passport, change of clothes, wash bag, laptop, the torch/stun gun – into an overnight bag, knowing that she might be gone some time.

She'd hoped what had happened wouldn't put her off this place. It was a similar assault in her old apartment that had led to her move here. But when she'd opened the spare-room door and seen what they'd done with the rocking chair she'd bought from the antique shop in the main street a few weeks before – the one she liked to sit in at night sometimes, looking out across the village – she'd almost been sick. They'd placed it next to the bed, and there were ropes attached to the legs and arms, while on the floor beside it were two full, unopened bottles of cheap red wine and a plastic funnel.

Bastards. Their plan had been to drug her, tie her to the chair, and force-feed her the alcohol through the funnel. By the time they finished she'd have been so drunk that she wouldn't have been able to resist as they stripped her naked and drowned her in the bath. No one would have suspected anything either. Tina had a history of alcoholism, had been diagnosed with stress on more than one occasion, and was prone to erratic behaviour. It wasn't something to be proud of, but that was the way it was. The conclusion her colleagues would clearly have come to was that she'd been sent over the edge by the suicide of the man she'd been having an affair with. No one would have checked for needle marks on her skin, and without any obvious injuries it would look like she'd simply chosen to go the same way. End of story.

The ruthless clear thinking her adversaries were obviously capable of was terrifying, but then Paul Wise had the money to pay for the best. She'd been lucky tonight, just as she'd been lucky in the past, but as she stood staring at the rocking chair, knowing that she would never be able to sit in it again, she was struck by the unwelcome fact that some time soon her luck was going to run out.

Either she got Paul Wise, or he was going to get her. It was that simple.

After returning to her room to grab the bug

83

finder from among the contents of the drawer that she'd chucked at her largest assailant, she pulled the overnight bag over her shoulder and left the house, looking both ways down the quiet street, in case her attackers were still around somewhere.

But the street was empty. The lights from the local pub, the Carpenter's Arms, shone brightly out of the darkness, the sign swinging in the cold February wind.

Her car, a black Ford Focus, was parked in front of the house and she ran the bug finder over it, looking to pick up any tracking devices they'd placed on the bodywork. The bug finder wasn't foolproof by any means, and wouldn't have been able to pick up an advanced device, but she didn't think they'd've had time to plant anything like that.

When it didn't buzz, Tina decided she was safe enough and got in the Focus. There were three roads leading out of the village, but only one led directly to the M25, junction 22, and if the two men who'd attacked her had decided to hang around, they'd be waiting for her there. So she drove in the opposite direction, heading down silent, hedgerow-lined B-roads that seemed to belong to another, altogether more innocent world.

And, as she lit a cigarette and took a long, hard drag, she felt a weird but intense feeling of euphoria – the kind she sometimes used to get from a few good hits of vodka. She'd almost died only minutes ago, yet the shock that she knew would have to come eventually was nowhere to be seen, and she almost wanted to laugh out loud because, by God, she'd survived. They'd tried to kill her and she'd survived.

She thought of that evil little runt Paul Wise, wondered how he'd be feeling when he found out that she was still standing, then pointed her cigarette at the bruised but unbowed reflection in the rear-view mirror.

'I'm coming for you,' she said out loud. 'This time I'm coming for you.'

CHAPTER 10

The man known by those who hired his services simply as Nargen picked up the payphone and waited while the man on the other end spoke.

'Is this line secure?' demanded the caller.

'Yes. It's a public phone, and I've swept the booth for bugs. There are none.'

'Good. What is the status of our situation?'

'Target One is dealt with,' answered Nargen, choosing his words carefully. 'The police officer in charge of the case has accepted that he took his own life. However, there might be a complication.'

The voice at the other end was impatient. 'What kind of complication?'

'Target Two.'

'What about her?'

'We were unable to carry out the termination. And our cover has been compromised.'

'What happened?'

'We waited for her at her house. We almost had her but she managed to get away.'

'You mean you failed.'

'The instructions we were given meant that it was a very difficult task,' Nargen countered defensively.

'That's why I chose you to perform it,' said the caller. 'You often boast of your reputation, and you charge very highly for your services because of it. Therefore, I do not expect failure. Nor will I tolerate it. Where is she now?'

'We don't know. We were forced to abort the operation.'

The caller cursed loudly. 'This is not good. She knows too much.'

'Not necessarily,' said Nargen. 'We left a listening device in the target's office. It picked up a conversation she had with the investigating officer. All she has are suspicions.'

'So she has no way of finding out what Target One knew?'

'We made him give us all the information he had. He deleted all the files on his laptop while I watched. He also gave me his back-up tapes and the phone he'd been using to make his calls to her. They are destroyed now, but Target Two knows about the phone, and has asked the investigating officer for the records of the calls made and received on it – a request he has agreed to.'

'Then you need to find her. And fast. Those are the orders. Do you understand?'

'I do. My associate is working on it.'

'Good. Keep me informed of progress.'

The caller cut the connection, and Nargen

replaced the receiver, before crossing the road to the hired Lexus.

In the passenger seat, his associate sat hunched over a laptop, a look of painful concentration on his face. Nargen had got him to run a location trace on the mobile number they had for Tina Boyd, using a specialist UK-based website that promised to give the current location of any mobile phone in the UK – a process known as reverse look-up, which only required the number itself.

Tumanov had the powerful build and the arrogant good looks of a young Dolph Lundgren; it was he who'd been standing with the knife outside Nick Penny's family home the previous night. Everything Nargen had told the journalist, Penny, about Tumanov was true. He wouldn't have hesitated to kill Penny's wife and children one by one. After all, he'd done such things, and worse, in Chechnya while serving as a paratrooper there, and it was known in the tight-knit circles they moved in that he enjoyed killing in a way that was sometimes considered unhealthy. Usually Nargen would have avoided such a man, but Tumanov was also a professional who could be relied on to carry out the kinds of tasks that other men would have baulked at.

'He's not pleased,' said Nargen, getting back in the driving seat. 'How far have you got?'

'I'm just waiting for them to come back to me with the trace,' Tumanov grunted.

Then, as Nargen switched on the engine and

pulled away from the kerb, Tumanov smiled. 'Got it,' he said triumphantly. 'She's on the move.' He stretched his bulk in the seat and lifted up his immense hands, slowly clenching and unclenching them. 'I want to see that bitch die.'

Nargen chuckled. 'You'll have your chance soon enough.'

CHAPTER 11

Chivas Regal Amora owed his first two names both to his father's love of whiskey and to the fact that by the time he came along, the youngest of thirteen children, the family had long since run out of preferable alternatives. Brought up dirt-poor, Chivas had had to work his way out of the ghetto the hard way. Now he drove a truck that he part-owned with his wife's two brothers, and was finally making ends meet.

But money was still tight. Chivas had seven children of his own to feed, and he had to split the profits and the jobs three ways, which was why when Benny Magsino had approached him with the business proposition, he'd said yes immediately. Benny was the foreman at a warehouse in Manila docks that Chivas and his partners regularly took deliveries from, and what he was offering seemed very simple.

All Chivas had to do was turn up at the warehouse and make one of his usual pick-ups – in this case, six pallets of materials for a building company he often delivered to in Angeles City. The only difference was that one of the boxes in the final pallet to go on the truck would be marked with a red cross, and Chivas's instructions were to drop this box off en route. He'd then be given another identical box and would continue with the delivery. For this small diversion, he was going to be paid twenty thousand pesos – a huge sum of money for someone in his position.

Chivas was no one's fool. He knew that whatever was in the box had to be illegal – drugs, or something similar. But that wasn't his concern. He considered himself an honest man and a good Catholic, but his first responsibility was to his family, and this money would help them greatly.

However, as he turned off the main road and began heading down a winding, dusty backstreet, the uneven, shoddy buildings of a shanty town on one side, and a high fence topped with barbed wire on the other, Chivas began to grow nervous. His truck, though far from new, stood out in a place like this.

The fence to the right ended, giving way to a stretch of garbage-strewn wasteland that sloped down to an ink-black river, beyond which were the broken concrete and corrugated-iron buildings of another shanty town. Even though it was four in the morning, a handful of ghostly figures, illuminated by the head torches they wore, moved in the darkness among the garbage hills, carrying bags in which they collected anything of value. Otherwise all was silent.

Ignoring the stench of rubbish and human waste

that seeped into the truck, and which reminded him of the grinding poverty he too had grown up in, Chivas drove slowly along the pothole-scarred track until he came to a turning next to a burnt-out shell of a building that looked like it might have been a factory once. A single dim light glowed in one of the first-floor windows.

This was the place.

Chivas stopped the truck and got out, looking round warily, wishing he was home with his family, fast asleep in bed, and telling himself that he would be as soon as he was finished here. And twenty thousand pesos richer too.

Forcing down his fear, he walked round to the back of the truck and unlocked the rear doors. The box with the red cross marked on it was on the top row of the nearest pallet, placed there deliberately for easy removal. Chivas took down his trolley, then climbed inside and used his pocket knife to cut the pallet's strapping. Carefully, he manoeuvred the box free. It felt heavy, but not excessively so, and with a grunt of exertion he got it first to the floor of the truck, and then, with a final heave, on to the trolley.

Looking inside the box was not an option. Chivas was as curious as the next man, and he couldn't deny that he was interested to know what it was he was handling, but he was also sensible, and didn't want to do anything that would jeopardize his twenty thousand pesos. So he did as he'd been instructed and, having relocked the truck doors, he wheeled the trolley round the side of the building, conscious of the loud noise it was making over the potholed ground.

A high cement wall, cracked and graffiti-strewn, bordered the rear, and in the middle of it was an open double gate. Taking a deep breath to suppress his nerves, Chivas wheeled his cargo through the gate and into an empty courtyard that was shrouded in darkness. Rats scuttled about in the shadows, darting among the piles of garbage and broken glass, but they appeared to be the only occupants.

Squinting in the gloom, Chivas spotted an identical box to the one he was wheeling propped up against the far wall. Such was his hurry to do the swap and get the hell out of there that when he parked his trolley next to it, his own box toppled over and hit the ground with a loud bang before he could grab hold of it.

That was when he heard a man curse in English from somewhere in the shadows behind him. 'Jesus Christ!'

Chivas jumped at the intrusion and only just managed to stifle an embarrassingly frightened yelp.

'Don't turn round,' hissed the man. He sounded American or English.

Chivas stood still, suddenly scared that he'd destroyed whatever it was that was in the box. 'I didn't mean to do nothing, boss . . .'

'Shut up. Leave the box there and take the other

one. Count to ten, then turn round and leave. I have a gun. If you look at me, I will kill you. Do you understand?'

'Sure, boss.'

'You didn't look inside, did you?'

Chivas shook his head urgently. 'No, boss. I've just taken it out now. See, it's still sealed.'

'Good. Now get moving. And I repeat: do not look at me.'

Chivas didn't need telling twice. The stranger had spooked him so much he'd almost wet his pants, so he shoved the new box on to his trolley and backed out of the gate as fast as he could, eyes fixed firmly to the ground as he silently prayed that the stranger wouldn't change his mind and put a bullet in him.

Barely a minute later, and with relief surging through him, he climbed back into the cab, having literally flung the new box in the back of the truck. He was already thinking about those twenty thousand pesos in his hand, and didn't hear the movement behind him until it was far too late, and the knife was already being drawn slowly and deeply across his throat.

His last thought as he saw his own blood-spray hosing across the windscreen wasn't about his children, his wife Mariel, his truck, or even his twenty thousand pesos.

It was what could possibly be in that box, and why he'd had to die because of it.

CHAPTER 12

Tina took another long look in her rearview mirror before coming to a halt, but the road behind her was empty, and she was certain she hadn't been followed. Her journey had covered a succession of back roads, several of them little more than tracks, and there was no way that she wouldn't have spotted a pursuing vehicle. Even so, she parked the car more than two hundred yards down the road from her parents' place, just to be on the safe side. It had taken her three hours to get here, almost twice as long as usual. She'd had to stop at one point as the shock of what had happened took hold, and had sat shivering in the driver's seat for ten minutes, fighting back the tears, an unlit cigarette in her hand, as the realization of how close she'd just come to dying washed over her, before finally pulling herself together and carrying on.

The clock on the dashboard read 9.31 as she cut the engine and got out of the car. She took a couple of deep breaths and started up the street.

She'd moved with her family to this quiet, tree-lined street on the edge of Winchester when she was just seven years old. Both her primary and secondary schools had been easy walks away, and she always felt happy coming back, because it felt so familiar and reminded her of the happy, easy days of childhood.

She heard a car turning into the road behind her and stiffened. The torch was in her coat pocket, but it was no longer a weapon of surprise, and she wasn't sure she had the strength for another fight.

A black Mercedes SUV rumbled slowly past and she looked as casually as possible inside, but the windows were blacked out and she couldn't see the driver. She cursed herself. The last thing she needed was to bring the demons from her own life into those of her parents.

But then the SUV turned into a driveway a few doors further up, and an attractive woman in her late thirties jumped out and flicked back her long, curly hair ostentatiously, before striding up to the front door of the house and letting herself in.

Tina sighed and told herself to stop being so paranoid. She'd taken every precaution possible, and there was no way her assailants would be able to track her down to here. There was nothing in her own home with her parents' address on it, and Boyd was too common a name to be of any use to anyone intent on finding her. Even so, she still looked round several times, checking those few cars parked on the street for occupants, before opening the gate to her family home.

Her mother was at the door in seconds. An older, slightly darker version of Tina, courtesy of some Spanish blood a couple of generations back, she looked fantastically fit and well for sixty-one, and Tina often hoped she'd look half as good as her mum at her age. She couldn't see it happening, though. Not the way her life was going. Making thirty-four was going to be challenge enough.

'Tina, how lovely to see you, darling,' said her mother with a huge smile, giving her a hug that was surprisingly painful after what had happened earlier. She took a step back and suddenly frowned. 'My God, what's happened to your hair?'

'I had it cut, Mum. People sometimes do that.'

'And that colour. You look . . .' She pulled a face. 'Well, you look like a man, Tina. You've got lovely hair. Why did you have to do that to it?'

'I fancied a change,' said Tina, thinking she should have expected this kind of reaction. She'd decided on a whim a few weeks earlier to have her hair cut ultra-short and bleached blonde, and whatever her mum might have thought, she liked her new look. It went with the new, leaner body she'd been working on with her new four-times-a-week gym regime – something that had stood her in good stead earlier that evening.

'And what's happened to your face?' continued her mother, noticing the cut and swelling on Tina's cheekbone where she'd been hit with the butt of the gun.

'It's nothing. I had a bit of an argument with a suspect, that's all.'

'It doesn't look like nothing,' she said, ushering Tina inside and closing the door. 'You know, I don't know why you do that job, darling, I really don't. You've had so many bad things happen to you. Why don't you think about doing something else? You've got a degree, a good one too. You could do anything.'

Tina smiled and said she'd think about it. Her mother's concern was hardly surprising, given all she'd been through in the past few years. As well as enduring the deaths of a number of people close to her, she'd also been shot twice in the line of duty; shot at by suspects a few more times than that; even kidnapped. She was therefore a source of constant worry to her staunchly middle-class suburban family, utterly unused to the violence that lurked on the streets of the capital. Her father was the retired finance director of an insurance company; her mother had been a midwife, then a housewife; her older brother, Phil, was a married quantity surveyor with his own business and two small children. All lived the kind of pleasant, uneventful lives that would have driven Tina insane with boredom, but she'd given up trying to tell any of them that.

And she was secretly pleased that she had people who cared for her so much.

'Look who's here, Frank,' said her mother as they walked into the lounge.

Her father got up from the sofa where he'd been watching golf on his new plasma TV. He and her mother tended to spend the evenings apart watching TV. in separate rooms, which seemed somewhat bizarre to Tina but appeared to suit them just fine.

He gave her a smile that couldn't quite hide the concern, and took her in his arms, holding her there for a few seconds longer than usual. Although not as overtly emotional as her mother, Tina knew he worried about her just as much. They'd always been close, and it felt good to have him hold her now.

'Good to see you, love,' he said. Tina sensed that he'd seen the state of her face but had decided to make no comment, though he nodded approvingly at her hair. 'To what do we owe the pleasure?'

'Just thought I'd pay a visit,' she answered, taking a seat in one of the armchairs and trying to look as natural as possible. It was hard being back in the comfort of the family home, with the same old photos on the walls of happier childhood times, knowing that only three or so hours earlier a man she'd never seen before had tried to drown her in her own bath, and come very close to being successful.

She had a sudden, intense urge for a real drink. To grab hold of a huge glass of silky Rioja – the sort she used to buy when she was feeling flush – and gulp it down in one fell swoop, allowing that sweet, drifting feeling of lightheadedness to wash away all her troubles. She hadn't been to an AA meeting for more than a week now, and felt her mouth watering at the prospect of booze. But her parents knew about the problem she'd carried around for much of the last six years – it had been well enough documented – so she felt safer knowing she wouldn't be able to relent here.

Instead, her mum offered her a cup of tea and Tina spent the next fifteen minutes chatting to them – not about the job, a subject her parents both tended to avoid, but about neutral subjects: the neighbours; her brother's family; her dad's golf handicap. Such conversation should have been comforting, but she found it difficult to concentrate. There was too much else to think about – most importantly: what was it that Nick Penny had discovered before he died? And why did his killers want her dead as well when she had nothing that could incriminate Paul Wise? These were questions that were going to need answering.

When a welcome pause broke in her mother's talking, Tina grabbed her laptop and asked her father if she could use his printer. Five minutes later she was sitting at the desk in his study, poring over hard copies of Nick Penny's phone records on the dedicated number he'd used for their investigation.

In the earlier bills, there were plenty of calls, including many to overseas numbers, where Wise's various holding companies held countless secret bank accounts. Wise had long been suspected of laundering money from the illicit businesses he was involved in – most notably drug smuggling, people trafficking and prostitution. She knew Nick had drawn a blank at every turn and, as she sat there, remembering his initial gritty determination to bring Wise to justice (a determination she'd found so attractive at the time), it struck her how naive they'd both been, thinking that they could ever find evidence where everyone else had failed.

As if to prove her point, the calls had gradually thinned out as the months passed, and the overseas ones had disappeared altogether. Nick had never let on to Tina that his determination was flagging, but it must have been hard to keep up his motivation as the doors to success had closed one after another.

In the week before she'd last spoken to him, he'd only made four calls on the phone, and had received none. Three were to UK-based mobiles, all of which he'd called before. The other was to a central London landline number, again one he'd called a number of times before. Nothing stood out.

She took a deep breath as she came to the calls for the last seven days, the crucial ones during which he must have made the discovery that had led to his death. He'd made eight calls and received two.

The last call he'd made had been to Tina's own mobile number the previous day at 4.45 p.m. Only hours, possibly even minutes, before he'd died.

She frowned. She didn't remember getting a missed call from him, although she'd been in a meeting for much of the previous afternoon and had had the phone off for its duration. Had he intended to tell her something? She pulled out her phone now, went back through the missed calls page, and sure enough, there it was.

'Jesus,' she whispered, surprised she'd missed it. But then she'd had half a dozen missed calls during that meeting, including three from her reluctant, now former, witness Gemma Hanson.

She shook her head sadly, wondering what it was he'd wanted to say, and knowing that she'd probably never know now, then pushed her emotions to one side and looked at his other calls. Three of the ones he'd made had been to the same number. It was a foreign mobile with the prefix +855, which was one she didn't recognize. Straight away, she noticed that two of the calls had lasted over ten minutes, and she felt that familiar excitement that came from stumbling on something interesting.

She Googled the +855 prefix, seeing immediately that it was from Cambodia. She tried to remember if Paul Wise had any connections there, but nothing came to mind.

According to the world clock on her phone, Cambodia was seven hours ahead, which made it five in the morning. Pretty damn early for a Saturday, but worth a try.

Her call was answered on about the tenth ring

by a man talking in the local language. His tone was brusque and he sounded as if he was some kind of official.

Tina asked him if he spoke English.

'Yes,' he answered stiffly. 'You are through to the Phnom Penh Police, Detective Bureau. Who is speaking please?'

'My name's Detective Inspector Tina Boyd from London's Metropolitan Police.' She waited while he wrote this information down before continuing. 'I am following up on a number of calls made by a UK-based journalist to this number on Monday and Tuesday of this week. His name was Nicholas, or Nick, Penny.'

'This is the main switchboard number for the Detective Bureau. Do you know what it was he wanted?'

Tina chose her words carefully, wanting to make clear the importance of the call. 'I'm afraid not. But I'm sorry to have to tell you that he was murdered here in the UK yesterday, and we're extremely interested in finding out whether it had anything to do with the calls he made to you.'

If this information fazed the officer, he didn't show it. 'I will see what I can find out, but we are a big department, and it is very early in the morning here.'

'I understand that. Anything you can do would be hugely appreciated by the British police.'

Tina was put on hold. But when the man finally came back on the line five minutes later, it was obvious he hadn't found anything out. 'I will circulate a memo and see if anyone remembers speaking to him, but that is all I can do. Do you have a number that you can be reached on?'

Tina gave him her mobile number, then took his name and thanked him for his time before hanging up. She wondered what Nick could possibly have wanted to talk to the Cambodian police about, and whether he'd actually got through to anybody who'd helped him.

He'd also made two calls to different numbers with the prefix +63 – another country code she didn't recognize. One had been to a landline, the other a mobile number. He'd also received a call from the mobile lasting more than twenty minutes. All three had been made at various points on Tuesday morning, just a couple of days before he'd died.

A quick search revealed that +63 belonged to the Philippines. Once again, off the top of her head Tina couldn't recall Wise having any business links there either, and for the first time it struck her that this might not have anything to do with him.

But if it hadn't been to do with Wise, then why had she too been targeted? It didn't make sense. He had to be behind this somehow.

Before she called the Philippines, she studied the only other number that Penny had called that week, which was also a number that had been used to call him. It was a UK-based mobile, which looked vaguely familiar, so she reckoned its owner was someone he'd been in contact with before. Whoever it was had also been the last person to call Penny before his number went out of service, at 11.30 on the morning he'd died.

Taking a deep breath, she punched in the number now.

'Satnam Singh,' said a well-educated voice at the other end after barely a ring.

Recognizing the name as someone Nick had mentioned before, Tina introduced herself, apologized for the time, and asked if he'd heard about what had happened.

'Yes,' Singh replied. 'I heard this morning. We worked together at the *New Statesman* a few years back. It's terrible news. I understand you were working with him on the Paul Wise case.'

'I was,' she answered, hoping that Nick hadn't mentioned anything to him about their affair. 'Although he was the one doing most of the work.'

'And do you think it was suicide?'

'No, I don't.'

'Interesting. Why not?'

Tina had no desire to get into a lengthy conversation with a journalist she'd never met, so she said that right now it was nothing more than a hunch.

'I don't think it was suicide, either,' said Singh. 'I spoke to Nick twice this week and both times he sounded fine. No sign at all that he was about to take his own life.'

'Can I ask what it was you spoke about?'

'Is this an official interview?' he asked guardedly.

'No. Nothing I've been doing on the Paul Wise case has been official, so this is just between us.'

'And is this line secure?'

'It is, I promise.'

'OK. Nick rang me on Monday night and asked me if I could find out if Paul Wise had travelled to certain countries on certain dates in the past.'

'And why did he think you'd have that information?'

'Because my brother works for a company that stores the PNR databases for a number of large airlines.'

'What's a PNR?'

'It stands for passenger number record, and it's a record in the database of an airline's computer reservation system that contains the itinerary of the passenger. Because of the size of the databases, they tend to be hosted by specialist companies like my brother's rather than on the airline's own systems. I'd got information about passenger manifests from him several years ago when I was researching a story, which is how Nick knew about the connection.'

'And I'm assuming your brother's not allowed to give out that information?'

'Correct. But he has access to it, and on that occasion he did it as a once-in-a-lifetime favour to me.'

'And this time?'

Singh sighed. 'Nick was desperate. He genuinely believed he was on to something that might help in his libel defence against Wise. Under those circumstances, and considering he'd always been a good friend of mine, it was difficult to turn him down.'

'What was it he was so interested in?'

'Whether Wise had travelled to Cambodia and the Philippines on certain, different dates. One was in 2007, the other in 2008.'

Tina felt her heart begin to pound as she asked her final question. 'And did he?'

'Yes, he did.'

Between 12 and 18 September 2007, Paul Wise had been in Cambodia, and between 11 and 26 June 2008, he'd been in the Philippines. That was the extent of the information Satnam Singh had given to Nick Penny. According to Singh, they hadn't discussed what Nick had needed it for. All Singh knew was that he'd needed it, and urgently.

Tina thanked him for his help, then called the Philippines landline number on Nick's bill. It immediately went to automatic message, telling the caller that he or she was through to the *Manila Post*, that the main offices were currently closed, and giving another number that could be called twenty-four hours a day to report a story.

Tina hung up. It was a quarter past six in the morning in the Philippines, and for a moment she considered calling the mobile, but stopped herself.

She had no idea who the number belonged to, and if she called it this early, the person on the other end might be reluctant to cooperate.

Instead, she fed the digits of the number into the Google search box, and pressed Enter.

And hit the jackpot.

A company called Aztech Direct Rentals came up. Beneath it was a short advert for a vacation apartment to rent in a place called Anilao. The owner was listed as a Mr Pat O'Riordan, a name that was unfamiliar to Tina. Next to it was the mobile number from Nick Penny's phone records.

She wrote down the information on the screen, and Googled the name Pat O'Riordan.

A long list of results came up on her laptop screen, and as she ran her eye down them she saw that there was a Pat O'Riordan, now retired, who manufactured high-quality concert whistles, whatever they were; another who was a tax accountant; nine who were listed on Linkedin, the business directory—

She froze. There it was, near the bottom. What she was looking for.

She double-clicked and started reading, a slow coldness creeping up her spine.

Because she now knew exactly why they'd had to kill Nick Penny.

CHAPTER 13

It was the deep grey hour before dawn when I arrived at the address I'd been given, a compact-looking two-storey detached house set back behind thick foliage and a high stone wall topped with a line of rusting razor wire. Situated about halfway down a narrow residential back-street, it looked like it had seen better days.

The house was dark and the street silent as I stopped at a solid iron gate. It had a sign on it which stated that the property was protected by a company called AAA Emergency Response Inc, which was no great worry since all it meant was that if my target got a chance to call them (which he wouldn't), there was still a good five minutes minimum before they could get to the house, by which time I'd be long gone.

Tipping the brim of my baseball cap down so that it better obscured my face – just in case there was a hidden camera somewhere – I slipped on plastic gloves then, having found the key I was looking for, very slowly opened the gate. Even so, it still squeaked loudly.

I stepped inside, shutting the gate behind me,

and slipped the gun from beneath the jacket I was wearing, screwing on the suppressor. I was in a small, secluded garden, well stocked with a variety of tropical plants. Sweet-smelling bougainvillea climbed up the walls of the house, and a table and chairs were arranged on a patio in front of locked French windows. The place looked like something out of the colonial era, and it struck me as I crept over to the front door, admiring the wooden shutters on the window, that they'd made a real effort with this place, and that if I had to live in Manila, I'd choose somewhere like this.

With the buildings next to it a good thirty feet away on either side, it also made it perfect for an assassination, since it was highly unlikely anyone would hear any shots.

I looked at my watch. 6.16. I'd managed to grab a few hours' sleep, and was feeling alert if not refreshed. Although I'd had the phone on silent, I had two missed calls from Schagel. One at 3.30, the other an hour later. Which wasn't like him at all. Calling me when I was on a job was both dangerous – just in case the phone went off at an inopportune moment – and a sign of impatience that I wouldn't have expected from a consummate pro like Schagel. It made me uneasy.

Checking once again that the phone was on silent, I used the two other keys on the ring to open the front door, and was pleased to see that the target hadn't deadbolted it from the inside. It was clear that Schagel was right, and he wasn't expecting trouble. Either that or he was very careless.

I moved through the hallway in the direction of the staircase, trying hard but without success to ignore the photos on the walls. They were family pictures, featuring the silver-haired man I was here to shoot, and an attractive, middle-aged Filipina woman, who I assumed was his wife. There were also two kids. Both boys. In some they were very young, but in the more recent ones they were adults in their early twenties. It crossed my mind that one or both of them might be at home, but I immediately dismissed the thought. Schagel would have known, and he would have told me. I might not have liked the guy but I trusted his information absolutely.

I didn't like the idea of killing a man in his own home. I liked the idea of killing his wife there even less. Together in the marital bed. It was all too personal, because it showed me exactly what I was destroying. Not just two lives. But their whole, shared history as well.

I'd only killed people in their homes twice before, and both occasions were a long time ago. Plus, my victims had been brutal, sick killers themselves and had deserved everything that was coming to them. But this time . . . This time the intended victim was a journalist, for Christ's sake. He'd dug something up on one of Schagel's clients, and now he was being made to pay. As Schagel had pointed out, more journalists die in

111

the Philippines than any other country in the world, and I doubted if very many of them were corrupt.

I could feel the doubts coming on, and I had to work hard to force them aside, something I was sadly getting better at as my body count grew.

But the stakes were higher this time. Do this, and Schagel had hinted that there might be a chance he'd let me retire and live out my life in my own secluded corner of the world, never hurting another human being again.

I mounted the stairs, gun out in front of me, listening hard to the silence, conscious of every squeak of the wooden steps.

And then, as I reached the top and found myself on a landing with doors to either side of me and too many photos on the walls, I heard it. Coming from the room at the end.

The sound of a mobile phone ringing.

I heard movement behind the door, someone climbing out of bed, cursing sleepily.

Now was the time. Do it now, I told myself, and I could be out again in two minutes. Back at the hotel in ten.

There's never any point in putting off the inevitable. It's one of the most valuable lessons I've learned over the years.

So I didn't. Taking deep, steady breaths, I yanked open the door in one movement.

The target, Patrick O'Riordan, was standing next to the bed. Stark naked, his silver hair all over the place, he was holding his trousers and rifling through the pockets, hunting for the mobile phone. The bed was empty.

He turned round as I raised the gun and his eyes widened. He looked so damn vulnerable, so shocked that his life had come to this sudden, abrupt point, that when he opened his mouth to speak, no words came out. His lips simply moved, and small burbling sounds came from between them. I could see first the fear, then the resignation in his eyes. And finally that first glint of hope as he realized I was hesitating.

The phone stopped ringing.

I pulled the trigger, twice, the gun kicking in my hand as he staggered backwards, hit both times in the chest. Then he fell back against the window, and slid slowly down it to the floor, his mouth filling with blood. And all the while he was staring at me as if he couldn't believe how cruel I had been.

Unable to stand the accusation in his stare, I took four steps over to him, lowered the gun and, still trying to avoid those eyes, shot him a final time in the top of the head from point-blank range.

He grunted once and slid down on to his side, his eyes closed. I didn't bother feeling for a pulse. Instead, I turned away and made for the door.

Which was when I heard the sound of a flushing toilet coming from the other end of the landing.

CHAPTER 14

I just had time to close the door and get behind it. Keeping my breathing low and even, I listened as the footsteps came closer, the pace of their owner too casual for her to have heard anything.

Except when the door opened and the figure came inside, I saw that the her was actually a him, and a young one too. Probably no more than twenty, at most. Like O'Riordan, he was stark naked, except his body was a lot more toned, the ravages of age still yet to catch up with him.

If they ever did.

The kid, a local Filipino, gasped as he saw what had happened to his lover, and put a hand dramatically to his lips. He had his back to me but I could see him tense as he sensed my presence.

It was decision time.

The first rule of contract killing is always get rid of witnesses if it's at all possible. It was perfectly possible now. I was already pointing the gun at him, and the fact that I'd pulled the trigger only seconds before made it a lot easier to do so again.

But I didn't. Instead I told him not to turn round, trying my best to disguise my voice.

'What have you done to him?' he said, his voice cracking with emotion. Even though I couldn't see his face, I could tell he was silently weeping. It was the way his shoulders were shaking. 'Why did you hurt him?'

'If you want to get out of here alive, you'll do what I say. Get on your knees and put your hands behind your head. I'm going to throw you your clothes, you're going to put them on, and then you're going to walk out of here.' Letting him go was madness, even if he hadn't seen my face, I knew that. Yet I was finding it unbelievably hard to pull the trigger. He was so young, and I knew that if I killed him, he'd haunt my dreams for ever.

'You bastard!' he spat, and for the first time I noticed that he had a hint of an American accent. 'You cold-hearted bastard!'

'This is your last chance. Get on your knees.'

The speed with which he spun round and lunged at me, his face a twisted mask of grief and rage, caught me off-guard.

But only for a moment. I may have hated what I did for a living, but I'd been doing it long enough to have swift reflexes and, even with a combination of jetlag and a lack of sleep, I fired instinctively, the power of the round stopping him in his tracks.

He went down hard and loudly, rolling over on to his front, his body going into spasms as he clutched desperately at the bed sheets.

I shot him twice more, my gun hand steady as my business side took over, and a few seconds later he lay still.

Gun smoke drifted up through the silent room, and for a long moment I stayed where I was, staring down at the two bodies, wondering why O'Riordan's lover had got himself killed when if he'd done what I'd told him, I'd almost certainly have let him live.

It was time to get out of there. I left the room, closing the door behind me, and headed back to the stairs, trying to push the brutal immensity of what I'd just done out of my mind. Instead, I concentrated on retirement, picturing myself on my balcony looking out across the tree line as it dropped towards the Mekong River, a beer in my hand, safe in the knowledge that I could live out my final days in peace.

If Schagel ever let me.

When I reached the bottom of the stairs, I noticed that the door to O'Riordan's study was ajar. I pushed it open further and stepped inside, curious as to why his killing had had such a specific time limit attached. By two p.m. that afternoon or the job was off. It had also occurred to me that I couldn't rely on Schagel to let me retire out of the kindness of his heart – since he didn't appear to possess either the kindness or the heart – so any information I could find to bolster my bargaining power would be useful.

O'Riordan's study was small and dark, even after

I'd flicked on the light, with brimming bookshelves surrounding a small, impeccably tidy desk with a PC on it, a couple of trays, and an A4-sized desk diary. The diary was open to Thursday and Friday, and was a mess of doodles, telephone numbers, and barely legible notes, with nothing of any obvious interest to the untrained eye.

But when I flicked overleaf to Saturday and Sunday, something interesting caught my attention. O'Riordan hadn't had a chance to deface the pages with his doodling, and Saturday was entirely blank. Except for an entry at three p.m. that afternoon.

It was only three words long, and I had to stare at it for close to half a minute before I could finally decipher those words. As far as I could tell, they read Cheeseman/Omar Salic. Clearly Salic was a person, and my guess was that O'Riordan was supposed to be having a meeting with him. Cheeseman could have been the venue, or possibly the name of someone else. But given the timing of the meeting, an hour after my deadline, I knew it had to be important.

I had no idea what I was going to do with the information, but I live by the philosophy that you can never have too much of it, so I ripped out the page, as well as the previous one, and pushed them into my back pocket.

Then, with a sigh, I pulled out my lighter and set fire to the diary. As the flames picked up, I threw it in the wastepaper basket, and added a couple of books. I felt bad for O'Riordan's wife. Not only had I killed her husband, I'd unwittingly exposed his affair with another man, and now I was going to burn down her house into the bargain.

Dawn was just beginning to break in the east as I slipped out of the front gate and headed back through the still sleeping streets in the direction of the guesthouse, leaving behind only corpses and shattered lives.

It really was a shitty business I was in.

CHAPTER 15

When O'Riordan didn't pick up, Tina left a message asking him to call her back urgently.

Next she called the dedicated story line of the *Manila Post* and eventually managed to get the young reporter who took the call to give her O'Riordan's home number, even though it was clear she didn't have a story to trade. But O'Riordan wasn't answering that either, although she let it ring and ring.

She told herself there was probably a perfectly simple explanation why she couldn't get hold of him, but in the light of the events of the last forty-eight hours, she was paranoid enough to check all the Philippines-based English-language news websites for any reports of his death. The problem was, she had to speak to O'Riordan urgently. He was the key, not only to Nick Penny's death, but also to finally bringing to justice the man she'd been after for so many years now. The link she'd discovered between Nick and Paul Wise was still tenuous, and it would require a lot more legwork, but it was definitely Wise's Achilles heel. Why else would he have killed Nick?

Tina knew immediately what she had to do. It was a big move – reckless, some would have said – but then she'd always been impulsive. In the past it had been both a strength and a weakness, and it had almost got her killed on more than one occasion. But she was finally on to something. And she owed it to all those Wise had murdered – including John Gallan, the man she'd been in love with, and the man she still thought about too many times, even now, six years on – to bring him to justice, whatever it cost.

Ten minutes later she'd set up a new, secure hotmail account so that she could send and receive emails without them being tracked, and ten minutes after that she'd done what she needed to do.

Taking a deep breath, she got up from her father's desk, feeling stiff from being bent over the laptop for so long, and walked outside for a cigarette. It was nearly eleven and the air was cold and damp as she stood on the porch, looking out over the beautifully tended back lawn where she'd often played as a young child. Good days – almost forgotten now. She'd been a happy kid, brought up in a happy, stable family unit. She'd done well in school, had indulged in only the most minor of teenage rebellions (smoking and a single fumbled bout of under-age sex the worst of them), and had gained decent A levels. University and a year's backpacking round South East Asia and Australia had followed. At that time, the world had truly been her oyster. The economy was doing well, there were plenty of jobs and money around. She could have done anything. Anything at all.

Yet she'd made the decision to join the police. Her parents had been shocked. It wasn't what they'd hoped for their bright, attractive daughter, but Tina had brushed aside their concerns. She hadn't wanted to work in an office. She'd wanted a job with variety, where she'd have a chance to actually do something useful, and have some excitement too.

Well, she'd had more than her fair share of that.

She thought back to what had happened earlier that evening, to those moments struggling in her bath while she'd been held underwater, only seconds away from unconsciousness, and death . . .

The back door opened behind her and she jumped, swinging round fast. Her mother stood in the doorway in her dressing gown, ready for bed.

'Tina, are you OK?' she asked uncertainly.

Tina nodded, giving her mother a reassuring smile. 'I'm fine. You scared me, that's all.'

'I was just coming to say goodnight. Your father and I were also wondering if you'd like to stay for lunch on Sunday? We could invite Phil and Wendy and the children over, have a proper family get-together?'

'Sorry, Mum, but I've got to be going early in the morning. I've booked a holiday.'

121

Her mother looked shocked. 'What? Just now?'

'You can do anything on the internet these days. I'm due a lot of leave, so I thought I'd take a week to get away from this weather.'

'But, where are you going?'

'Thailand,' Tina lied, knowing her mother would only worry if she knew she was going to Manila. 'It was a last-minute deal. I'm booked on tomorrow morning's flight.'

CHAPTER 16

From behind the trees at the back of the garden, Nargen watched the two women talking. He waited until they'd both turned and gone back inside, having heard all he needed to hear, then slipped over the wall and walked the short distance to the car.

'So, do we take the bitch out?' asked Tumanov with barely disguised excitement as Nargen climbed inside.

'It's not our decision,' Nargen told him firmly. 'Now drive.'

Five minutes later they were outside a public phone box on the edge of a nearby village. Nargen called the number he'd been given at the beginning of the job, leaving a short message on the voicemail, then replaced the receiver.

Two minutes after that, the payphone rang.

'We've located her,' said Nargen into the receiver. 'She's currently staying at her parents' house, and they are both in residence. She's also made the connection from the phone records.'

'Do you know what she intends to do about it?'

'Yes. She's going to Manila, flying out of

Heathrow tomorrow morning. I don't know the flight number or the airline yet but we'll be able to find out.'

'Where's she staying in Manila?'

'That information may be harder to gather. She's using a different email address for her booking. One we haven't got access to.'

There was a pause as the caller digested this information.

'Do you want us to go in?' Nargen asked. 'We could neutralize the parents as well. It will be no problem. They will all be asleep shortly.'

The caller was silent for a few moments. 'No,' he said at last. 'It will only cause problems for our people. It will be much easier to deal with her in Manila. She will be vulnerable there, and it won't matter so much how she dies.' The caller chuckled – an unpleasant, high-pitched sound. 'In fact, it will probably work out perfectly.'

CHAPTER 17

When I woke from a dreamless slumber, bright sunshine was seeping through the cheap hotel room curtains.

My back ached as I sat up in bed and checked my watch. It had just gone midday, and my mouth felt thick and dry. I'd sunk three beers in rapid succession to help me sleep when I'd got back, and I was tasting them now. I picked up the iPhone from on top of the pile of clothes I'd worn for the hit. I was going to have to get rid of them today, as well as the gun and the phone itself, but for now I checked it for messages and saw that I'd missed five calls from Schagel.

I didn't know what the hell was wrong with him. I'd texted him as soon as I'd got back to the room to let him know the job was done, so there was no need for him to be chasing me, especially as he'd told me to get rid of the phone afterwards anyway.

I knew he'd be expecting a call back, but he was going to have to wait. I needed to wake up a bit first. Drinking the last of my mineral water, I took a shower, cleaned my teeth, and threw on some

fresh clothes, finally feeling a little more human –
at least physically.

Mentally, of course, it was a different story. Now
that I was awake I couldn't stop thinking about
the two men I'd killed, haunted by what I'd done
in a way I wasn't used to. I'd broken my self-
imposed rule of never targeting the innocent. I
was pretty certain O'Riordan wasn't corrupt or
wicked yet I'd gunned him down in cold blood.
And I'd killed his lover too, a man who was barely
more than a kid and whose only sin had been to
be in the wrong place at the wrong time. It all left
me feeling deeply in the wrong.

I sat down on the bed and called the number
I'd texted earlier, confirming once again that the
job was completed.

I wasn't surprised when Schagel called me back
barely two minutes later, sounding in good spirits.
'Any complications?' he asked – his standard
opening phrase whenever I'd done some work for
him.

'A small one. There was someone else at the
address when I arrived.'

'His wife?'

'No, another man. I think he and the target were
lovers.'

Schagel laughed. 'What a naughty boy. And you
dealt with the other one, of course?'

'Of course.'

'So, it was a clean job, yes? The house is no
more?'

'I did everything as instructed.'

'Good. Because I want you to stay in Manila for a day or two longer.'

I was immediately on my guard. It wasn't like Bertie Schagel to make changes to his plans when I was already in the field, and I wondered, not for the first time, whether he'd finally decided that it would be safer to be rid of me, and was setting me up. 'Why's that?'

'We're expecting a visitor to the city who you may need to deal with. For an extra fee, of course. Are you still in possession of the box?' he added, referring to the gun.

I told him I was.

'Good. Keep it for now. I will try to organize another one, but I might not be able to at short notice. In the meantime, get rid of the phone as we arranged and get yourself a new one. Then call and leave me the new number.'

'Who's the visitor?' I asked him.

'I'll send the details to the email account in the next few minutes. We are expecting her to arrive in Manila tomorrow morning, and you'll need to be there to meet her. I'll confirm the time later.'

'Her?'

'Yes. It's a woman.'

This was a big problem for me, especially the way my guilt was going today. I'd only ever killed one woman in my life, and she'd been a monster. I didn't want to have to kill any others.

When I didn't say anything, Schagel sighed

loudly. 'Look,' he said, sounding almost conciliatory, 'I know how you feel about women. But if you agree to do this one job, I'll bring your retirement plans forward. OK? One last job, and you'll be free.'

I couldn't believe what I was hearing. This wasn't like Schagel at all. 'If you're bullshitting . . .'

'I'm not. I know you want to retire, and this is an extremely important task. Do it and our business relationship is over, and you can do whatever you want.'

Now it was my turn to sigh. I thought of my place in Laos, of being able to live out the rest of my life in peace. 'OK,' I said at last, forcing down the sick feeling I was getting in my gut. 'I'll do it.'

And in that moment, I sealed my fate.

CHAPTER 18

It was 2.30 p.m. and I was standing in the stifling heat, waiting for my new gun. Schagel had decided, after some thought, that it was too risky to use the one I already had, and it was now broken up and lying at the bottom of a nearby canal.

The street I was on was hot, dirty and poor, the stink of exhaust fumes and gutters pervading everything. On either side, three- and four-storey cobbled-together buildings loomed, their corrugated-iron roofs leaning precariously over the tarmac and blocking out what light there was in the smog-choked sky. Drying clothes hung from every available space, and streams of unwashed, half-naked kids dodged the traffic as they played on the uneven, lumpy tarmac, while the women, many holding babies, sat round on chairs, boxes or whatever was to hand and gossiped as they looked on. The men, sour-faced and bored, simply loitered and smoked, those who could be bothered eyeing me suspiciously.

Westerners stood out more in Manila than in many other Asian cities. There were fewer of them as a proportion of the population, and, unlike me, those that were here didn't tend to hang round in areas like this. A couple of passing hawkers had already tried to sell me their wares, and though I'd shooed them away, they still hung back at a distance, like vultures, waiting for my resistance to sap.

I'd never liked Manila, and had avoided it during the three years I'd lived in the Philippines. In fact, I'd only ever stayed here the once, when I came to kill a paedophile – a contract job that had been organized by my old friend and business partner Tomboy Darke.

A bit of history here. Back in the old days when I was still a London copper, Tomboy Darke had been one of my top informants. He was a small-time career criminal, dealing mainly in stolen contraband, but even so, I'd always liked him. He was a gregarious character and good company, and we'd often gone out drinking together. He was also sensible enough to know that the kind of business he was in, particularly the informing part, was never going to be a long-term option, so when he'd saved up enough money from his various nefarious activities he'd upped sticks and disappeared to the Philippines. It was a testament to our friendship that we'd remained in touch, and once my world in London had finally fallen apart, I'd come here and looked him up.

And he hadn't let me down, either. Tomboy had helped me when I'd needed him. He knew what

I'd done and could easily have turned me in to the authorities in the Philippines, probably gaining a sizeable financial reward for doing so, but he hadn't. Instead we'd gone into business together running a dive operation, first on the southern island of Siquijor, then after that in the resort of Puerto Galera, a few hours south of where I was now. It had been a lot of fun, too. We'd got drunk together, laughed at each other's jokes, been almost like brothers, even if, now and again, he'd wanted me to kill the occasional bad guy to help raise funds for the business.

But then, six years ago, something had happened, something that had changed my opinion of him for ever. The last words I'd ever spoken to him, made in a phone call from England after I'd gone back there to sort out some unfinished business, were a coldly uttered threat: 'Just pray I never come looking for you.'

We hadn't spoken since, and in the interim I'd tried to forget about him and the terrible thing he'd done. But, standing on that hot, polluted street, I thought about him now, and wondered whether he was even still alive.

Somehow I reckoned he would be. Tomboy had always been a survivor.

A wiry little guy in a scraggy T-shirt weaved through the traffic on a moped. As he saw me, he nodded and, without slowing down, pulled a satchel from his shoulder and held it out with an outstretched arm.

I took it in one casual movement and put it over my own shoulder, then I was walking one way and he was riding the other.

And that was it. A two-second exchange, and once again I was ready to commit murder.

I'd changed hotels, not wanting to stay too close to where I'd killed O'Riordan and his lover the previous night, and had booked myself into the Hilton on Roxas Avenue – the main thorough-fare through the upmarket bay area of the city. It was costing me a lot of money, but I figured that I'd be able to claim it back from Schagel as a justified business expense. After all, I was doing him a favour by hanging around a place where I'd just committed two murders.

On the way back to the Hilton, I stopped off at an internet café that promised fast broadband connections and air conditioning, and bought an hour of time from a kid with a funky haircut who didn't even look up from the bowl of noodles he was vacuuming up. I found a spot in the corner, away from the two other surfers, and logged into the hotmail account I shared with Schagel.

As promised, there was an email in the drafts section with a single jpeg attachment. I opened it and found myself looking at a photo of the head and shoulders of an attractive white woman in her early thirties. Her bleached-blonde hair was cut very short and gave her a confident, almost aggressive look that made me wonder, inappropriately, what she'd be like in bed. She was partly turned away from the camera, an expression of concentration on her face, and it was clear that she wasn't aware the shot was being taken. It was still a good one, though, and I knew I'd have no trouble recognizing her again – especially with that hair.

I closed the attachment and returned to the body of the email, reading it through quickly. According to Schagel, the woman's name was Tina Boyd and she was expected in Manila the following day on an as yet unspecified flight. As soon as he had the flight number and time, he would contact me. My instructions were to be at the airport when she arrived and to follow her to her destination. ON NO ACCOUNT (Schagel's capitals, not mine) was I to lose her. I would then receive further instructions. He signed off the mail by telling me to delete both it and the attachment.

I did as I was told, but remained seated at the PC. Tina Boyd. The photograph wasn't familiar but the name was. I'd definitely heard it before, a long time ago.

And then I frowned, because I remembered where. A cold winter's night just over six years ago, back in London. The last time I'd been there. And I recalled all too well what it had been in connection with.

So a London-based police officer – a DS, if I remembered rightly – was coming to Manila, and her arrival had clearly ruffled the feathers of the wrong kinds of people. I Googled her name and rank – which was when I learned she was now a

DI – and skim-read the slew of articles about her that immediately came up.

My hour had almost run out when I finally got up, having found out plenty about Tina Boyd's controversial, on occasions death-defying, career, but still no nearer to knowing why she had to die, or even whether she had any connection to Patrick O'Riordan.

But I was suddenly very curious to find out.

CHAPTER 19

Omar Salic needed the reward money the *Manila Post* man, Pat O'Riordan, had promised him. He needed it badly. It meant he could leave Manila with Soraya and set up the carpentry business he'd been dreaming of back home in Mindanao. It meant escaping the malign influence of the men he'd been working with – men he'd thought initially were his friends, but who were now turning into devils. If he carried on with them, he'd be dead soon, there was no question about it, and Soraya – his beautiful Soraya – would be left all alone to bring up their unborn child. A child Omar would never see.

O'Riordan was the man who'd promised to help Omar escape, yet he hadn't turned up at the meeting, and nor had the other guy he was supposed to bring with him, the American, Cheeseman. Omar had obeyed O'Riordan's instructions and not written anything down but he'd memorized every last detail, and had waited for him and Cheeseman at the agreed location for more than two hours before finally, and reluctantly, leaving.

The walk back home had been one of the most

painful of his life. Every five minutes he'd tried O'Riordan's mobile – a number the reporter had told him he could be reached on any time of day or night – and every time it had gone straight to voicemail. Omar hadn't left any messages. He hadn't seen much point. O'Riordan, the man who was going to change things for him and Soraya, had given up on him, even though Omar was sure that the information he had was worth thousands, maybe even millions, of dollars. The problem was, he was running out of time to find someone else willing to pay for it, and if this opportunity slipped through his fingers, as it now looked like it would, then there would almost certainly not be another like it again.

It was a quarter to six and the sun was beginning to go down amid the smog as Omar reached the grim apartment block in Manila's Tondo district where he and Soraya had lived for the past three years while he scraped a living in this city they both despised. On the ride up in the elevator he told himself that he would find someone else to sell the information to, that he shouldn't give up just yet. He also forced himself to cheer up. He didn't want to worry Soraya, not in her current condition. She knew nothing of his double life, nor of the meeting with O'Riordan. As far as she knew, he'd been out with friends that afternoon, and that was how he wanted it to stay.

But the moment he stepped into the apartment he could see that it was too late for that.

Soraya was sitting in her favourite chair, but there was something terribly wrong. Her mouth was gagged and her arms and legs bound. Above the gag, her eyes were wide and terrified.

Omar gasped, unable to comprehend for a moment what was happening, but even in her terror, Soraya was gesturing behind him with her eyes.

Before he could turn round, he was grabbed from behind by firm hands, and felt a knife being pushed hard against his throat. 'On your knees, traitor,' hissed a voice he recognized in his ear, and he was shoved roughly to the ground so that he was lying on his front. From the position he was in, only a few feet away from the chair, he could see, with a growing sense of dread, that Soraya's black dress was wet with blood.

At least two men were holding Omar down, and though he felt a terrible rage at what was being done to his beloved wife, he knew there was no point resisting, not with the knife against his throat. 'What's going on?' he gasped, trying to regain some control of the situation, even though he could feel his bowels turning to water. Because he knew what these people were capable of.

'You know what's going on,' hissed the voice. 'What have you said to the journalist?'

'Nothing, I swear it,' replied Omar, just about managing to make eye contact with Soraya, and giving her a look that said he would sort this out and stop these men from doing any further harm to her. 'Please. Let my wife go. She's pregnant.'

But as he spoke he saw a third man come out of the tiny kitchen, a nail gun in one hand and a butcher's knife in the other. It was Anil, and he looked perfectly calm. But then he always did. Even when he was killing.

'Please Anil,' whispered Omar, feeling the knife cut his skin as he spoke. 'Let Soraya go. She has done nothing.'

'But you have, haven't you, Omar,' said Anil slyly. 'Who have you told?'

'No one.'

'What about the journalist?'

Omar had no idea how they'd found out about O'Riordan. He'd covered his tracks with extreme care, and the only reason he'd approached O'Riordan was because he thought that a journalist with his experience would have done the same. But in the end none of this mattered. Because the point was, *they knew*. Which meant that Omar was going to have to tell the truth. He was finished, he knew this. But if there was any chance of getting Soraya out of this alive, he had to take it.

'Look, we just arranged to meet. That's all. But the journalist didn't show up.' He pushed his head up from the floor, ignoring the pain from the knife, so that he was looking at Anil man to man. 'I know I've done wrong—'

'You have, Omar. You have.'

'But Soraya has done nothing, and she's pregnant.'

'So you keep saying.'

'Please don't hurt her, Anil. I swear no one knows the details. No one.'

Anil looked at Omar with distaste, then signalled to the men holding him.

Suddenly, Omar gasped as he felt a knife being inserted deep into his side. At the same time the knife at his throat was removed and a piece of duct tape was slapped roughly against his mouth. He felt no pain, just shock as his blood dripped down on to the dirty tiles of the floor, and he thought that if this was dying, it was a great deal less painful than he'd imagined.

Except it wasn't death. It was just the beginning.

Because after that they made him watch as Anil went to work on his wife.

And by the time he'd finished, the anguish Omar was experiencing was so great that he would have rather died a thousand times over.

CHAPTER 20

After I left England at the end of 2004, having burned my bridges with Tomboy in the Philippines, I headed back to the Far East, unsure of what I was going to do next. Although my relationship with him was finished, Tomboy still owed me money – more than twenty thousand dollars to be exact – and I needed it to start over again somewhere else.

That somewhere else turned out to be Thailand.

Stopping in Bangkok, I'd bought a tourist book, read through it and decided to head down south to the island of Ko Lanta in the Andaman Sea. I chose Ko Lanta because it was comparatively underdeveloped, with no airport, and could only be reached by ferry. It was also less popular with Brits, who tended to congregate in the more touristy destinations like Phuket and Ko Samui, so I was less likely to be recognized. What swayed it for me was the quality of the diving, which was supposed to be some of the best in the country.

As a qualified instructor with more than fifteen hundred dives under my belt, I quickly found work at a small operation, the owners of which were also in need of some investment to buy new equipment. I emailed Tomboy and, luckily for him, he didn't kick up much of a fuss when I asked him for the money he owed me. I got it transferred over, pumped it into the business, and immediately became a part-owner.

And so, within a few months, I'd settled down once again, put the past behind me, and was enjoying life under the assumed identity I'd been using for the previous three years, that of Marcus 'Mick' Baxter. No one questioned my past. In the Ko Lanta diving community, people were only interested in the here and now. It suited me perfectly, and I could probably have lived like that for the rest of my days.

But life has a way of throwing up surprises, and the surprise for me was that I fell in love.

I met Emma Pettit when she came down from Bangkok with a female friend for a long weekend to do some diving, and chose our outfit to go out with. The boat rides from Ko Lanta to the best dive sites were typically between two and four hours, which left plenty of time for the dive staff and their guests to get talking, and Emma and I just seemed to gravitate to each other. She was a real livewire, with twinkling eyes, a huge smile, and a host of tales to tell. Although originally from Somerset, she'd been living overseas for most of the previous five years, teaching English as a foreign language in various locations in Africa and Asia, and was now based in Bangkok, where she taught at a private school. She loved to travel and sample other cultures, and she talked of all the places she wanted to see both in Asia and beyond. She was also interested in me, wanting to know my background and how I'd ended up where I was.

'You don't seem the type to be a dive instructor in a place like this,' she said as we sat together on the side decking of the boat, our feet dangling over the edge.

'What's the type?'

'I don't know. More shallow.'

I laughed. 'How do you know I'm not shallow?'

'I can tell. You've got sad eyes.' She grinned. 'A lot of dark secrets in there.'

'I wish,' I said, and proceeded to give her my revised background – the one I'd learned off by heart for just this kind of eventuality. How I'd grown bored in my job as an IT software salesman and had one day pooled together all my savings and simply taken off round the world, settling first in the Philippines, then here.

Emma bought the story. In the end, there was no reason for her not to. I'm a good liar, and it was a plausible enough tale. I was mildly concerned that she might twig who I was because she would have been in the UK when my face was splashed across the front pages there, but I trusted in the effects of time and the plastic surgery I'd had in the Philippines, and found myself relaxing in her company, enjoying the fact that for once I was having a non-diving conversation.

At the end of the day, as the boat pulled up in the harbour, with the sun setting behind us, Emma asked if I'd like to join her and her friend for a drink. I should have said no – it would have been safer that way – but life in paradise can be very unfulfilling, and I felt a real yearning for good company. So I told her I'd love to, and offered to bring a couple of the dive staff along too, thinking that I didn't want Emma's friend to feel too left out.

We met up at a beach bar near where they were staying, and as the evening progressed it became more and more obvious that Emma was interested in me. I was interested in her too. At thirty-six, she was only six years younger than me, and she had a hell of a lot going for her. She was fun; she was interesting; she was attractive. She was, I realized to my surprise, everything that I'd been missing over the years, and I ignored my innate instinct for caution and let the moment take me.

After we'd walked Emma's friend back to the beach bungalow they were sharing, the two of us went for a walk along the beach, hand in hand. We kissed, we touched, we carried on talking, and it was three a.m. when I finally dropped her back.

The next day they didn't come diving. The friend wanted to hire a car and drive round the island, but we met up again in the evening, and again we managed to slip away alone and wander down the beach, enjoying the warm breeze and the silence. By the time I dropped Emma off again that night, I knew that this was something special.

A week later I was in Bangkok with a week's leave and staying at her tiny apartment in the heart of the city.

It was, without doubt, the happiest week of my life. We ate, we drank, we made love. We were the only two people in the world. In forty-two years on the planet, I'd never been truly in love. Until that point. Now I was absolutely smitten. I'd finally discovered the swirling, intense, gut-wrenching feeling that encompassed excitement, passion, helplessness and sheer terror all in one go, and it was unstoppable.

I started seeing Emma whenever I could. It wasn't that easy, because being a dive instructor can often be a seven-day-a-week job, but I had the advantage of being a part-owner in the place and, although money was tight, I got to Bangkok at least once a month, while Emma got down to see me at similar intervals, often for no more than a couple of days at a time. One time we even managed to get ten days off together and took off to Borneo to go diving and trekking.

Everything was rosy. The world, finally, offered a future of hope and contentment.

Which should have been a warning to me. Life can never be rosy for too long, at least not for a man like me – a man for whom freedom has always been a fragile, desperate gift. But I'd become complacent, so when the end came I still couldn't quite believe it. In fact, I still can't quite believe it now, three years later.

It all started when Emma fell pregnant a little over a year into our relationship. It was a complete accident. At least I thought it was. Perhaps she'd been secretly planning it. After all, she was well into her thirties and her biological clock would have been ticking pretty fast. But the fact was, when I found out I was happy. Nervous too, because it meant a huge commitment, but I also felt that it would bring Emma and me together and move our relationship up to a new level.

And at first it did. She was incredibly excited and we talked of our plans for the future.

Unfortunately, it seemed that our plans were very different. I wanted her to move down to Ko Lanta and have the baby there, because with my stake in the business I had enough money to support us all. But Emma wanted us to return to England. Her family were all still there, as were a few of her close friends, and she felt that it would be a better place to bring up a baby. She even suggested that I could get a job back in software sales.

'Come on, Mick, you didn't want to do this for ever, did you?' she asked incredulously when I'd knocked that particular suggestion. 'You're too good for this.'

But the point was, I did, because the alternative – going back to the UK – simply couldn't happen. I suppose I'd always known in the back of my mind that something like this was inevitable, yet I'd chosen to ignore it. We argued and, with her being strong-willed, she announced that she was going back anyway, telling me that if I loved her, I'd come back too.

It was a terrible position to be put in. I tried to persuade her to change her mind, saying I was the owner of a business, that I was happy here in the sunshine, and that she and the baby would be too if we only gave it a chance. For her part, she continued to try to persuade me that England offered the best, most secure future for us and our unborn child.

Eventually, we settled into an uneasy détente, neither of us wanting the arguments to destroy our relationship before it had had a chance to grow, and life continued with the two of us living apart. But then Emma announced that her parents were planning to visit, and wanted to come with her to Ko Lanta for a short holiday, and to meet me.

So it was with a heavy heart and growing feeling of dread that I met them off the ferry a couple of weeks later.

Straight away, I knew her father didn't like me. A short, rail-thin man in his late sixties who dressed like he'd just come from the eighteenth hole, he regarded me with barely suppressed suspicion from the moment we shook hands, his eyes scouring me for confirmation of my unsuitability. His name was Stephen, and he made a point of emphasizing the second syllable as if I might forget myself and insult him by calling him Steve. Emma's mum, Diane, was the complete opposite, a cheery, smiling woman a few years younger who gave me a welcoming hug and a kiss on both cheeks; but I hardly noticed because I was too worried about the old man. An accountant by profession, he was the classic retired busybody who read the papers from cover to cover, doubtless bemoaning the state of the country, someone I knew would have devoured every detail of a story about a renegade police officer implicated in at least six murders.

Emma, on the other hand, seemed hugely happy to be introducing her parents to me, and talked with pride about our relationship, my business, and the good time we'd had together. Three months into the pregnancy, she was blooming, her face a picture of health, the bump not yet showing. Acting like a woman without a care in the world.

After they'd settled into their hotel, half a mile down the road from where I had my bungalow, we went for a late lunch, and then I drove them round the island in a jeep I'd borrowed from a friend, showing them the various sights. It turned out to be quite a pleasant afternoon, mainly because I managed to avoid talking too much to the old man. At the same time, he seemed to be on his best behaviour, asking me the odd question about the business and my background, but mainly keeping his own counsel.

But when we met for dinner that night, I could

tell he knew that something wasn't quite right about me. He asked me more in-depth questions about my background – what I'd done in England; who I'd worked for; where my family were – a forced casualness in his tone that contrasted with the cold suspicion in his eyes. Diane playfully told him to stop interrogating me. Only Emma seemed to notice that something wasn't quite right with her father.

I tried to shrug it off, turning on the charm full throttle, asking questions of my own, discussing current affairs, putting my hand in Emma's to demonstrate our closeness. But inside I was rattled, a situation that grew steadily worse as the evening progressed and I caught Stephen watching me out of the corner of his eye when he thought I couldn't see him, as if he knew he'd seen me before and was trying to remember when and where.

It was then that my panic gave way to something else. A numb resignation that my relationship with Emma and our unborn baby – my one true shot at happiness – was over. Her father might not have made the connection yet, but it was only a matter of time before he did. And then I wouldn't just lose Emma. I'd effectively lose the rest of my life.

Lying in bed that night, with Emma's head nestled in the crook of my shoulder as I listened to the chirping of the cicadas in the long grass outside the window, I made my plan.

The next morning, I told her I was feeling sick, and said that if she didn't mind, I'd stay in bed a little longer and see if I could sleep it off. We'd only arranged to go to the beach with her parents so I could walk down to meet them later.

'Of course,' she said, touching my brow and looking concerned. 'Take your time. I think they'll be disappointed though. Especially my mum. She likes you.'

'I like your mum too,' I said, pulling her in closer, holding her for one last time, taking in her scent, the smell of shampoo in her hair, my hand running gently over the tiny bump as I silently said goodbye to a child I'd never meet, before finally letting her go.

I'll always remember how low and empty I felt as I watched Emma disappear out of the door with a grin and a wave, knowing that as long as I lived I could never set eyes on her again.

Ten minutes later I was out of the bungalow carrying a holdall full of possessions, not even leaving a note behind. Using the car I'd borrowed the previous day, I drove down to the port and on to the car ferry, making my way to Krabi Airport. Six hours after that I was on an Air Asia flight from Bangkok to Phnom Penh in Cambodia – the kind of destination where I'd be able to lie low while I worked out my next move.

But things didn't quite go according to plan. When I arrived at Phnom Penh Airport I was stopped at immigration, and before I knew it I was being taken down an adjoining corridor and into a windowless room by two silent men in uniform, who told me I was under arrest. When I asked on what charge, I was met with blank faces.

I was locked inside the room and left to stew for what was one of the toughest hours of my life. I knew that somehow they'd found out who I was. I didn't know how – although I suspected that my prospective father-in-law might have had a hand in it somewhere – but that was irrelevant right then. All that mattered was finding a way out of the situation. The problem was that there was no way out of it. I was trapped in an unfamiliar country with no weapon, no friends, and definitely no escape route.

The door finally opened, and I remember my stomach lurching as a hatchet-faced Cambodian in the uniform of a military officer came in and sat down at the table opposite me.

'My name is Lieutenant-Colonel Thom of the Royal Gendarmerie,' he said in heavily accented but perfect English. 'And your name is Dennis Milne.'

'No,' I said firmly, determined not to show any sign of the panic that was tearing up my insides. 'My name is Marcus Baxter. It says so in my passport.'

His face remained impassive. 'You are Dennis Milne, and you are wanted by Interpol for murder. We can take a DNA swab from you and it will match the DNA of your family members back in Britain. You will be held in prison here in Phnom Penh while we await the results, and then you will be extradited back to your own country to face trial.'

I felt the whole world closing in on me. This day had always been coming, but now that it was here, its true ramifications were still impossibly hard for me to comprehend. Only twenty-four hours earlier I'd been driving round the paradise island of Ko Lanta in an open-top jeep with the woman I loved sitting next to me. Now my life was effectively over, because as soon as they got me back in the UK I'd be behind bars for the rest of my natural life. Even death was preferable to that, and it took every ounce of self-control to stop myself from breaking down.

So much so that I hardly heard Lieutenant-Colonel Thom's next word.

'Unless . . .'

I stopped. Looked into his dark eyes. Wondered if this was a trick to get me to admit who I was. 'Unless what?'

'Unless you do exactly what I say. There is a possibility that things do not have to . . .' He paused, as if choosing the right word. 'Escalate. If you are in agreement, then we are going to walk out of this door and go for a drive. Your passport will be left here. It will be destroyed. It is no use now anyway as the name on it has been identified as an alias used by you.'

'But how will I be able to move around?'

'You must ask no questions. You just do what I say. Yes?'

I had no idea what I was getting myself into but figured that it had to be better than the situation I was already in. So I said yes.

I felt as though I was in some kind of dream as Lieutenant-Colonel Thom led me down a series of corridors, through the baggage area where the holdall containing what few possessions I owned was waiting for me, through doors marked No Entry, and past grim-faced officials who simply nodded deferentially at him before finally emerging into a rear car park outside the main terminal building. A military Land Rover pulled up almost immediately and we both got in the back.

As we drove out of the airport, I saw that the surrounding area was very different from the lushness of Thailand that I'd become used to. It was very flat and very dry, a patchwork of parched fields that were little more than red dust, with emaciated-looking palm trees poking up at various intervals like scarecrows, and scrawny cattle grazing by the roadside on what scrub they could find. This was the land of the Killing Fields: the barren, terrible place where the bones of thousands of victims of the Khmer Rouge genocide – men, women, children, even babies – lay buried beneath the soil. Thirty-plus years on there was still a vague, lingering feeling of evil in the hot, close air, as if the ghosts of the past had yet to be fully exorcised, and my mood continued to darken as we drove into Phnom Penh.

The jeep wound through a maze of squalid, crowded streets until we came to a narrow, tree-lined boulevard of attractive brick and timber townhouses dating back to the French colonial era, the kind of architecture that Manila could only dream of. We stopped at a set of high double-gates, and a couple of seconds later they were opened from the inside by an armed guard in a blue uniform, with a rifle strapped to his back.

A western man in a suit came out of the house and led Lieutenant-Colonel Thom and me into a sumptuous, classically decorated entrance hall. We were then split up, he and the man in the suit heading off into a backroom while I was directed through a side door and on to a pretty covered veranda that looked out on a small but beautifully kept and watered garden.

I sat down in one of the wicker armchairs, and immediately my thoughts turned to Emma. I'd tried not to think too much about how she must be feeling now that she knew I'd gone, the look on her face as she slowly realized that I'd left her without a word of explanation. And then her dad putting two and two together before informing her that the father of the baby she was carrying was nothing more than a brutal murderer who'd spent the previous six years living a lie. I swallowed hard, fighting to keep down my emotions as I thought about the extent of my betrayal. How, in the space of a few hours, I'd managed to leave her life in utter ruins. I could imagine her weeping and inconsolable. The woman I loved. The woman I'd vowed to protect.

I've hated myself many times in my life – that's the cross you bear when you've sinned like I have – but never as much as I hated myself then, and I was shocked by the speed with which the intense wave of self-loathing enveloped me.

'Good evening, Mr Milne,' said a voice, interrupting my thoughts.

And that was the moment I first met Bertie Schagel.

'It's good to meet you at last,' he continued, squeezing into the wicker armchair next to mine, a glass of what looked like G&T in one meaty hand. 'I've read a great deal about your exploits.' He smiled in the vulpine manner I've since become used to, the smile of a man who knows he's holding all the cards.

'I don't know what you're talking about,' I said instinctively, but there was no conviction in my tone.

'There is no point lying,' he told me. 'I received a phone call from a contact in Bangkok who said you were on the plane. It seems that every police officer in South East Asia is suddenly after you. The photo of your face taken at Thai passport control has now been passed on to police forces across the region. You are in a very dangerous

154

position, with no room for manoeuvre at all.' He paused to take a sip of his drink, eyeing me over the rim of the glass.

I didn't say anything.

'I can still help you though, Dennis.' His cunning eyes, an icy blue, glinted. 'Do you mind if I call you Dennis?'

I shrugged.

'If you accept my offer, the following will happen. You will remain here for the next three days. There is a reliable staff here who will endeavour to make your stay as comfortable as possible. None of them know who you are, and Lieutenant-Colonel Thom can be trusted not to tell anyone. During this time, a whole new identity will be prepared for you, including a passport and driving licence. I will also organize a prosthetics expert to make some further cosmetic changes to your features so that you will be able to move around freely again. Finally, I will supply you with a Panamanian bank account into which ten thousand dollars in cash will be deposited to – what is it you English say? – get you back on your feet.'

'It sounds a very attractive offer, Mr Schagel,' I said at last, my voice cracking just a little.

'It is. The best, in fact the only one, that you are going to get.'

'And what do you expect in return?'

He put his drink down on the table and regarded me closely. 'Sometimes I have a need for the type of service you provide – the elimination of certain people who have become a threat or a hindrance to certain other people. I will only need such services on occasion, and will pay you a fair market rate each time that I do. The remainder of the time you will be free to do as you please, although I insist on always knowing where you are based. I am a fair employer, and prefer my employees to be happy, but should you decide at any point that you do not like working for me and try to disappear, then I will make the authorities fully aware which alias you have been travelling under and will put all my resources into making sure you are either imprisoned or eliminated. Do you understand?'

I nodded. It was pretty self-explanatory.

He put out a hand. 'So, you will agree to work for me, yes?'

The fact was, he had me over a barrel and, as he'd pointed out himself, I wouldn't be getting any other offers. I felt mildly nauseous at the prospect of going back to killing people for money after I'd left that whole life behind and started afresh back in the legitimate world, but in reality I had little choice. Needs must when the devil comes calling, and right then he was sticking his hooves straight through my front door.

With a heavy heart, I'd put out my own hand and we'd shaken on the deal.

And now, three years later, here I was sitting on a bed in yet another hotel room, although somewhat superior to the one I'd been in the previous night. It was 11.30 p.m. and I was drinking a San Miguel – the local Filipino brew. I was tired, but also restless, and thinking far too many melancholic thoughts. I was wondering whether O'Riordan and his partner had been in love, in the way I'd been with Emma, and concluded from the way the partner (a man whose name I would never know) had gone for me in a grief-stricken rage that they must have been. And I'd destroyed it.

'I'm sorry, hon,' I said aloud to the wall, addressing Emma as I still did sometimes when I was alone.

I wondered once again where she and our child were now. Emma would have found someone else, I was sure of that. She had too much personality, too much spirit, to be on her own for too long. Our child – for some reason I always imagined him as a son – would be two now. I imagined the three of them together. A tight-knit family tucked up round a warm, roasting fire, the kind I hadn't seen for years now. I pictured Emma and her new man kissing; making love in front of that roaring fire; my son, walking now, smiling and calling him Daddy . . .

I drained the beer, knowing I had to stop torturing myself, and got myself another. I drank that one far too quickly. Then I picked up the copy of the *Manila Post* that had been left in the room and skimmed through it, conscious that there was no mention of the murder of one of their journalists yet. That would come tomorrow. I concentrated on the articles, working hard to keep the black cloud of melancholy at bay, though it continued to sit waiting on the edge of my field of vision.

The new mobile I'd bought that afternoon to replace the iPhone rang. Since only one person other than me had the number, I knew the caller would be Schagel.

He asked me if I'd picked up the email message with the details of the new target.

I told him I had.

'Good. I can now confirm that she is arriving tomorrow on Singapore Airlines flight SQ910, landing at Ninoy Aquino Airport Terminal L1 at 1.25 p.m. local time.'

I found a pen and paper on a desk by the window and wrote the information down, the booze making my handwriting shaky.

'I want you to meet her there, follow her to whichever hotel she goes to, and make sure she checks in. It's imperative you don't lose her. Understood?'

He seemed more agitated than usual, his cold arrogance noticeably absent, and I wondered yet again if everything was OK.

'Understood. But how do we know she's not being met by officials at the airport?'

'She isn't. Her business in Manila is unofficial.'

I was surprised at how much Schagel knew about

her movements but didn't say anything. I knew he had his methods.

'And remember, if you do what needs to be done on this job, you can leave my service afterwards. You have my word.'

I thought about Tina Boyd – a woman, a police officer, someone who doubtless had loved ones of her own. People whose lives would be crushed savagely and permanently by my actions if I carried out the job.

And then I thought once more about the prospect of retirement. Of running my business in the hills of northern Laos, safe from prying eyes; of never having to be at the beck and call of anyone again.

'I'm on it,' I told him. And hung up.

PART II

THE AXE STEADIES

CHAPTER 21

The flight from London to Singapore was long, bumpy and full. Tina had managed to get an aisle seat, but the man sitting next to her had been overweight, far too free with his elbows, and had snored loudly on the few occasions he'd dozed off.

Consequently, by the time she arrived at Changi Airport at 8.30 on Sunday morning, after thirteen painful hours in the air, she was exhausted. She changed into a T-shirt and long shorts in the toilets, got herself a large espresso from the Starbucks in the terminal, managing to pay using US dollars that she'd changed at Heathrow, then found a seat and checked the messages on her phone.

The first was from Bob Levine at CMIT, in response to the message she'd left for him the previous morning in which she'd said that, following on from his kind offer to give her a week off, she now wanted to take two weeks of outstanding leave, starting immediately. Levine's message was an annoyed one in which he said she needed to give him more notice if she wanted to take time off like that, and telling her to call him on Monday to discuss her request. He was going to be even more annoyed when he realized she was calling him from the other side of the world, but she'd worry about that later. Tina knew that she was considered to be a generally reliable cop. She was rarely off sick (except through on-duty injury) and, apart from Christmases, she hadn't gone on leave since the month-long trip she'd taken to central America the previous summer. She was due a bit of slack and, at least on this occasion, she had a good reason.

The second message was from a blocked number, and the line wasn't good, but even so she recognized the voice of the Phnom Penh police officer she'd spoken to on Friday night. On the message, he introduced himself formally as Lieutenant Hok Ma of the Royal Gendarmerie of Cambodia, and said that he'd located the officer Nick Penny had spoken to.

Tina listened carefully while Lieutenant Ma left the details of the conversation that the two men had had, and those details confirmed what she already knew. Tina wanted to find out if the Cambodian police had taken any action as a result of Penny's conversation with them, even though the tone of the message suggested they hadn't. Lieutenant Ma had only phoned an hour earlier, and she found his number in her bag and tried calling him back, but there was no response.

No matter. Because she knew now she was definitely on the right track.

She finished her coffee and slowly made her way over to the departures gate to begin the next stage of her journey.

And that was when she saw him.

Coming out of the first-class lounge, twenty yards ahead. A small, hunched man in his fifties, with thinning hair dyed an obvious black, and sharp, pointed features on a pale, pudgy face, he reminded Tina of an overfed rodent. He was wearing an unfashionable cream suit and a white open-necked shirt that was stretched tight over a prominent pot belly, and he would have looked like any other ordinary middle-aged traveller with his duty-free bag and carry-on luggage if it hadn't been for the fact that he was accompanied by a powerful-looking bodyguard in a dark suit who was looking round with the studied, humourless air of a professional.

But there was nothing ordinary about Paul Wise. Nor about the terrible things he'd done.

For a moment, Tina was too shocked to react. She'd read so much about him, seen so many photos of his face, had spent so many hours making her own savage plans for revenge. Yet in all that time she'd never seen him in the flesh. Seeing him now, and knowing that she was powerless to do anything about it, filled her with an almost sickening rage. She wanted to grab him by his flabby throat and squeeze with every ounce of strength she had, enjoying the look of terror in his eyes, telling him how long she'd waited for this moment, that it was payback for all the people whose lives he'd ended, until the last of his rancid breaths came and went, and he finally went limp in her arms.

Instead she turned away and quickly took a seat, keeping her head down and pretending to look for something in her bag. Paul Wise knew exactly who Tina was – after all, he'd tried to have her killed barely twenty-four hours earlier – and she couldn't risk him seeing her now.

He headed with his bodyguard towards the departures gate, and she waited a full minute before getting up and following, wondering what on earth he was doing here.

It didn't take long for the question to be answered. He turned left at gate 70 and was ushered past the long queue of economy-class passengers before disappearing down the tunnel to board Singapore Airlines flight SQ910.

Paul Wise was on the same flight as her, and he was going to Manila.

The question was, why?

CHAPTER 22

anila's Ninoy Aquino Airport is a tatty and confusing place that was thankfully less busy than usual that Sunday afternoon. Non-travellers aren't allowed in the arrivals area. Instead, they are forced to wait behind a long fence that's separated from the main terminal building by a pedestrian tunnel and two access roads. As with most things in the Philippines, however, security's pretty inefficient and it wasn't hard for a western man like me, who looked like he knew where he was going, to slip through the crowds and get inside the security cordon.

I found a seat in the corner at the front of the building from where I could see the passengers exiting through an open double doorway, but where they were unlikely to see me. There were a dozen or so Filipino guys hanging about holding signs who acted as a useful screen between me and the doorway, but no sign of any security.

I sat back and waited with a copy of the *International Herald Tribune* open in front of me. I wasn't reading it, though. I was thinking about Bertie Schagel's offer of retirement. Lying in bed the previous night, it had crossed my mind that it was a trick of some sort – that he couldn't risk letting me go, but would have me killed instead to make sure I never talked of our association. Since waking up at ten o'clock that morning, however, feeling refreshed and reinvigorated, and with the brilliant tropical sun shining in through my hotel window, my maudlin mood had largely dissipated and I'd spent much of the intervening time convincing myself that he'd meant what he said. Granted, Schagel's word was hardly his bond, and I wouldn't trust the guy as far as I could throw him. But on the plus side, killing me would be a hassle. It would be far easier to pay me the money I was owed and let me disappear from the scene. Even if I was arrested further down the line, I knew so little about Bertie Schagel it was unlikely in the extreme that I could provide the authorities with any information that would even identify, let alone convict, him.

With the money I earned from this job, I could retire in style. And if I ever got bored in Laos, I could always head somewhere else, maybe even buy a new ID so that there was no way Schagel could ever track me down, should he change his mind about letting me go. The point was, if I did this last job, I'd have options, opportunities. I could start a new life.

A thin stream of people was emerging from the arrivals doorway now, and I positioned the paper so that I could only just see over it, while trying to maintain as casual a pose as possible, knowing that as a copper with more than ten years' experience Tina Boyd was going to be keeping her wits about her and looking for anyone out of place.

And then she was walking out in front of me – a lean, pale-skinned figure, her body well-toned beneath the shorts and T-shirt, the shock of blonde hair making her stand out. Although clearly exhausted, she was prettier and younger than she'd looked in the photo, and she had the poised, confident gait of the longterm copper, yet with a hint of latent aggression beneath, as if she was constantly expecting trouble of some sort or another.

Straight away, I knew I was going to have to be careful around her. She wasn't the sort of person you should underestimate.

My eyes returned to the paper as I heard her ask one of the local guys in the hall where she could get a taxi from. I waited while she walked out on to the access road before getting to my feet and following her through the doors, keeping ten yards and several people back.

When she was through the tunnel and at the taxi rank on the second access road, she took a casual look round behind her. I wasn't sure if she clocked me or not, but it wouldn't matter if she had. I was carrying my holdall and looked just like any other passenger. Although she'd once been a police officer at the same station in London as me, she'd joined after I'd gone, so we'd never met.

It was possible that, because of the crimes I'd committed, my face, as it was all those years ago, would be familiar to her, but I looked a different person now – age, plastic surgery and the tropical sun having all done their work on me.

I got in the queue for the taxis one person back so as not to make it too obvious that I was following her. Luckily, there was a long line of drivers waiting and my cab was on the move only ten seconds after hers. I greeted the driver with those immortal words 'Follow that car', and offered him a two-thousand-peso tip as an incentive.

It worked. He kept the target cab in view the whole time but was sensible enough not to stick too close to it, and half an hour later we saw it pull up outside the front of the Bayview Hotel on the harbour front, barely half a mile from where I was staying.

I told the driver to pull up a hundred metres further on, and gave him his money. I'd already changed in the back of the cab, putting the old stuff in the holdall, and was now wearing a T-shirt, new sunglasses and a New York Yankees baseball cap. The driver raised his eyebrows but didn't say anything as I stepped outside.

By the time I'd walked back to the front of the hotel, I was five minutes behind her. As was always the case in the Philippines, there were security guards on the door but, true to form, it never occurred to them that a western man like me was any kind of threat, and they let me through with a wave and a smile.

Tina Boyd was at the check-in desk filling in a registration form. As I wandered slowly past, acting as if I was waiting for someone in the lobby, she handed it back to the receptionist, who then told her she was in room 927 on the ninth floor. I carried on walking, before crouching down and rummaging through the holdall, pretending to look for something as she came past on her way to the lifts.

Only when the doors had closed behind her did I get back to my feet and walk out the hotel's main entrance, before turning into a quiet side street and dialling Bertie Schagel's number. I left a message, giving him the target's current location, and walked up and down the pavement while I waited for him to call back.

Five minutes later he did, and I listened while he gave me my instructions.

Then I cut the call and, conscious of the feel of the new gun – a short-barrelled Taurus pistol with a ten-round magazine – pushing into my back beneath my jacket, I started back towards the hotel.

CHAPTER 23

It had just turned three p.m. when Tina finally climbed out of the shower and walked back into her poky little bedroom, rubbing herself dry. She felt a lot better than she had done, but she was still tired and more than a little nervous. She'd seen a western guy at the airport and thought that she'd seen him again down in the reception area. She couldn't be absolutely certain, but she was concerned enough to consider swapping hotels.

The thing was, who the hell even knew she was here? She'd booked the flight and the hotel from a new and secure email address and had run sophisticated anti-virus software on her laptop, so there was no way it had been bugged. Maybe she was just being paranoid. After all, she hadn't slept properly for more than twenty-four hours, and was utterly exhausted.

She picked up her phone and looked at it. She wanted to make a call to Mike Bolt, her ex-boss at the Serious Organized Crime Agency, and ask him whether he knew of any reason why Paul Wise might have been in the Philippines. For a long time, Mike and Tina had been very close. He'd recruited her to his team when she was going through a bad time, and had done more than anyone else to get her back on her feet. Their friendship had almost ended in an affair, which was the main reason Tina had left Soca and rejoined the Met, but their paths had crossed a number of times since. On one of those occasions, Mike had saved her life, risking his own in the process. On another, she'd got him to break all the rules and risk his job in order to get her some information she desperately needed. He'd been disciplined for the help he'd given her then, and although he'd kept his job and rank, Tina still felt extremely guilty about it. Afterwards, she'd called and apologized for putting him in such a difficult situation and he'd told her it didn't matter, that he'd been happy to help; but something in his tone suggested he regretted it. She also knew he considered her to be a loose cannon these days, ruled by her obsession with Paul Wise and her desire for revenge.

They'd only spoken once since then, the previous September, when at Nick Penny's request she'd called him with some questions about Wise's business interests in Panama. On that occasion, Mike had told her that he'd been explicitly ordered not to give any information about Wise to anyone outside Soca without prior approval from its Director General. He'd added that they were still actively investigating him, but something in his voice had told her that they were no longer trying that hard, which was no great surprise. A great deal of resources had been channelled into bringing Paul Wise to justice, yet Soca were no nearer their goal than they had been when they'd first started looking into his affairs more than four years ago. It was inevitable that they would eventually move on to other, easier targets.

Tina could imagine Mike's reaction now if he found out she was in the Philippines chasing yet another obscure lead in her hunt for justice, so she dropped the phone back on the bed, finished drying herself, and slowly got dressed. It was time to explore her new surroundings, get her bearings, and begin her search for Mr Pat O'Riordan.

'You don't need anyone else,' she said to herself as she got up from the bed, experiencing that familiar mix of excitement, determination and defiance that had characterized her career so far, and which always seemed to lead her into danger.

Which was ironic, really, because she'd only taken a single step when she stopped. Dead. Staring at the door as the handle was turned from the outside and slowly began to open.

CHAPTER 24

I stopped outside room 927 and looked up and down the corridor. It was empty. I listened at the door, but couldn't hear anything. I was guessing the target was still inside, hopefully sleeping off the jetlag, which would make my job a lot easier. If she was awake, I was going to have to be silent and very quick. There'd be no time for hesitation, or second thoughts. Get through this and a new life awaited. Mess it up and I became a liability to Schagel. The stakes were that high.

In my line of business, you need to know how to break into places, and it's amazing how easy it can often be. The standard credit card trick of forcing the bolt doesn't tend to work with a lot of the new locks, but a variation of it still does. I pulled an old iTunes gift card from my wallet. It had an angled, square-inch divot cut out of the bottom and I slid it into the narrow gap between the door and the frame just above the lock. Next I lowered the card so that the bolt slotted comfortably into the divot. Finally, I gave it a couple of hard pushes, and the door clicked open.

Slipping the gun out of my waistband and screwing on the suppressor as surreptitiously as possible, I turned the handle and crept inside, thinking as I so often had before how sad it was that I'd become so proficient at burglary and murder after years spent trying to fight both.

I was in a short narrow hallway with the bathroom to my right and the bedroom beyond. The bathroom door was open but the light was off. I took a step forward, peering inside. Empty. I took another step forward. I could now see the bottom half of the bed. There was an open case on it, but no sign of the target. She must have gone out, which meant I was going to have to wait. Never a nice task, to spend time sitting amid the personal effects of someone you're going to kill, but at least it offered the element of surprise.

Relaxing a little, I stepped into the bedroom proper, catching sight of her only at the last possible second. She'd been waiting against the inside wall, and before I had a chance to pull the trigger, she slammed the butt end of one of the bedside lamps right into my jaw.

My head was knocked sideways from the force of the blow, the pain sudden and excruciating, but I did the only thing I could under the circumstances and kept hold of the gun.

But this girl was fast. She dropped the lamp and threw herself into me so I couldn't get a shot off, one hand grabbing my gun arm at the wrist and yanking it to one side, while she used the other to deliver a series of short, sharp punches to my already tender jaw.

Dazed, I stumbled back towards the other wall, with her still clinging to me, trying to knee me in the groin. But I kept my legs tight together, knowing I was going to have to do something soon to turn this around, because she was twisting my wrist with surprising strength, and I was only just managing to keep hold of the gun.

As I hit the wall, I pushed backwards and launched myself off it headfirst, trying to butt her in the face. She turned away from the blow, so that it only glanced her, but my momentum caused her to stumble and trip over the lamp she'd dropped. She went down, and I managed to yank my gun hand free of her grip. Unable to steady myself I fell over her, landing on the bed and rolling over on to my back.

She was on her feet in an instant and ready to spring at me again.

Until she saw that I still had the gun, and I was holding it outstretched in both hands, the end of the suppressor only five feet from her chest.

She froze. We both did. Staring at each other. Her expression neither defiant nor scared.

I thought of retirement again. If I just did this one last bloody task . . .

My finger tightened on the trigger.

Time slowed, then seemed to come to a complete stop as I realized that this was it. My choice. My crossroads. If I pulled the trigger, I was free. But the price would be truly heavy. Murdering a female police officer in cold blood. How would I be able to enjoy the peaceful evening sunsets knowing what I'd done?

What would Emma think? And our child?

I'd played hard and loose with my moral compass for far too long. Turned a blind eye to the rules I'd broken. Could I do it again one last time, when the victim was so clearly innocent of any crime?

The answer was no. I couldn't. Not even for the reward on offer.

And so it was with a feeling of relief, mixed with the first sign of trepidation, that I lowered the gun and placed it on the bed beside me.

CHAPTER 25

'You followed me from the airport, didn't you,' said Tina Boyd, staying where she was, her eyes lingering on the gun on the bed beside me.

I frowned, taken aback that it had been that obvious. 'Yeah, I did.'

She sighed and ran a hand through her short, spiky hair. 'I need a smoke, so I'm going to go over to the dresser and get my cigarettes. OK?'

I nodded, and watched as she retrieved her pack and lit one, thinking that this was a hugely surreal scene. Here I was having a polite conversation with someone who up until a few moments ago I'd been determined to kill. Now my retirement plans, so fresh and exciting only moments earlier, were fading in front of my eyes. Yet I knew I'd made the right decision. Killing her would have been a crime I'd have found impossible to live with, however hard I might have tried to convince myself otherwise.

Tina took the kind of long, slow drag on the cigarette that made me want to start smoking again. I noticed then that she was looking at me strangely.

'Do I know you from somewhere?' she asked.

'No,' I said firmly, starting to get up from the bed, knowing I had to leave before I made this situation any worse.

Tina retreated warily.

'It's all right,' I told her. 'I'm not going to hurt you.'

But my promise, unsurprisingly, didn't count for a great deal, and she kept going until she was backed up against the wall.

'Who sent you?' she asked.

'A man called Bertie Schagel. He organizes contract killings on behalf of other people,' I answered, sitting back down. 'When he finds out I haven't done this one he'll send someone else. You're not safe. You should leave.'

'Thanks for the advice,' she said, still staring at me in what seemed like a bizarrely intimate moment.

But then her eyes narrowed, and I saw the recognition in them.

'You're Dennis Milne, aren't you?' She paused. 'You look different. But not different enough.'

I should have picked up the gun and walked out right then. Left her behind and taken my chances. Thought of an excuse I could give to Schagel why I hadn't been able to kill her. But I didn't.

'That's right,' I said slowly.

'You murdering bastard. You were going to kill me, weren't you?'

'But I didn't,' I said, rubbing my face self-consciously where she'd struck it. It still hurt.

'Why not?'

'One, because you're a cop. And two, because I didn't think you deserved it.' Which was pretty much the truth.

Not that my admission did me much good, because the next second, she took a few quick steps forward and slapped me hard round the face.

'Jesus,' I said loudly, leaning back. 'Haven't you hurt me enough already?'

'That's for all the shame you've brought on the Met. And for nearly killing me.'

I rubbed my cheek, eyeing her warily in case she decided to continue the assault. 'Shouldn't you be trying to find out who it is who wants you dead? Schagel's only a broker. He works for other people.'

'I know full well who wants me dead. But why the hell should I tell you of all people?'

'Because I might be able to help,' I said.

But even as I spoke the words, I wondered why I was offering to get involved. Maybe it was a desire to atone for past sins. Maybe it was something more shallow, like rescuing a pretty damsel in distress, even though Tina Boyd didn't look or act much like she needed rescuing. Either way, I genuinely meant what I was saying.

Tina nodded slowly, then in one sudden movement, she reached down and grabbed the gun from the bed, pointing it at my chest, just like I'd done to her only a few minutes earlier. 'I ought to hand you straight in.'

I faced her down. 'Like I said, I might be able to help you.' I looked around the room. 'You're in Manila for a reason, and it's definitely not official business.'

'How do you know?'

'Because I was told by Schagel.'

She looked shocked. 'He knew? How?'

'I don't know, but whatever you're here for, you need to be very careful. This is a dangerous city.'

'So I'm finding out. And how did you get to be working for someone like him?'

'It's a long story.'

'I've got a long time.'

'OK. Put the gun down and I'll tell you.'

She hesitated for a moment, then placed it back on the bed.

I got up and moved away from where it lay, taking a seat by the desk in the far corner. Then I started talking.

I told her about my life in the early days in the Philippines; the move away to Ko Lanta; how I'd met Emma; and, finally, how I'd met, and ended up working for, Bertie Schagel. I missed out the bit where I'd returned to the UK to avenge the death of a former colleague (a man she may well have known), because a lot of people had been killed then, and I didn't want to incriminate myself any more than I already had.

'That's some story,' Tina said when I'd finished. She lit another cigarette, blew out a thin plume of smoke, and turned to face me properly. 'You know, I still can't quite believe that I'm having a conversation with a man who's just tried to kill me.'

'Well, believe it. And believe this too. The man who's after you knows you're here, which means you're in a lot of danger. But not from me.' I sensed that her stance was softening. 'Look, you're not going to get far in this town on your own, and I'm offering to watch your back. If you don't trust me, you keep the gun.' I nodded towards where it lay on the bed. 'Now it's your turn. What are you doing here?'

Tina sighed. 'The man I'm after is called Paul Wise. He's the one who I think ultimately hired you. He's a gangster, a drug dealer, and a child killer.'

'Sounds like a nice guy.'

'The problem is, he's also extremely wealthy, with friends in some very high places. So even after everything he's done, he's still walking free, and the British police are giving up on ever bringing him to justice. But I'm not going to. I've been after him for six years, ever since he had my boyfriend murdered. And I'm not going to stop.' She fixed me with an iron gaze. 'No matter what he tries to do to me.'

I liked her determination. I could relate to it. She was the kind of copper I'd once aspired to be, a long, long time back. I asked her why Wise had killed her boyfriend.

'John was a detective, and he'd found some

information about a gang of paedophiles that included Wise as well as several other high-profile figures. Wise wanted to make sure that the information was suppressed at any cost. They made John's death look like suicide. But I always knew it was murder.'

A tight knot began to develop in my gut. 'Your boyfriend. Was his last name Gallan?'

She nodded slowly. 'How did you know?'

'Because,' I said, 'I was the one who gave him the information.'

CHAPTER 26

Paul Wise was sitting on the villa's rear terrace watching the sun go down over the clear blue waters of the South China Sea when the phone call came through.

'Has the package arrived?' asked Bertie Schagel.

'It has,' said Wise. 'It's being kept safe in Manila for the moment. I don't want it brought down here until the last minute.'

'When is the meeting scheduled for?'

'Tuesday at eight p.m. Will you be sending your people to collect the package?'

'My two best men will be in the country tomorrow. They will pick it up and bring it to you on Tuesday morning. They'll also remain there until the meeting is concluded.'

'Are these the same two best men who failed to deal with our mutual friend when they ambushed her in her home?' asked Wise testily.

'They made a rare mistake,' replied Schagel with matching testiness. 'They will not make it a second time.'

'And what's happening about our mutual friend now? I understand she was on the same plane as me coming into Manila.' He chuckled. 'I thought that was a nice irony.'

'She's being dealt with by one of my other operatives. I'm currently awaiting confirmation that it's been done.'

'If he hasn't seen to her, how easy would it be to get hold of her alive?'

'No, no, no,' said Schagel impatiently. 'It would be far too difficult. It might jeopardize everything. Neither of us can afford that.'

'I understand, but if the opportunity presents itself, I'll pay another hundred thousand dollars.'

'How about we make a compromise?' said Schagel, ever the businessman. 'If she hasn't already been dealt with, I will tell my operative to make it as painful as possible. OK?'

'Please do. And if he could get me a souvenir – a photo, perhaps, or even better, some footage – I would be most appreciative.'

Schagel chuckled down the line. 'I will see what I can do.'

When the call had ended, Wise poured himself a glass of Château Coutet 1989 from the bottle in the chiller and took a tiny sip, savouring the taste. A good white wine sipped while watching the sun make its slow descent towards a calm azure sea was one of life's great pleasures.

As was revenge. Tina Boyd had been a thorn in his side for far too long now. He'd left her alone, thinking that to take her out would only gain him unwanted attention, but still she'd persisted in

186

aggravating him. It was only when her new lover, the journalist Penny, had started poking his nose into affairs that had nothing to do with him that he'd finally concluded enough was enough. Even then, though, she'd managed to weasel her way out of what was coming to her.

But now Tina Boyd had made a huge mistake. She was coming into territory that Wise knew well, and considered his own. So much so that he was planning to base himself here permanently in the near future, now that his bitch of a wife had demanded a divorce after hearing some of the allegations levelled against him. He had a network of contacts in the Philippines, and even though he'd had to have some of them eliminated for the sake of security, there were plenty of others to call upon.

He took a deep, relaxed breath, savouring the smell of the bougainvillea coming from the garden below, and allowed himself to fantasize about getting his hands on Tina Boyd. He imagined taking her down to the basement beneath the villa where he could use his instruments to beat, humiliate and torture her until he'd debased her to such an extent that her spirit was completely broken. Only when he'd tired of the game would he remind her of his role in the death of her loved ones while he slowly squeezed the last of the life from her. And then, finally, she'd join the others, in a shallow grave among the acacia trees beyond the lawn.

He took another sip of his wine and placed the glass on the marble coffee table.

It was time to talk to Mr Heed, the man looking after the package for him in Manila, and tell him to expect a visit.

CHAPTER 27

'What the hell are you talking about?' demanded Tina, shocked by the revelation that Dennis Milne, the man who only minutes earlier had been on the verge of killing her, knew something about the murder of her lover John Gallan.

She took another pull on her cigarette, suddenly feeling very claustrophobic in this airless little hotel room thousands of miles from home. A wave of nausea hit her. She knew it was shock. When she'd been staring down the barrel of Milne's gun, she'd been convinced it was the end of the road, that her luck had finally run out. Strangely, she hadn't felt any fear. Just a sense of inevitability, as if violent death had always been her destiny. Even so, her heart was still thumping, and her legs felt weak.

'But John died years after you went on the run,' she said, forcing herself to focus on this new information.

'I know,' said Milne, who was still sitting in the chair by the desk on the other side of the bed. 'But I came back to England a few years back. I wanted to find out who'd murdered an old colleague of mine. It turned out to be a gang of paedophiles who called themselves The Hunters. I killed them all, except for a man called Tristram Parnham-Jones, who was the Lord Chief Justice at the time. Because I couldn't get to Parnham-Jones, I contacted John Gallan, because I knew he was a man I could trust, and I gave him a dossier with all the details of what these guys had done. I heard later that Parnham-Jones committed suicide as well.'

'He didn't,' said Tina, stunned that Milne was somehow involved in all this. 'Parnham-Jones's suicide was Wise's doing too. You might have thought you'd killed all The Hunters, but you were wrong. You left the worst one of all alive.'

'That's what I can't understand,' said Milne, looking puzzled. 'I had it on extremely good authority that, apart from Parnham-Jones, there were no survivors.'

'What kind of authority?'

Milne took a deep breath, as if he was reluctant to say. 'I interrogated the most senior of The Hunters, a man called Eric Thadeus,' he said at last. 'I made him give up the names of everyone. He was under a lot of pressure to tell me the truth.'

Tina could believe that. There was a hard yet haunted look about Milne. His face was thin; the lines on the heavily tanned skin deep and pronounced; and his pale grey-blue eyes reflected the darkness that he'd inhabited at times these past nine years, and the terrible deeds he'd done. He was still good-looking, but in a brutal, intense way, and with his greying hair and the signs of plastic surgery round his eyes and nose, he easily looked his age.

Milne frowned suddenly. 'Hold on. Thadeus did tell me something. I remember now. He said that there'd been a man called Wise in The Hunters, but that he'd died a few years earlier.'

Tina shook her head. 'No, Paul Wise is very much alive, but I've found out something that could destroy him.' She wondered then whether she was making the right move by opening up to Milne. But she needed allies, and right then, they were very thin on the ground.

'And what's that?' he asked.

'If you know about The Hunters, then you know Paul Wise's background. He was involved in the abduction and murder of a young girl back in England.'

Tina watched as he nodded, the memory crossing his face like a shadow. 'Her name was Heidi Robes,' he said. 'Thirteen years old. I'll remember the details about her as long as I live.'

'Well,' she said. 'In September 2007, a twelve-year-old girl from New Zealand went missing in Phnom Penh and was never seen again. The following year, a thirteen-year-old Danish girl went missing here in Manila. Again, no trace of her was ever found. But in both cases, Paul Wise was in the country when they disappeared, and in both cases he'd flown in forty-eight hours before, and left within a week.'

'And you think he was the one who abducted them?'

'He wouldn't have done it himself. He'd have got other people to do it. That's the way he operates. But I know he's involved.'

'Any proof?'

'The man who found out this information, a journalist called Nick Penny who Wise was suing for defamation, was murdered three days ago.' Tina had to fight to stop her voice from cracking as she pictured Nick, and recalled what had happened to him. 'Then there was an attempt on my life twenty-four hours later. Definitely not the actions of an innocent man, and definitely no coincidence.' She paused. 'And now Wise is in Manila.'

'And you think he's going to take another girl?'

'He's definitely up to something. Nick Penny was in touch with a journalist here, a guy who wrote a number of articles about the disappearance of the girl in Manila in 2008, and a possible link to western paedophiles. I can't get hold of the journalist, which is one of the reasons I came out here. To interview him.'

Milne gave her a strange look. 'His name wouldn't be Patrick O'Riordan, would it?'

Tina frowned. 'O'Riordan, yes,' she said uncertainly, wondering how on earth he'd known.

'Then I'm afraid you've got a problem.'

'What do you mean?'

'Schagel sent me here to kill O'Riordan. I did it yesterday.'

Tina felt a lurch of shock that was almost physical. It was the calm, even way the man in front of her had just confessed to the murder. He was looking at her now with a mildly regretful, almost hangdog expression, as if he'd done nothing more than traipse dog shit across her living-room carpet, and she was suddenly filled with an intense, unstoppable fury.

Without thinking, she strode across the room, grabbed Milne by his shirt, hauled him to his feet and slammed him into the wall with a force that surprised even her. He made no move to resist as she brought her face close to his. 'He was just a bloody journalist doing his job!' she yelled. 'Like Nick was doing when they murdered him!'

'I know,' he said quietly. 'I wish I hadn't done it.'

'And that's meant to make it all right, is it? It's murder! It's permanent! Don't you understand that? What's wrong with you?'

She let go of him and turned away, unable to look at him any more.

'Jesus Christ, you disgust me. And you've probably ruined the last chance of bringing a brutal child killer to justice. I hope you're fucking proud of yourself.' She grabbed another cigarette from the pack by the bed and lit it angrily, keeping her back to him. 'Get the hell out of here. Now. Before I call the police.'

But he didn't move. 'You won't be able to get your revenge without me, Tina,' he said softly.

'Don't flatter yourself.'

'I've got leads. Real ones. You haven't.'

The problem for Tina was, he was right. Without O'Riordan, she had nothing. And that was the other problem. Milne was a cold-blooded murderer. Even being in the same room as him sickened her. And yet . . . In the end, the most important thing, as it had always been, was to get Wise. Even if it meant using the services of characters as unsavoury as Dennis Milne.

She turned round to face him, curiosity getting the better of her. 'Go on then. What leads have you got?'

'One: O'Riordan's wife. I had the keys to his house. They came from somewhere. And O'Riordan had a male lover. It looked like it was serious, which suggests it had been going on a while. So, it's possible his wife paid him back by setting him up on behalf of Wise, or Schagel. At the very least it means she knows something. There was a report about O'Riordan's death in the paper this morning which said that the wife had been staying with relatives just outside Manila for the weekend, which is why she wasn't there when he was killed. And that also strikes me as very convenient. If we can track her down, then she might be able to give us some information.'

'We?'

'I told you, I want to help.'

'And why exactly should I trust you?'

'Because it's not going to take long for Schagel to realize that I haven't killed you. And as soon as he does, he's going to come looking for me. We're both fugitives, Tina.'

She considered this for a moment, again knowing that he was right, and that whatever sins he may have committed, he was risking his neck now by not killing her. 'OK, O'Riordan's wife is one lead, and I suppose it has potential. What else?'

'O'Riordan had a meeting planned for yesterday. I'm sure it had something to do with the reason he had to die. It was scheduled for three p.m., and I had a time limit of two o'clock for killing him. I was also ordered to burn down his house, to get rid of any evidence.' He reached into his pocket and pulled out a couple of crumpled pieces of paper, which he carefully unfolded. 'These are the actual pages from his diary. I've got the name of the man he was meant to be meeting. I don't recognize it, but you might. Omar Salic?'

'I don't,' she said, shaking her head, still shocked by the matter-of-fact way in which Milne was talking about O'Riordan's murder. But she took the proffered pages. 'I can look into it.'

'How about Cheeseman? It's there next to Salic's name. Mean anything to you?'

Again she shook her head. Neither name was remotely familiar to her. 'We're not getting far here, are we?' She made no effort to disguise the contempt in her voice.

If he noticed her tone, he didn't show it. 'There's one more thing. I was booked into a crappy hotel on my first night here and the gun I used for the O'Riordan job was already there, under the bed in my room. Whoever put it there probably could not have done so without the hotel owner's knowledge, which means we need to speak to him.'

'What makes you think he'll cooperate?'

Milne fixed her with a hard stare. 'He'll cooperate, don't worry about that.'

Now Tina knew it was her turn to make a decision. Milne had made his by not pulling the trigger. Now she had to decide whether to continue her investigation alone, or throw in her lot with a wanted hitman.

'You don't have to come with me,' he said, seeing her hesitation. 'I can go alone, and update you later.'

Tina gave him a grim smile and picked up the gun from the bed. 'No thanks,' she said, accepting what she had to do. 'I'll come with you. We're fugitives together, remember?'

CHAPTER 28

Dusk was beginning to make its presence felt, and the hawkers were still hanging round outside the guesthouse I'd been booked into when I first arrived in Manila. As Tina and I got out of the taxi on the other side of the road they immediately swarmed round us and I had to literally swot them away, but still they followed, undeterred, thrusting their fake Rolexes and packs of cigarettes under our noses as we made our way over to the gate.

I pressed the buzzer, and after a lengthy pause the owner's voice came over the intercom, sounding just as morose as it had when I'd first checked in. I identified myself as Robert Mercer, a guest from the previous day, and said I needed a room for the night again, confident that in a dump like this one there'd always be a room free. I was right, because he grunted an OK, and then a few seconds later I heard his slow footfalls, and the sound of the gate being unlocked from the other side. I gave Tina a look that said that for the purposes of this interview she should leave the questioning to me.

The owner poked his head out and said something uncomplimentary to one of the hawkers in the local Tagalog dialogue, before giving us a quick once-over, his eyes lingering on Tina just a little longer than necessary. Then he let us inside.

The narrow little yard was empty, and I didn't hesitate, pulling the gun from beneath my jacket and thrusting it into his side. His eyes widened as he looked down, and out of the corner of my eye I saw Tina turn away.

I fixed him with a cold glare. 'Let's go back to your office. We can talk there. If you do anything stupid, I'll kill you. Do you understand me?'

'Yes, yes,' he said, nodding frantically, and I slipped the gun back under my jacket, motioning for him to lead the way.

We walked through the poky little lobby with the empty reception desk facing us, and into a cluttered back room that was part office, part storage area. It smelled of sweat, and the ceiling fan did little to alleviate the hot mustiness.

The owner turned to face us as I brought the gun back out. 'What do you want, boss? I haven't done nothing.'

'Sit down.'

He slumped down into a creaky chair, and I took a step forward so I was standing above him, the gun pointed down towards his belly.

'You remember me, don't you?'

'Yes, boss,' he said uncertainly, clearly trying to work out what answer I wanted to hear. He was sweating profusely as he stared at me, looking like he might burst into tears at any moment.

I felt sorry for him then, but this was no time for weakness.

'When I stayed here the other night, there was a gun under the bed in my room waiting for me. Who put it there?'

'I don't know what you mean, boss.'

Moving fast, I grabbed his flabby chin and thrust the gun in his face, ignoring his gasp of terror. 'Tell me. Now. Someone must have come here. Who?'

Behind me, I could hear Tina shifting her weight uneasily from foot to foot. I'd told her on the way over here that I might have to be a little rough with my interrogation techniques, and she'd acquiesced on the proviso that I didn't hurt him. I knew I wouldn't have to. Most people will tell you what you need to know when they've got a gun pointed in their face, and this guy was no exception.

'A man came here the other night,' he said hurriedly, his eyes almost crossed as he focused on the gun. 'He said he wanted to leave a package in the room where you were going to stay.'

I pushed the gun harder against his skin, pulling back the hammer, my eyes cold. 'Give me a name.'

'I don't know his name. Honest, boss. He was an *extranjero*. He used to stay here sometimes a long time ago. That's why I said yes. I didn't know what was in the package, I promise.'

199

I believed him. He was crying now, and I didn't dare look back at Tina.

'Tell me what he looked like,' I said.

'He was a white man. English. Your age maybe, boss. Blond hair, like your friend. And tattoos. He had tattoos. One on his neck. Like a snake or something.' He tapped a dirty finger on his jugular to demonstrate. 'Honest, boss. That's all I know. Please.'

That was when I heard the trickling sound and looked down to see a small puddle of urine forming on the dirty floor. Poor bastard, I thought, reholstering the gun and taking a step back.

'Thanks for your time,' I said quietly. 'And if you ever say a word to anyone about this visit, I'll come back and I'll kill you.'

He didn't reply. He was sobbing silently, urine pooling round his cheap shoes.

I turned away, ignoring Tina's accusing expression, and together we walked out of there in heavy silence.

Only when we were back on the street did Tina finally speak. 'That was horrible,' was all she said as we walked down towards the main road, ignoring the hawkers.

'It had to be done.'

'Did it? I don't see that we're any further forward. That kind of description hardly narrows down our list of suspects.'

'Well, that's where you're wrong,' I said, turning

towards her. 'I know exactly who he's talking about.'

'Who?'

'My old business partner. Tomboy Darke.'

CHAPTER 29

I'd booked us into separate rooms in a small, family-run guesthouse in one of the less touristy areas of Manila, paying in cash so we couldn't be traced. On the way there I told Tina about how I'd fallen out with Tomboy.

'He was always a rogue and a liar. But he was a character too, and I never had him down as anything more than a petty criminal with a bit more ambition than most. We were good mates as well as business partners. But when I went back to the UK to find out who killed my old colleague, I discovered a link between Tomboy and the group of paedophiles Wise was involved with. As far as I'm aware, he was never one of them, but it was Tomboy who got rid of the body of Heidi Robes. If it had been anyone else, I would have gone after him. As it was, I told him that if I ever clapped eyes on him again, he'd be a dead man.'

'So he knew Wise?'

I let out a deep breath, still thrown off-balance by what I'd just found out. 'I guess he must have done.'

'Do you think he knew it was you he was delivering the gun to?'

I'd been wondering about that. 'No,' I said. 'Otherwise I don't think he'd have done it. But the thing is, he's involved, which means we need to pay him a visit.'

'Have you any idea where he's based these days?'

'He used to live in Mindoro. We both did. It's about three hours south of here, so it's as good a place to start as any.' I looked at my watch. We were outside the guesthouse now and it was dark, 'It's a bit too late to go now, but do you want to take a trip down south tomorrow morning?'

She eyed me warily, as if still unsure of my intentions. In all honesty, I couldn't blame her. Finally, she nodded.

I asked her if she fancied joining me for a bite to eat, keen to demonstrate that I wasn't some kind of monster, but I wasn't surprised when she said no.

'I'm tired and jetlagged,' she said. 'I just need to sleep.' As if to reinforce the point, she yawned. 'I'll meet you here in the morning. Make it nine. That'll give me time to get myself together.'

'Sure. And, Tina? Trust me. Please. I know it's not easy right now, but I'm not going to do anything to harm you. I promise.'

'I'm going to have to trust you, aren't I?' She was looking me in the eye, her face set hard. 'Look, I appreciate the fact that you didn't pull the trigger when you had a chance, but that doesn't change the fact that I despise you for all the things you've done. And I always will. Make sure you don't forget that.'

And with that, she turned away and walked inside.

I watched her go in grim, shameful silence. I was a pariah, a man who could expect sympathy from no one. It was a painful thought, but one I'd become used to; yet sometimes I still felt misunderstood. Because the fact was, I had a conscience. I'd always had one. I was no socio-pathic killing machine, whatever the tally of the men who'd died by my hand might suggest. I'd been a good cop once. I still wanted to make the world a better place, even in my darkest moments. And, in the end, it was because I still cared that I found myself in the position I was in, defying the one person with the power to destroy me.

Bertie Schagel not only knew my true identity, it was he who'd created my fake one as well. He knew what I looked like, and on more than one occasion he'd suggested that he'd had photos taken of me at our meetings that could easily be released to the police if he wanted them to be. I suspected he also tracked my movements through the ID, which wouldn't have been that hard, and meant that he knew I lived in Luang Prabang. In short, he owned me, and without his help or the fake ID I was effectively trapped in the Philippines.

My only hope was that he wouldn't want to betray me to the police, just in case it somehow backfired on him. That said, he would certainly want me out of the way, and the best way to do that would be to kill me. I knew I wasn't the only killer on his books, and certainly not the cruellest. The decapitated Russian woman in Kuala Lumpur was a perfect illustration of that. If I were Schagel, I would send someone else to kill Tina, then me as well.

All this meant we had to move fast. But as I checked the phone I'd bought the previous day, I saw that I had three missed calls from blocked numbers, which meant Schagel had been calling me, no doubt hunting for an update on Tina's status. I'd had the phone on silent, because I'd been putting off talking to him for as long as possible, but I knew I couldn't wait any longer. It was only a matter of time before he found out that I'd gone over to the other side.

Before I called him, I went to an internet café across the street and got online. It had always been a habit of mine, since I'd begun to work for Schagel, not to read anything about the individuals I'd killed once the job was done, because I never liked to know too much about those whose lives I'd ended. But tonight I was making an exception. I needed to reassure myself that, by sparing Tina's life and effectively destroying any hope of a comfortable retirement in the rolling hills of Laos, I'd made the right decision.

I Googled O'Riordan's name and read everything I could about him, concentrating

205

particularly on the articles that, if Tina was to be believed, had ended up getting him killed. He'd written three on the disappearance of the thirteen-year-old Danish girl, Lene Haagen, from her Manila hotel room in 2008, all within a month of her disappearance. A photo of Lene appeared in one of them. She was pretty, with lots of blonde curly hair, and had a big gap-toothed smile. Although no trace of her had ever been found, O'Riordan stated in his two later articles that she'd almost certainly been snatched to order on behalf of a western paedophile gang with strong connections to establishment figures within the Philippine judiciary. He provided a number of pieces of evidence to back up his claims, including the disappearance of two local girls of the same age in the previous eighteen months. Most damning of all was the death, five days after Lene's disappearance, of the nightwatchman at the hotel from where she'd gone missing – a man O'Riordan claimed police sources had told him was a prime suspect in the case – who'd been shot dead outside his home during an apparent robbery. It looked a hell of a lot like O'Riordan was on the right track. But then the articles stopped, just like that, and as much as I tried, I couldn't find anything more that he'd written about Lene. It was as if the world and O'Riordan had simply decided it was time to move on. I guessed that he'd been warned off by someone.

Finally, after close to half an hour on the PC, I logged out, feeling sick about what I'd done to

Patrick O'Riordan. I'd murdered a decent man. I remembered Tina's parting words, the hardness in her voice as she'd said how much she despised me, and thought once again how badly my life had gone wrong.

When I got back up to my room, I called Bertie Schagel's number and left a message.

He was back on the phone in the space of a minute. 'News?' he demanded tersely.

I kept the hatred I felt for him firmly under control. 'I've lost her.'

'How?'

I explained that when I'd got to Tina's room, she wasn't there. 'I must have missed her on the elevators. I stayed inside her room for the best part of the last six hours, but she still hasn't come back.'

Schagel cursed. 'This I do not need. Where are you now?'

'In the hotel lobby. That's why I'm talking quietly.'

'OK, here is the deal. If you want to retire, make sure you find her before midday tomorrow and eliminate her. Otherwise I will use someone who can, and our deal will be off. Call me the minute it's done.'

He cut the connection and I stood staring at the phone for a long time, knowing I'd now burned all my bridges, and wondering if I'd made a terrible mistake. It even crossed my mind, for just a split second, to go down to Tina's room and do what Schagel was paying me to do. But I recognized the feeling for what it was: a moment of weakness. This wasn't the time for regrets. For the first time in a long time, it felt like I was doing the right thing.

I switched off the phone and removed the SIM before throwing it in the bin. I had no further use for it now. Then I opened the window, bent the SIM in half, and sent it fluttering into the warm night air. I stood there looking out over the vast cluster of lowrise buildings, interspersed with the occasional tower block, that was the Manila skyline. It was an uninspiring sight that only added to my sense of utter loneliness.

In truth, I'd been upset that Tina wouldn't join me for a meal. It had been months since I'd had female company for dinner, the last person being a middle-aged German woman called Ilsa who was on a year off following a messy divorce. She'd stayed in Luang Prabang for a month and during that time we'd had an uneasy, rather unsatisfying fling. Both of us were in need of some kind of physical closeness, and were going for the nearest available option, but there were no tears, and only the briefest of goodbyes, when she moved on to her next destination. Other than that, there'd been no one since Emma.

Emma. I started thinking about her again, as I did so often, but forced the thoughts aside. I couldn't change the past. It was gone. Finished with. All I could do now was change the future.

Paul Wise. A man I'd never known, and whose

name before today I'd heard only once. That had been on a cold winter's night in England more than six years earlier, when I'd been told by a bleeding, broken man that he was dead. Except he hadn't been dead. Instead, he was linked somehow to my old friend Tomboy. Linked to me too. Inextricably.

And not just for my actions of the past forty-eight hours.

You see, the first job I'd done for Bertie Schagel, shortly after he bribed the Cambodian police to release me from their custody, had been in Phnom Penh. It had involved killing a western man called Robert Sharman. All I'd known about Sharman was that he was a private detective who was snooping around where he shouldn't have been. At the time I was just grateful to be free, and knew that there was no point in worrying too much about what I had to do.

I'd shot him in the back of the head using a nine-millimetre pistol with suppressor, not far from the world-famous tourist bar the Heart of Darkness. He'd been drunk at the time and an easy target, stumbling into the night having just had a shouting match with a rickshaw driver. He seemed a rude, obnoxious sort, which was how I justified his killing to myself.

But when I was in the internet café earlier, I Googled the name Robert Sharman and discovered that he'd been hired by the family of missing twelve-year-old Letitia McDonald, the girl Tina

209

claimed had been murdered by Wise, to investigate her abduction from a hotel in Phnom Penh six months earlier on a family holiday, after the local police had drawn a blank, only to be shot dead in an apparent robbery three days after arriving in the country.

That was when I realized that for the last three years, I'd been working on behalf of a cabal of child killers.

Now was my chance to make them pay for their sins.

Whatever it cost me.

CHAPTER 30

Tina Boyd lay stretched out on her hotel bed, and laughed out loud.

A wanted man had tried to kill her today, and had come close to succeeding, and not only had she not handed him in to the local police, she'd actually gone into partnership with the guy. Even in a life as dramatic as hers had become these past few years, the day's events would take some beating.

Although exhausted from all the travelling, she was still wired from the adrenalin punch of having to fight for her life only a matter of hours earlier. Once again she'd come within a whisker of death, yet somehow her luck had held out. Bizarrely, she trusted Milne. She even felt sorry for him after what he'd told her about his years on the run, particularly the woman and the unborn child he'd had to leave behind.

It was possible he could have been spinning her a yarn, of course, but Tina didn't think so. She might have become something of a cynic over the course of her career – an inevitability, given the violence and the tragedies that the job had flung in her face – but the heartfelt manner in which Milne had told his story rang very true. If it was an act, it was a damn good one. And the thing was, nobody she'd ever spoken to who'd known Dennis Milne had ever described him as a psychopath. They'd thought him a flawed, bitter character who'd betrayed his colleagues and his profession terribly, but still a man who'd been brought low by circumstances, rather than having started off that way.

And he was a useful, if dangerous, ally. Tina might not have agreed with his methods – putting a gun to the head of a man and scaring him so much that he wet himself was brutal in the extreme, and she'd almost intervened – but the fact was, they worked. The man had talked. Others would too. At home, Tina was constrained by a constant stream of rules and regulations, and the rights of suspects were paramount. Out here, and especially with Milne helping her, everything was far more flexible. She knew she would have to watch herself, so she didn't cross the same line that he had all those years ago. And she knew too that she had to keep her distance from him emotionally. Milne was a criminal. She wasn't. Their partnership was a marriage of convenience. Nothing more.

And after it had run its course, what would she do then?

That was a question for later.

Hungry suddenly, she ordered a pizza from room

service, and while she waited for it to arrive she booted up her laptop. She got out the pages from O'Riordan's diary that Milne had given her and examined them before Googling the name Omar Salic. There were no relevant matches. The same with Cheeseman. But Milne was right. The meeting had to have had a bearing on O'Riordan's death, and she wondered if Salic was some kind of pimp with information about the abductions.

Lighting a cigarette, she looked at the tangled mess of doodles and phone numbers that made up the other diary pages, thinking that it was highly unlikely she'd find anything of use there. But then she spotted a phone number running along the top of Friday, and next to it a scrawl which on closer inspection looked like 'Marie at Jean-Pauls'. Tina remembered Milne telling her that Mrs O'Riordan had been staying out of town with relatives at the time of her husband's murder.

A visit to a Philippines-based website providing census information and a single credit-card payment quickly elicited a copy of O'Riordan's wedding certificate, and confirmation that his wife's maiden name was Marie Gomez. Twenty minutes, one pizza and several more credit-card payments to various reverse look-up sites later, Tina had found out that the number on the top of the page belonged to a Mr and Mrs Simangan of Ternate, a coastal town about fifty miles south-west of Manila.

Tina sat back on the bed and rubbed her eyes,

pleased that she'd found a possible location for O'Riordan's wife. That didn't mean she'd cooperate, though, particularly if she'd had any involvement in her husband's death, and Tina wasn't sure if she could allow Milne to put his gun to the head of a defenceless and recently widowed woman who might well not be guilty of anything.

The lead that Milne had to his old business partner, Tomboy Darke, might also be worth something, but Tina knew better than to rely on it. She needed more information, something that linked Wise directly to the killings she was convinced he'd committed. Now that he was back in the Philippines, she wondered if he had a house here. Because if he did, it was possible that Lene Haagen, who'd disappeared in Manila in 2008, had died there. And if she had, there would still be evidence, however microscopic, at the scene. Evidence that could be used to incriminate him.

She knew who she had to call.

It was early Sunday afternoon UK time, and Mike Bolt picked up after three rings. There was no small talk.

'What can I do for you, Tina?' he asked warily, as if half expecting that she'd got herself in trouble and needed his help – which, to be fair, had been characteristic of their relationship over the last few years. 'I'm out with Claire at the moment. Is everything OK?'

Claire was his girlfriend, now fiancée, a woman Tina had never met, and didn't want to know too much about. Even so, Mike had still taken her call, which she supposed counted for something (although she wasn't a hundred per cent sure what).

She told him she was fine.

'Where are you? It sounds like you're somewhere abroad.'

There was no way round it, so she told him she was in the Philippines.

'Christ, Tina.' He paused briefly. 'Have you heard about Nick Penny?' he asked uncertainly, clearly thinking she hadn't.

'Yes. It wasn't suicide.'

'I thought you'd say that.' He didn't add that he'd heard she'd been having an affair with Penny, even though she was sure he would have done.

Having got this far with the conversation, Tina gave Mike a brief rundown of the events of the past forty-eight hours, including what Penny had found out about the two missing girls, as well as the attempt on her life and the fact that she'd seen Paul Wise in the flesh at Singapore airport. Sensibly, she made no mention of the fact that she'd now teamed up with a man wanted in the UK for mass murder.

When she'd finished, Mike let out a loud, frustrated sigh. 'If you were attacked, why the hell didn't you report it?'

'Who's going to believe me, Mike? There were no witnesses. No obvious evidence. And you know my history. The leave for stress, the drinking . . .'

'So instead you disappear off to the Philippines, a dangerous country you know nothing about, on a one-woman crusade that's either going to be a complete waste of time, or in the worst-case scenario might even get you killed.'

'I need your help,' she said, in no mood to tolerate a lecture, even though she knew what he was saying was true.

'You always need my help.' Again there was that hostility in his tone that she'd detected the last time they'd spoken.

'This time it won't get you into trouble. I promise. I need to know if Paul Wise has property in the Philippines. And if so, where it is.'

'Why? So you can go round and have it out with him? Demand that he confess to his crimes? It's not going to happen, Tina, don't you understand that?'

He was right. Even if she and Milne did track down Wise to whatever bolthole he was using, in reality there was nothing they could do about it. It was something she'd been conveniently trying to forget.

She sighed. The phone call to Mike had been a stupid move.

'I understand everything you're saying,' she told him, 'but I'm following up a couple of separate leads and it would help me if you could find out what property and connections Wise has here.' She thought about adding that it would also be helpful if he could find out if the name Bertie

Schagel came up on any of the intelligence databases, but decided against it, concluding that the answer might raise too many difficult questions. For the moment, she wanted to be as straight as she could be with Mike.

He told her that he'd see what he could do but was unable to promise anything. Off the top of his head, he didn't know of any obvious link Wise had to the Philippines, or even Cambodia. The Soca investigation into Wise had, he admitted, been scaled down on orders from high up, due to the lack of any concrete evidence linking him to any crimes, and the fact that he was prepared to sue anyone who suggested otherwise.

His tone angered Tina. 'Don't you want him caught?' she demanded. 'After all he's done? His actions could have had you killed as well, you know.'

'I know all that,' he snapped back. 'And I've done everything I can to bring him to justice, including risking my neck to help you, and paying the price for it. But I'm also a pragmatist. You can't continue to pour all your resources into catching one man if you've got no evidence.' He stopped his rant, took a couple of deep breaths, and told her he had to go, that he'd get back to her when he could. His last words to her were 'be careful'.

Tina had never been careful in her life, and it was unlikely she was going to start now. She and Mike both knew that; it was one of the things that had finished their relationship before it had even started. As always, she'd rely on the potent mixture of cunning, determination and luck that had kept her going this far.

As weariness finally overtook her, she put the chain on the door and got ready for bed, hoping that she wasn't making a terrible mistake by trusting the man who, only six hours earlier, had come to her room with the express intention of killing her.

CHAPTER 31

The house was immense. Set back behind a high wall, fronted with a line of mature mahogany trees, it sat on an isolated stretch of road a few miles to the north-east of Ternate town. It was built in Spanish colonial style, over three floors, with a tiled roof and shuttered windows, while long sprawling fingers of ivy and bougainvillea climbed up the sand-coloured walls. It spoke confidently of money and taste, and I wondered if we had the right place, because whoever lived here had serious wealth.

I knew better than to question Tina's information, though. In truth, I was impressed by the way she'd hunted down a location for Mrs O'Riordan so quickly, and had told her so – a compliment that she'd accepted with a single nod of the head. It was fair to say that our relationship was stuck fast on a cold, professional level, and would probably remain that way for its duration, however long that might be.

Tina had hired the car we'd come down here in, and had insisted on driving. Our plan was to see what we could find out from Mrs O'Riordan, then continue along the coast in the direction of Mindoro, where Tomboy hopefully still resided. I'd tried to break the silence and make conversation during the hour-and-a-half-long journey down here, but Tina had made it clear she wasn't interested in small talk.

I'd found it an uncomfortable journey, and not just because Tina didn't want to speak to me. By now, Bertie Schagel would have realized that I'd betrayed him. Either he would give me up to the authorities or, more likely, he'd send someone else to take out Tina, and probably me as well. Either way, we were now racing against the clock to find evidence that would bring down Paul Wise. But even if such evidence did exist, and we found it, what would happen afterwards to me? Even if Tina didn't turn me in – and there was no guarantee of that – my future still looked pretty damn uncertain.

It had just turned 11.30 a.m. as Tina drove through the open gates towards the house, the car's tyres crunching on the newly gravelled driveway. On either side sprinklers were spraying the emerald-green lawn, and a middle-aged Filipino man in overalls was pruning a hedge. As we got out of the car, he approached us, shears in hand, a less than cheery expression on his weathered features.

'What do you want?' he demanded, stopping in front of us, his grip on the shears just a little too tight for comfort.

Unfazed, Tina held up her British warrant card. 'My name is Detective Inspector Tina Boyd from the British police, and this is my colleague . . .'

She hesitated briefly, so I piped up with my current pseudonym. 'Detective Robert Mercer.'

'We're here to speak to Mrs Marie O'Riordan. Is she here?'

'What do you want with her? My sister is very distressed at the moment. Her husband has just been murdered.'

'We know,' said Tina, softening her voice. 'And we're very sorry to hear it. We need to speak to her about the murder. We believe it has something to do with a related crime in the United Kingdom.'

'She was staying with me at the time, and she has already spoken with the police. She knows nothing about any of it.' He swept a hand back towards the gate. 'Now, leave.'

'Sir,' I said, taking a step forward and looking him right in the eye. 'If we leave, we will only have to come back with representatives of the Filipino police. Both our countries are cooperating in this case. We believe Mr O'Riordan was investigating a matter of great seriousness as part of his job, and that's why he was murdered. We need to find out if your sister knows anything, however small, that might help us. Please. It'll only take a few minutes.'

He seemed to relax a little, and thankfully, so did his grip on the shears. 'Wait here. I will see if Marie is willing to talk.'

When he'd gone, I gave Tina a sideways glance, risking a small smile. 'I think your haircut scared him. It makes you look like Brigitte Nielsen.'

'Who the hell's Brigitte Nielsen?' she said.

'She was an eighties film star, very Amazonian-looking. Married to Sylvester Stallone?'

'Ah, long before my time, I'm afraid.'

We looked at each other. She didn't return my smile, but nor was she frowning, and I thought I detected the first hint of a thaw in her demeanour. Or maybe I was just hoping.

Mrs O'Riordan's brother reappeared in the open doorway. 'Marie will see you for five minutes, but I don't want her upset. She is very emotional at the moment.'

He led us through a beautifully tiled hallway with high vaulted ceilings and into a light and spacious lounge, with old-fashioned furnishings and a huge bay window looking out on to the back lawn. Seated stiffly on an uncomfortable-looking chaise longue was a Filipina woman in her late forties, dressed all in black. She was clutching a tissue, and it looked like she'd been crying recently.

Straight away I thought she was trying too hard.

The brother stood behind the chaise longue, a protective hand on the recently widowed Mrs O'Riordan, while I made the introductions.

'It's a nice place you have here,' I said, looking around admiringly.

'It's not ours,' she said distractedly, waving an

arm in the direction of some chairs. 'Jean-Paul looks after it for the owners. I stay with him sometimes.'

'It's lucky you were staying here this weekend,' said Tina as we sat down in chairs opposite her.

'It isn't,' said Mrs O'Riordan vehemently. 'My husband is dead. I wish I was with him now.' Her face creased up and I thought she was going to cry, but she evidently stopped herself.

'Do you have any idea who might have killed him?' I asked.

'Who are you? And what is your interest in Patrick?'

When Tina and I had discussed how we were going to play this interview on the way here, we'd decided to come straight to the point and tell Mrs O'Riordan everything we knew. The theory was that if she was involved in setting up her husband, she'd be overcome with guilt when she found out that the reason for his murder was because he was on the brink of exposing a group of western paedophiles involved in child abductions, and would tell us everything she knew.

So Tina spelled out the details of the disappearance of Lene Haagen in 2008, and how it linked to other earlier disappearances, before culminating in the murder of Nick Penny, and of course Pat O'Riordan himself.

Unfortunately, our theory didn't work, because when Tina finished speaking, Mrs O'Riordan looked at us both blankly and said she knew nothing about any of that.

'Did your husband ever talk to you about his work?' I asked her.

'No. That was always his business.'

I raised a sceptical eyebrow. 'Never? You were married twenty-three years, and he was a journalist that whole time. And you never discussed his work?'

'Maybe in the early days, but not for a long time.'

She looked me dead in the eyes as she spoke, as if defying me to disbelieve her, but she seemed uncomfortable, and I noticed that she was rubbing her hands together anxiously, and tapping her foot. My police interview training was a long way out of date, and it was obvious that with the death of her husband she'd suffered a huge shock to her system, but even so, something in her tone felt wrong.

She knew something. I was sure of it. So, it seemed, was Tina.

'When did you come here, Mrs O'Riordan?' she asked.

'On Friday. For the weekend.'

'My sister will be staying here longer now,' said Jean-Paul. 'After everything that has happened.'

Tina nodded. 'That's understandable.' She smiled reassuringly at Mrs O'Riordan. 'And when was the last time you stayed here with your brother?'

Mrs O'Riordan frowned. 'What has that got to do with anything?' she asked testily.

Tina feigned surprise. 'I'm sorry. I was just interested.'

Mrs O'Riordan shrugged dismissively. 'I can't remember. Some time before Christmas, I think.' She looked up at Jean-Paul, and he smiled down at her. 'I don't stay as often as I'd like.'

'Do you know what your husband was planning to do last weekend, Mrs O'Riordan?' I asked, breaking their moment.

She shook her head. 'No. Working, I think.'

I looked at Tina, and she gave a tiny nod. It was time for Plan B. Provoking a response.

'Do you know who the man killed along-side your husband was? We have his name as twenty-six-year-old Vincent Baltar,' I added, quoting from the newspaper report.

'No. He must have been a friend of Patrick's.' But I could tell by the flash of anger in her eyes that she knew exactly who he was.

'Vincent Baltar was your husband's male lover,' I said, wanting to rattle her.

It worked. She stared at me as if I'd just slapped her. So did Jean-Paul, who looked like he wanted to slap me back. Twice as hard.

'How dare you!' she yelled. 'What are you talking about? Patrick was not homosexual!' Again she looked up at Jean-Paul, who still had the protect-ive hand on her shoulder. 'Jean-Paul, make them leave. They are lying.'

Jean-Paul started to come round from behind the chaise longue, an enraged expression on his face.

Tina and I both got to our feet, knowing our time was running out. 'Mrs O'Riordan,' said Tina firmly. 'The people behind your husband's murder are responsible for killing young children. You have children. Imagine what it would be like if you'd lost one of them to paedophiles. If you have any idea who could have killed your husband, please tell us now, and it won't go any further, I promise.'

'No,' snapped Jean-Paul, grabbing me by the arm and pushing me roughly towards the door. 'You must leave now.'

I had a gun beneath my jacket, in the waistband of my jeans, and I was sorely tempted to produce it now, but I held back.

He tried to grab Tina as well, but she shoved his hand away angrily. 'I'm a police officer,' she snarled. 'Don't you dare touch me.' She then turned to Mrs O'Riordan. 'This is your last chance to help us, and to help yourself. Because if you have anything to do with this, I'll find out. I promise you that. Now, I'm going to put this card with my number on it on the table here, and I'd strongly advise you to call it.'

Mrs O'Riordan began to sob loudly, and as Tina placed the card on the coffee table, Jean-Paul started to go for her again, but this time I got in the way. 'All right,' I said, 'we're leaving,' and I ushered her out, with Jean-Paul bringing up the rear and telling us not to come back.

But as we came out on to the driveway, we all stopped. A police patrol car was coming through the gates, and as we watched it pulled up behind the rental car, effectively blocking us in.

I stiffened as the two cops got out, suddenly very conscious of the gun in my waistband, and my lack of any police ID. The driver was short and squat – late twenties probably, and already balding fast – and he had a wide, pudgy, frog-like face. His partner was late forties and whip-thin, with horn-rimmed glasses and neatly pressed trousers that were pulled up so high they must have come close to castrating him. He looked an officious sort, while Frogface, who had big, dead eyes and lips set in a lazy sneer, had the air of the psychotic about him.

They sauntered over, Mr Officious frowning at us sceptically. 'What are you doing here?' he demanded.

'We were just visiting Mrs O'Riordan,' replied Tina, meeting his gaze.

'They were bothering her,' said Jean-Paul, coming out from behind us. 'And making accusations about Mr O'Riordan's death. They claimed they were police.'

Tina pulled out her warrant card and held it up. 'We are police. I'm Detective Inspector Tina Boyd.'

Mr Officious inspected the card carefully, his lips pursed with disapproval. 'The British police have no jurisdiction here. Why were you questioning Mrs O'Riordan?'

'There's a connection between her husband's death and a murder in the UK.'

'What connection?'

Tina hesitated. It was clear she didn't want to elaborate too much. 'Mr O'Riordan had a number of phone conversations with a journalist in the UK shortly before his death. That journalist is also now dead.'

'No one told us about any of this,' said Mr Officious. He turned to me. 'Where's your ID?'

I noticed Frogface watching me with those dead eyes, his fingers gently touching the handle of his holstered gun, as if he suspected I might try something. In my admittedly limited experience of dealing with the Filipino police – particularly local, out-of-town guys like these ones – I'd usually found them to be slow and lazy. But these guys were different. They were alert, they were confident, and for the first time I wondered how they'd got here so fast and where they'd come from.

'I'm not a police officer,' I said. 'I'm a cousin of the journalist murdered in the UK.'

Mr Officious's frown grew so deep it made his face shrink. 'Passport,' he snapped, holding out a hand.

I handed him my fake one, and he opened it at the photo page, gave it the once-over, and handed it back. I was hoping he'd leave it at that, but he didn't. He stood staring at me for several seconds, and I felt the hairs on the back of my neck stand on end.

I could take them. If I was fast. I knew I might have to. Because if they searched me and found the gun, I was finished. Out of the corner of my eye, I saw Tina staring at me as well. The message in her expression seemed to be 'don't do anything stupid', but I ignored it. They were all staring at me, and at that moment I was only a hair's breadth from committing at least two more murders.

My hand started to move ever so slowly towards the gun in the back of my trousers.

'I don't care who you are,' said Mr Officious loudly, jolting me out of my preparations. 'Either of you. You don't come here and question people on Philippine soil. Now, leave this place, and if you come back, we will arrest you. Do you understand?'

Relief surged through me, but outwardly I remained completely calm. 'Don't worry,' I told him. 'We're going.'

Tina said the same, and this seemed to mollify Mr Officious, although Frogface continued to watch me closely as we got back in the car and waited while they reversed their patrol car out of the drive.

They followed us back on to the main road, and it was only when they turned off half a mile later that Tina finally broke the silence.

'You would have shot them, wouldn't you? If they'd tried to arrest us? I could tell.'

I saw no point in lying. 'If it'd come to it, yes.'

She shook her head. 'Jesus. What the hell am I doing with you?'

'I didn't do it though, did I? Why don't you

worry about things after they've happened rather than before?'

Her eyes flashed with anger. 'Because it's too late then, isn't it? The people are already dead. Like Pat O'Riordan. How did it feel seeing his widow?'

'It didn't feel good, Tina, all right? Is that what you want to hear? I'm just trying to make amends, that's all. Give me a chance.'

'Christ, if anyone found out I'd teamed up with you, a wanted fugitive, I'd end up losing every-thing. My career, my liberty. Everything.'

'I already have lost everything, Tina. Because I didn't kill you.' I looked at her. 'We need each other for the moment. So let's work together, OK?'

She sighed loudly. 'OK.'

'Mrs O'Riordan knows something.'

'I agree. But it's too risky to go back there with the local police around.' She rubbed a hand across her scalp, making her bleached-blonde hair stand up in tufts – a habit I'd noticed of hers. 'Let's hope your friend's more cooperative.'

I thought about that one. 'If I find him, then I promise you, he'll have no choice but to be cooperative.'

CHAPTER 32

They moved through the airport in silence, taking their places in the queues for immigration and then customs. Two seemingly ordinary western men. One big, powerfully built and blond; the other, shorter, balding, but with a confidence about him that commanded respect.

Both men were tired, having flown all the way from the UK, but they were used to lack of sleep from their military days, and were able to cope with it better than most. This last part of the job was comparatively routine. They were to pick up a package from Manila and take it to an address a few hours outside the city, then provide security for a meeting that was to be held there. Nargen knew what was in the package, and if he was honest with himself, its contents scared him. But he and Tumanov were being paid fifty thousand dollars each to make sure it reached its final destination – a lot of money for less than a day's work. It was for that reason, and that reason alone, that he'd decided to take the job.

As they walked out of the arrivals hall into the stifling midday heat, crossing the access roads and making their way through the waiting crowds, a large man in a burgundy suit, his face partly hidden by a black panama hat, stepped into their path, blocking their way.

The man tipped his hat, and Nargen's immediate reaction was one of distaste. The man's parched, flabby skin was an unhealthy shade of yellow, and looked as if it would disintegrate if it were ever exposed to the light of the sun. He was wearing an unpleasant, leering smile that showed off stained, uneven teeth, and even from feet away Nargen could smell his rancid breath. He looked like a walking corpse, except for his fish-grey eyes, which glinted with a malignant cunning.

'Gentlemen,' he said in a sonorous voice. 'My name's Mr Heed. I've been sent here to meet you. I have a package for you to collect.'

Nargen didn't bother shaking his hand. 'Where is it?'

'I have it kept securely. Come with me.'

They followed as he led them to an old black Cadillac parked in a restricted zone nearby, and got in the back. The interior smelled strongly of air freshener and disinfectant, but there was another odour beneath it that Nargen recognized all too well, and which made him wonder what had gone on in this car.

When they were out on the highway, Heed removed his panama hat, revealing hair the colour of a nicotine stain, and made a call on his mobile. He spoke quietly into the phone before passing the handset to Nargen. 'It's for you,' he said, as the car slowed in the morning traffic.

It was Bertie Schagel. 'I have another job for you.'

'Yes?'

Nargen was irritated. Like most professional killers, he didn't like changes being made to jobs when he was out in the field, but knew better than to argue with the man who'd been his boss for the best part of the last ten years.

'The target you missed in England—'

'You mean the target you told us to spare when we had the opportunity to deal with her.'

'I'm not interested in semantics,' grunted Schagel. 'As you know, she's in Manila, and we need to deal with her quickly. You also need to deal with the man she's with. He's armed and potentially dangerous. Until a few hours ago, he was working for me, but now he seems to think that he is better off siding with her.'

'Do you have their location?'

'I will have it very soon. They have just been to see an informant of Mr Heed's. She will make sure that they go back there. In the meantime, Mr Heed will provide you with the tools you will need to do the job.'

'Do you want them dealt with before we collect the package?'

'Yes. Their presence threatens the whole operation. I want them dealt with today. Can you do that?'

'If you get us a location, then of course. But it will cost you. The lack of preparation time means it will be risky.'

'How much?'

'Another hundred thousand dollars.'

Schagel grunted. 'Just do it,' he said, and hung up.

CHAPTER 33

From Ternate we drove south and joined the main South Luzon Highway, heading to Batangas, which was the main ferry port to the island of Mindoro – the place that had once been my home.

I'd been happy then. Running a sleepy little dive operation in the palm-fringed paradise of Big La Laguna Beach, along with my old mate Tomboy. Taking people out every day to dive the myriad sites that peppered the craggy, volcanic coastline; coming back to watch the sun set every evening at the beach bar and guesthouse we also owned. Letting life slip by in that warm, familiar ex-pat fog of drink and sand and heat, enjoying the occasional affair, never thinking too much about what the future might hold.

Until that one day when it had all ended. When I'd decided to go back to England to find out who'd murdered an ex-colleague of mine, and by doing so had ended up opening a Pandora's box that's given me nothing but regret and heartache ever since.

I often wondered what would have happened if

I hadn't gone back. I wouldn't have met Emma, of course, a thought that even now was difficult to bear. But life would have been good all the same, I was sure of that. Dull perhaps, but my conscience in those days had purged itself of guilt, and I would have been content. I would never have known about Tomboy's past – his single, terrible crime – and our friendship would have been untainted.

It seemed strange to think that I was coming back here now, fully prepared to kill him if it came to it.

It was gone two p.m. by the time we'd wound our way in hard, thoughtful silence through the sprawling, semi-industrial maelstrom that was the port of Batangas, and parked the rental car near the ferry terminal in the shadow of one of the giant oil refineries that bordered the city.

The terminal was quiet, with just a few families sitting round under shelters lining the gangplanks, and a couple of boats bobbing up and down in the water. After some asking around, followed by a bout of haggling, I found a guy who agreed to take us on his outrigger direct to Sabang, the small tourist town on Mindoro where Tomboy and I had been based, for two thousand pesos, as long as we didn't mind travelling with a party of holidaying South Koreans.

It was a glorious sunny day with barely a cloud in the sky, and the journey across the clear blue waters of the Verde Island Passage that separated the main island of Luzon from the mountainous majesty of Mindoro passed quickly. The sea was calmer than I remembered and halfway across we were joined temporarily by a pod of bottlenose dolphins, much to the delight of the South Koreans on board, although their presence did little to lift the continuing tension between Tina and me.

I watched her looking out to sea, and I could see the stress she was under. For a young and attractive woman in her prime, she'd experienced far more than she should have done in life, and the frown that seemed to be her default expression sat far too easily on her pale features, now showing the first deep lines. Maybe I should have left her in the hotel room the previous day after I'd failed to pull the trigger, because by staying with her I was only adding to her pressure. And yet for all her toughness, I wasn't sure she could do this alone. She was in a dangerous foreign country, up against well-organized enemies. I figured that with me alongside her we at least stood a chance of success.

Or maybe I was just kidding myself. Maybe I was with her now because I was attracted to her in a way I hadn't been attracted to anyone since Emma.

'That's Verde Island,' I said eventually, pointing to a large rocky landmass swathed in green and dotted with the occasional building that appeared to our left as we got closer to Mindoro. 'There are a couple of rocks a few hundred metres off the southern end. They barely stick out of the water, but they're the pinnacles of two underwater mountains, and the diving down there's magnificent. I used to take people there all the time.'

'That's nice,' said Tina, before turning away, and I fell silent again, wondering how long she was going to keep this up for.

And then, a few minutes later, Sabang Bay opened up in front of us, with its thin white line of low-rise buildings nestling between the sea and a mountainous green backdrop, and I felt a lump in the back of my throat as my memories finally took on a physical dimension. Over half a decade, and little had changed. Kids still played on the narrow strip of beach amid the outriggers pushed up on the sand; music still blared from the floating bar in the middle of the harbour, and its few square yards were still filled with drunken, pink-looking westerners swaying in the mid-afternoon heat. It struck me then that, although it was nice to have the smell of the sea in my nostrils once again, I'd outgrown this place, and actually missed my new home in the landlocked hills of northern Laos.

The ferry manoeuvred its way through the boats bobbing up and down in the bay before pulling up at the shoreline. There were no piers in Sabang so we had to take off our shoes and paddle ashore in the warm knee-deep water. I looked around to see if there was anyone I remembered. But too much time had passed, and those few locals sitting on the stone steps that led up to the pavement running down the front of the buildings didn't even bother to look my way.

I thought back to the last time I'd seen Tomboy. It had been a warm, balmy night and we'd been sat having a drink together outside our old place, while he tried to persuade me not to go back to England. He'd told me that no good would come of it, and of course, in many ways he'd been right. We'd parted with a hand-shake, and he'd looked in my eyes and wished me luck; and the thing was, I knew he'd meant it. He'd cared for me. I'd cared for him too, far more than I'd admitted to myself these past six years, and even now I felt vaguely nauseous at the prospect of pointing a gun at him.

The dive operation and guesthouse we'd run together on Big La Laguna Beach was a ten-minute walk along the coast, and I led Tina along the narrow path round the nearest headland to Small La Laguna Beach. The Point Bar – a lovely open-air place that sat on a rocky promontory overlooking the bay, which I used to go to sometimes – was still there, but as we rounded the corner I saw that someone had built a high-rise monstrosity at the end of the beach that completely dominated the view. So, mass-market tourism had finally come to this part of the Philippines. It was a pity. There'd always been something quaint and off-the-beaten-track about the beaches of northern Mindoro; it was one of the reasons why, as a fugitive, I'd found it so easy to settle there. But it was clear by the growing numbers of westerners, particularly young ones, we were encountering as we walked that it was now part of the backpacker trail.

A group of sunburned English gap-year girls – pretty in a wholesome, Home Counties way – came past, clad in skimpy bikinis, forcing us to move aside to avoid them. Chattering excitedly among themselves, they didn't give me a second glance. But then, of course, they wouldn't. These girls would have been young children when my misdeeds had been dominating the news. In the ultra-fast world of the twenty-first century, I was nothing more than ancient history.

We cut through a gap in the headland by the big hotel and emerged on Big La Laguna, the best of Sabang's three main beaches, which to be honest wasn't saying much since none of them was that much cop. Even so, it was busier than I remembered, with groups of backpackers and tourists clustered along the sand. One guy with a huge afro was playing the guitar and singing some folky number, while half a dozen girls sat round him in an admiring semi-circle passing a joint from one to the other.

Tina stopped and looked around, taking in a big deep breath of the fresh sea air. She tipped up the sun hat she was wearing, and when she looked into the sunlight, her eyes gently closing as she finally relaxed, I thought she looked beautiful. She held that position for a few seconds before looking back at me, all business once again. 'Is it much further? I'm dying of thirst.'

'It's just up here,' I said, feeling a nervous trepidation as I walked along the sand.

But then I stopped.

Tina stopped beside me. 'What is it?'

'It's not here any more,' I said, looking at the spot where the Big La Laguna Dive Lodge had been, and where a hotel at least five times the size calling itself Anglo-Danish Divers, with a big PADI dive centre out front, now stood.

For a few seconds I just stood there, sweating and feeling foolish, as it dawned on me that we'd made this whole journey for nothing. I looked beyond the hotel, wondering if I'd made a mistake with the location, and saw a second new hotel beyond it. No, I was definitely in the right place. It was just that the world – and, it seemed, Tomboy – had moved on without me. The emptiness that was always squatting in my heart seemed to grow just that little bit bigger.

'Come on,' said Tina quietly, the first hint of sympathy in her voice. 'I need to get out of the sun. Let's grab a drink.'

We made our way over to an adjacent, and thankfully quiet, beach bar and took a seat at one of the tables.

Which was when someone called my name. Or more accurately, they called me by the name I'd been known by during my time in the Philippines.

241

'Mr Mick?'

It was the barman. He was waving at me from behind the bar, a big grin on his face, and I recognized him immediately. His name was Frankie and he'd worked the bar at our place when I was there. He still didn't look a day over sixteen, although he had to be at least thirty by now. It unnerved me how easily he'd recognized me.

I walked over, Tina following.

'Frankie. How are you doing?'

We started to shake hands, but then he leaned forward and hugged me, pulling away reluctantly. 'Where have you been, Mr Mick? You've been gone for years.'

'Away,' I said with a weary smile. 'This is my friend Tina.'

'Not your wife?'

'No. Not my wife.'

They shook hands, and Frankie smiled nervously at her, vaguely intimidated, I think, by Tina's short bleached-blonde hair, and her lean, muscular body.

'Why did you never call or write? Why did you never come back?' He looked at me, genuinely perplexed. 'We all missed you. Mr Tomboy missed you a lot. He wasn't good at running the place without you.'

'What happened to it?' I asked, looking over to where Anglo-Danish Divers now stood.

'Mr Tomboy sold it to the arsehole who runs that place,' he said, wrinkling his nose in distaste.

'How long ago?'

He thought about it for a moment. It looked like it was quite an effort. 'A long time back. A year. Two years. Maybe even longer.'

I hid my disappointment. 'Do you know where Tomboy is now?'

'Sure. He's still here. He lives up past the headland.' He motioned vaguely over his shoulder. 'Nice house. Good views. You want me to show you where?'

'No, it's OK. You're working. Just tell me where it is.'

He gave me the name of the house and rough directions, and I memorized them.

'It'll be a nice surprise for him,' said Frankie.

Somehow, I didn't think so. It wasn't going to be all that pleasant for either of us. But there was nothing that could be done about that.

I ordered two Cokes from Frankie and we went back to our table.

'I want to go up there alone,' I said to Tina, taking a huge gulp of my drink. 'I think it'll be easier that way.'

Tina looked into my eyes, as if she was trying to gauge what was beyond them. 'Are you going to kill him?'

'I hope I don't have to, but this time I'm going to get answers.'

She seemed to think long and hard about that, before eventually speaking again. 'Do what you have to do. I'll wait here.'

I finished my drink and got to my feet. 'I'll be back as soon as I can.'

'One other thing,' she said as I moved away.

I turned round, but didn't say anything.

'Be careful.'

I managed a smile. 'Don't worry about me. I'm always careful.'

Which was bullshit of course, but for the first time that day, her words made me feel good.

CHAPTER 34

It was a fifteen-minute walk up to Tomboy's place, past landmarks that had once been familiar but that had now changed beyond all recognition. Where once there'd been a ramshackle collection of shacks, peopled by extended families of locals who liked to do all their cooking on spits outside, and where chickens, even the odd pig, roamed the narrow streets, there were now rows of bland single-storey chalet-style cottages, with tarmac walkways between them. Only when I got up past the headland and into the quiet woodland that surrounded the coastal resorts did I see traces of what Mindoro had been like before the tourists had come.

Frankie was right. Tomboy's place was nice. A two-storey white-washed villa set back on its own behind mature teak trees, nestled close to the edge of the cliff with views back across towards Sabang, it was a damn sight better than anything he'd owned six years back. I very much doubted whether the proceeds of selling our small dive business would have paid for the Mitsubishi Shogun sitting in the drive, let alone anything else.

Suddenly feeling terribly nervous, I walked up to the front door and rang the doorbell.

For a few seconds there was no answer. Then I heard footsteps.

'Who is it?' he called out, but even as he spoke the words he was opening the door.

'Hello, Tomboy.'

He recognized me instantly, just like I knew he would. 'Jesus Christ, Mick,' he said, an expression of utter disbelief on his face. He took a step backwards. 'What are you doing here?'

'I need a favour. Can I come inside?'

He looked at me warily, and I thought that the last few years hadn't treated him at all well. He was only in his mid-forties, a few months older than me, but his face was soft and bloated, and even the deep local's tan couldn't disguise the meandering network of broken blood vessels that swarmed across his upper cheeks and over a nose that had grown noticeably more bulbous. His shoulder-length blond hair was a lank, thinning, tangled mess, and his eyes were bloodshot and weary. He was dressed in a pair of shorts and a loose-fitting white singlet with food stains on it that was tightening at the gut.

'What kind of favour?' he asked, clearly reluctant to let me over the threshold. 'The last time we spoke you told me to pray that you never came looking for me. Is my time up, then, Mick?' He looked away as he spoke, remembering no doubt the reason why I'd said those things. The old swagger he used to exude was long gone. Tomboy Darke looked like a man in terminal decline, and I felt a little sorry for him in spite of myself.

'You were my friend a long time, Tomboy. I've never wanted to kill you. But we do need to talk. Inside.'

He looked scared, confirming what I already knew. 'I don't see how I can help you. I haven't seen you in six years.'

'Take my word for it, you can,' I said, and slipped the gun from the small of my back.

He looked down, saw it. Inhaled loudly. Then he took a step back and allowed me inside, never taking his eyes from the gun.

'Turn around. Let's talk somewhere more comfortable.'

Slowly, as if each step was physically painful, he led me through the narrow hallway, past a very messy kitchen that smelled of old fish, and into an equally messy lounge dominated by a huge plasma TV hanging from the wall. Half-open French windows led out to a sheltered patio, but even so, the air con in the room was blowing out cold air so hard you could have hung meat in there.

He turned and faced me, his shoulders already slumping. 'Whatever I've done in the past, it was a long time ago, and I feel awful for it. I really do.'

'You mean, getting rid of the body of a thirteen-year-old girl murdered by paedophiles, then framing her father for it? Because that's what you did, isn't it?'

His soft jowly face creased into an expression of terrible guilt, but I wasn't fooled. Tomboy Darke had always been a good liar. It was why he'd been such a successful informant back in the day. Even the other criminals trusted him.

'It was a long time ago, Mick. I needed the money.'

'You're right. It was a long time ago. But there've been other crimes since.'

'What do you mean?'

'Don't bullshit me, Tomboy. You work for Paul Wise. You delivered a gun on his behalf to a hotel room in Manila three days ago. It was used in a hit.'

His eyes widened. 'Jesus, Mick. Was that you?'

I nodded. 'I work for a guy called Bertie Schagel. But his client's Paul Wise. Wise wanted the journalist Patrick O'Riordan dead.'

Tomboy looked puzzled. 'And you killed him, did you? I read about it in the papers.'

'I did. But I realize now I made a mistake. I've got to make amends, Tomboy. And that means finding Paul Wise – the last of those bastards responsible for the death of that little girl, Heidi Robes, back in England – and putting him in the ground.' I raised the gun so it was pointed at his head, and he flinched involuntarily. 'So, where is he?'

'Look, Mick, please,' he said, putting his hands

up defensively, 'I don't know any Paul Wise, I promise.'

I came forward fast, making him back up against the wall, and shoved the barrel of the gun in his face. A sour smell of sweat was coming off him in waves, and his bloodshot eyes were bulbous with panic.

'Please, Mick, I'm telling the truth, I promise.'

I kept the gun where it was, knowing how effective my silence combined with the feel of cold, deadly metal on skin could be. It didn't take long for him to start babbling.

'I've heard the name Paul Wise, I've got to admit that, but I don't know who, let alone where, he is. I swear it. I do my work for a man called Heed. He's the one who told me to deliver the gun. He might work for Paul Wise, but I can't even say that for sure. You've got to believe me, Mick.'

'Where did you meet Heed?'

'It was a long time back. He used to come down here sometimes. We got talking. I said I was always after work – it was when the dive business wasn't doing so well – and he said he might be able to put some my way.'

I quickly made a show of looking round the room, but I never took my eyes from him. 'It looks like this Mr Heed pays well.'

'I don't do stuff just for him.'

'So, who did you kidnap that little girl for, then?'

'What are you talking about?'

'I read a report yesterday about a thirteen-year-old girl called Lene Haagen who was abducted from a hotel in Manila in the summer of 2008. The report was written by Pat O'Riordan. It said that a witness saw a western man hanging round the hotel in the days before she disappeared. The description fitted you perfectly. Overweight, long, thinning hair, red face.' I was punting in the dark here, coming up with a theory for which I had no evidence, but something in his eyes, not guilt so much as real fear, told me I was on the right track. 'You kidnapped a little kid from her parents on behalf of Paul Wise, knowing exactly what was going to happen to her. You're a bastard, Tomboy. But then you knew that, didn't you?'

'I didn't do it,' he whined.

I felt a wave of pure hot rage flow through me. 'Don't lie. It won't save you. Nothing's going to save you unless you tell the truth.' I cocked the gun, the click loud in the dull silence of the room.

'Don't kill me, Mick. Please. I saved your life all those years ago, remember? I could have grassed you up, but I didn't. I let you go into business with me—'

'You did it though, didn't you? Took that little girl from her parents?'

'Oh Jesus.' His voice was degenerating into sobs, his whole body shaking with emotion. 'I know I did wrong, but Heed made me do it.'

'Don't bullshit me. You could have said no. Why did you do it? Money, or are you one of them too? Are you a child rapist, Tomboy?'

'Course I'm not,' he howled with indignation, as if this somehow made his actions justifiable. 'I was broke. Totally. Heed offered me fifty grand to do it.'

My finger trembled on the trigger. I was still finding it difficult to take in what he was telling me because it meant that Tomboy, my old friend, was a monster. The anger burned inside me.

'Where do I find Heed?'

'He owns a nightclub in Manila, the Juicy Peach.'

'And you delivered Lene Haagen to him?'

'Yes,' he said quietly. 'I did.' He looked at me, and his eyes were full of tears. 'I'm sorry, Mick, I really am. There's not a night I don't think about what I've done.'

'Is that right? While you're sitting in your nice big house paid for with her blood. You've got to stop lying, Tomboy, you really have.'

I stepped away from him, wanting to get his sour, terrified stink out of my nostrils, but kept the gun pointed at his head.

But now that I'd got Tomboy talking, he wouldn't shut up. 'I didn't want to do it,' he continued, 'I swear. But I'd been doing other stuff for Heed, getting young girls for clients down here, and he said he'd grass me up to the law if I didn't do what he told me. You know what it's like. You get dragged in.'

I did know. But even so, I'd never been dragged in that deep. And the problem was, Tomboy had form. He hadn't been corrupted. He was corrupt already.

I glared at him. 'Tell me everything you know about Heed.'

'He's an Aussie in his fifties. I don't even know his first name. He's lived in Manila for years, and been involved in the under-age sex trade for most of that time. He's scum, Mick. A horrible-looking bloke. He stinks of death.'

'I'm sure he's just as complimentary about you. Where else does he frequent?'

'He doesn't these days. He just hangs about the Juicy Peach like some kind of vampire. He lives in the basement, in a place with no windows. You reach it through a door in the club.'

'Give me the address.'

He reeled it out by heart. I memorized it.

'Turn round and face the wall.'

'Mick, please don't kill me.'

'Turn round.'

Slowly, very slowly, he did as instructed, until he had his back to me. I could see his knees trembling, and I felt sick, even though I knew what I had to do. If I left him alive, there was a good chance he'd tell Heed I was coming for him, and I couldn't have that. Time was running out. For me, and for Tomboy too. Although right now, his was running out faster.

'Oh God, Mick, no . . .' His voice was a low, cracked wail that seemed to echo round the room. He craned his neck so he could see me, willing me not to pull the trigger.

I snapped at him to face the wall, hearing the tension in my voice as I took the suppressor from where I'd been storing it beneath my shirt and screwed it on to the end of the pistol.

Which was a mistake.

Men will act in very different ways when they're waiting to die. Most will beg; some will accept their fate in stoic, dignified silence; very few will overcome the torpor of fear and fight back. I didn't think Tomboy would be one of the latter group, but unfortunately he was. And his desperation made him fast.

He launched himself at me with a ferocious bellow and was on me in a second, punching and kicking, his weight and momentum sending me crashing to the floor. The suppressor flew out of my hand, but I kept hold of the gun, my finger tense on the trigger, and it went off with a deafening retort.

Tomboy wasn't hit, though, and he launched a punch into my face before scrambling over me and running for the French windows, with very little coordination but plenty of speed.

I knew I had to move fast. Ignoring the pain from where he'd hit me – the second time I'd been laid into in little more than twenty-four hours – I jumped up and ran after him.

As he crossed the patio, making for the low wall at the end, he snatched a look behind him, saw me coming, and let out a little yelp of fear. He jumped the wall, caught his foot and rolled over, then scrambled to his feet again.

But I was gaining, and we both knew it.

He raced through the trees, but suddenly they opened up into a rocky clearing with a single bench on it looking out to sea, and beyond that, the edge of the cliff. It was the end of the line, and this time he realized it.

He stopped and turned round to face me, the breeze whipping up his thin, straggly hair.

For a few seconds, neither of us spoke, each lost in his own thoughts. I was thinking about the old days when we were friends; the drinks we'd shared together; the laughs we'd had. I think he was hoping that was what I was thinking, so that I might finally let my emotions get the better of me, and not pull the trigger.

But he was wrong. He deserved to die far more than many other people I'd killed.

I raised the gun, and he took a step backwards, coming perilously close to the cliff edge.

Then his expression changed. It became calmer. As if he was accepting the inevitable.

'Are you going after Heed?' he asked.

I nodded. 'And Wise. I'm not going to stop until they're all dead.'

'Make sure you get them.'

'I will.'

'I picked up a package for Heed the other night and delivered it to the Juicy Peach. It was a big briefcase hidden in a box that came from Manila docks, and it was bloody heavy. I have no idea what was in it, but I know it was valuable. Very valuable. And illegal. Heed was taking delivery of it on behalf of someone else.'

'Wise?'

'I don't know. But I'd ask Heed about it before you kill him. And tell him that it was me who gave you the information, and that I did it willingly.'

'I will. Thanks.'

He sighed. 'It's not enough to save me, is it?'

I didn't say anything. I didn't have to.

'Please, Mick. Come on. I've given you something here. Something that you can use. I won't say a word to any of them, I promise. For old times' sake. Please.'

Again, I didn't speak. Keeping the gun steady.

He swallowed. 'I wasn't always a low-life, you know.'

'I know. Neither was I.'

'What happened to us, Mick?'

'We made the easy choices, Tomboy. Now it's time to make the hard ones.'

He just had time to see the tears in my eyes, and then I pulled the trigger, sending him hurtling over the edge and into oblivion.

CHAPTER 35

Tina was watching a group of a dozen or so backpackers – young, tanned, and sporting new tattoos – chatting and drinking together on the beach. Their easy laughter carried across the sand to where she sat smoking and sipping from her second glass of Coke as the late afternoon sun began its slow descent towards the headland.

Her mood was bleak. All day she'd been finding it hard to come to terms with the fact that she'd effectively teamed up with a mass murderer in an attempt to bring another mass murderer to justice. It felt utterly wrong to her, not only for moral reasons but also because she had no real control over the situation. For all his protestations to the contrary, Dennis Milne was unpredictable and extremely violent. When they'd been stopped and questioned by the two local uniforms earlier, she'd seen the cold look in Milne's eyes, and knew that if it had come to it he would have killed them.

And if he had, Tina would have been an accessory to murder. It was as simple as that. In her conflict with Paul Wise, the stakes had always been high, but now with Milne on the scene they'd reached almost intolerable levels. It was why she'd been keeping a distance from him all day, and why ever since he'd left to find Tomboy she'd been thinking about making a break for it, and striking out on her own.

But an hour after he'd gone, she was still sitting in the same spot, because in the end she knew she needed him if she was ever going to bring Paul Wise to justice. In truth, she knew too that she was using him. Because Wise was going to have to die. Gathering enough evidence to haul him before the courts was no longer a viable option, if it ever had been. Tina had killed once before. She had deliberately run down a suspect. But that suspect had been a brutal killer who'd kidnapped and tortured her, and the killing had happened in the heat of the moment while the suspect was brandishing a gun and trying to escape, having just shot a young mother. Cold blood was different. If it came to it, she didn't think she had the necessary brutality to pull the trigger. But she knew Milne had.

From the beach came a peal of laughter. A pretty blonde girl, no more than twenty, jumped to her feet, pulling up a young, unfeasibly good-looking Italian guy with her, and they kissed passionately, much to the delight of the rest of the group of back-packers, before saying their goodbyes and striding up on to the path hand in hand, laughing and whispering together.

They walked past Tina, not giving her even the

slightest of glances. They were only interested in each other. Two kids on the cusp of life, with no fears or responsibilities, enjoying everything that life had to offer.

Their happiness made Tina jealous, and she hated herself for it. She'd been like them once. Backpacking round South East Asia; drifting from one beach to the next; soaking herself in the pleasures of the moment. She'd even had her own romances. There was Morgan the muscular Kiwi, whom she'd met in Bali. They'd watched the movie *The Beach* together on an outside screen under the stars, then, drunk and laughing, had made love back at his beach hut to the sounds of the sea. Tina could still recall how good it had been. It had been a short and intense relationship, two weeks only, while they travelled first to Lombok then to Cairns, where they'd said their goodbyes. It hadn't been love. It hadn't even been infatuation. They'd known they were never going to see each other again. It had simply been seizing the moment. Living for the day. Something that Tina had almost forgotten. Since then her life had been torn and twisted, and she'd seen so many things she wished she hadn't.

As she watched the couple disappear down the beach, she hoped that they never had to suffer like she had. She hoped they continued to have fun, got fun jobs, married other fun people like themselves, had lots of beautiful little kids and lived happily ever after.

She heard a movement beside her and looked up. It was Milne. He was carrying his jacket over one arm, and he looked tired. Sweat-stains had formed on his shirt round the armpits, and his nose and cheek were red and puffy. With a sigh, he sat down beside her, a bottle of San Miguel in his hand.

Tina eyed the bottle hungrily, but only for a moment. For some reason she had no desire for a drink.

'Did you see him?'

He nodded slowly. 'Yeah, I saw him. He works for a guy in Manila called Heed. It seems Heed's the one who has direct contact with Wise.' Milne didn't look at her as he spoke but stared out to sea, his shoulders slumped, the lines on his face looking more pronounced than usual.

Tina knew what had happened. It was written all over him. But for once she didn't feel like judging him. Instead, as she watched him, she felt a wave of sorrow wash over her. He looked broken, and her hand moved towards his shoulder in a comforting gesture. But at the last second, she brought it back.

'That girl who was abducted in Manila,' he said quietly, 'Lene Haagen. Tomboy took part in the abduction. He delivered her to Heed. I'm assuming it was on behalf of Wise.'

'Jesus. And he was your friend?'

'I still can't believe he could do something like that.' He looked at her then, and his eyes were full of pain. 'I guess I just didn't know him.'

They were both silent for a while, then Milne spoke again. 'I killed him,' he said, 'but before I did, he told me that the other night he delivered a briefcase to this guy Heed. He didn't know what was inside, but he was sure it was valuable. Now, I haven't got a clue what it could be, but it does coincide with Wise's arrival in Manila, so it's got to be connected in some way.'

Tina frowned. 'And it's got to be connected with the meeting O'Riordan was going to have with Omar Salic. I'm guessing Salic had some information he was going to give to O'Riordan. Perhaps he was involved in the abduction of Lene Haagen as well, and wanted to come clean.'

'But why incriminate himself? And if Wise's people knew O'Riordan was meeting with Salic, then Salic is probably dead as well.'

'I checked yesterday's papers. His name wasn't mentioned.'

'Which leaves us back with Heed. He's the man we've got to get answers from. He may still have that briefcase. I've got an address for him in Manila. We'll pay him a visit tonight.' Milne sat back in his seat, looking out to sea. 'I'd forgotten how beautiful it is here. I've missed it. And now I'm going to miss it all over again.'

Tina looked at him, realizing with a sense of shock that she was beginning to sympathize with his predicament. She tried to picture him coldly executing Patrick O'Riordan and his lover – two entirely innocent men – and yet she couldn't manage it. Nor could she work up any anger towards him. He looked like he was carrying enough of a burden as it was.

She felt a vibration in the pocket of her shorts. It was her mobile and she didn't recognize the number, although it was local.

'Is that Detective Boyd?' asked the voice at the other end in heavily accented English.

'Yes it is, Mrs O'Riordan,' said Tina, experiencing a stab of excitement.

'I've been thinking about what you said today, and I need to see you. I have some information about my husband's death that might help you. It's very important.'

'Can you tell me what it is?'

'Not on the telephone. Can you come here? Jean-Paul is out for the evening. He wouldn't want to hear what I have to say. It's not nice.'

Tina was tempted to probe for further details but the nervousness in the other woman's voice stopped her. She glanced across at Milne, who was listening avidly. 'OK, Mrs O'Riordan. But we're some way from you at the moment.' She looked at her watch. 'We could be with you by about seven thirty. Is that OK?'

'Yes. That is fine. I'll see you then.'

Tina replaced the mobile in her pocket, and gave Milne the details of the conversation.

'It could be a trap,' he said when she'd finished. 'Personally, I think it's a little bit too convenient that she's suddenly decided to cooperate.'

'So what do you think we should do?'

He thought about it for a few seconds. 'I think we ought to go.'

'I do, too. But we need to work out what to do if it is a trap.'

'Do you know how to use a gun?'

Tina nodded. She'd taken the firearms course in her early days in Islington CID, although she'd never had to fire one in anger. 'I'm rusty, but I know what I'm doing.'

'I took this from Tomboy's place,' he said, pressing something cold and metallic against her leg under the table. 'If we're going into what could be a hostile environment, I'd be happier if you had the means to defend yourself.'

Tina should have made him take it back, but she didn't. Instead she slipped the .22 pistol into her handbag, knowing that by taking the gun of a dead man she was taking matters to a whole new level.

CHAPTER 36

Nargen removed the gun from Mrs O'Riordan's head, and took the phone from her free hand. 'You did well. They are coming, yes?'

She nodded her head vigorously, the terror in her eyes obvious. 'Yes. She said they would be here by half past seven. Please, can you let us go now? I have done everything you told me to, and my brother is very badly hurt.'

He was hurt too. In these kinds of situations it was always good to establish dominance early, which was why Tumanov had gone to work on the brother hard while he'd been strapped to the chair next to his sister, blindfolded and helpless. He'd been brave, there was no doubt about that. When Tumanov had snapped two of his fingers, one after the other, he'd refused to scream. His breathing had quickened and his face had gone red, but the stubborn ox hadn't made a sound. But Tumanov was highly experienced in causing terrible damage to the human body. He knew every pressure point, every sensitive nerve, every soft place, and within minutes he'd had him howling for mercy. Now

263

the brother sat quietly in the chair, his eyes wet with tears, his face flecked with saliva and blood where he'd bitten right through his lip, still conscious, but only just.

Nargen gave her a reassuring smile. 'We won't hurt him any more, I promise you. I'm sorry that we had to do it in the first place, but it was very important that you take us seriously. And very important that you were convincing on the telephone. You understand why we had to do it, don't you?'

Again she nodded her head vigorously.

'You and your brother are going to be fine, Mrs O'Riordan,' Nargen continued in a soothing voice, re-tying her free hand as he spoke.

He could tell she trusted him. The reality was, she had little choice. Right now, she was so desperate for her life that she would cling to any scrap of hope, however small, and the fact was, unlike Tumanov, who wore his bleak savagery like a badge, Nargen looked just like any other ordinary middle-aged western man, the type you feel can't be all bad.

'Can you let me help him, please?' pleaded Mrs O'Riordan. 'He's a good man. He won't say anything.'

'Soon,' said Nargen, standing back up behind Mrs O'Riordan's chair, taking a step backwards and raising the gun so it was pointed at the back of her head. He signalled with a nod to Tumanov, who slipped a knife from his pocket. 'Very soon.'

CHAPTER 37

It was nearly eight o'clock when we arrived at the house where we'd interviewed Mrs O'Riordan earlier that day. We drove past the tree-lined avenue it sat on, and carried on along the main road for another hundred yards until Tina found a sheltered spot to park up a track beneath a scraggy-looking palm tree, where the rental car was hidden from view.

The night was silent, bar the gentle chirping of the cicadas and the distant hum of traffic from the coast road, as we slipped quietly from the car and made our way cautiously back in the direction of the house. On the way up here, I'd thought about Tomboy and what I'd had to do to him – not regretting my actions exactly, but wishing that they hadn't been necessary. Now, though, I pushed all thoughts of him from my mind. I needed to be alert.

There was no street lighting on the avenue, but two lanterns on either side of the open front gate burned brightly. Behind the gate, the top floor of the house loomed, but its windows were unlit.

We kept close to the trees as we walked, watching

for any signs of an ambush, but there was nothing. No cars, and no people.

Back in the car, I'd offered to go in alone and check the place out to make sure it was safe, but it hadn't surprised me when Tina had poured scorn on that idea. 'I don't need mollycoddling,' she'd said with a glare, and I'd left it at that, but as we stopped at the border wall of the house listening to the silence, I began to get an uneasy feeling. I drew my gun and screwed on the suppressor.

Tina gave me a look.

'Better to be safe than sorry,' I whispered, meeting her gaze.

Instead of going in the front entrance, we followed the border wall, round to the rear of the property. The going wasn't easy. The house sat on land that had once been marshes, and there were narrow dried-out channels, some several feet deep, criss-crossing our path, disguised by the thick foliage that had probably been left to grow wild and high as a security measure. Swarms of insects assaulted us as we moved slowly like amateur explorers, and it was a good ten minutes before we made it round to the rear wall.

The wall was about ten feet high but, unlike a lot of the properties further north in Manila, it didn't have barbed wire running across the top, which made life a lot easier. I handed my gun to Tina, and half jumped, half scrambled up, until I was straddling the top. A line of trees obscured my view of the back garden, but I could make out the lights beyond.

Tina gave me back the gun, and I helped her up with my free hand.

Without speaking, we slid as quietly as possible down the other side of the wall, then poked our heads out from behind the trees.

A large, well-manicured lawn with a swimming pool in the middle stretched out in front of us, and beyond it lay the house. The curtains on both floors were drawn, but there were several lights on the right-hand side of the ground floor, suggesting someone was inside. Further to our left was a pool house, and next to it a compact two-storey outbuilding, set back behind a hedge. Both were unlit.

We kept our position for a few moments, watching and listening. If this was an ambush, then any assailant would be expecting an approach from the front, which meant he – or more likely they – would be concealed round the front of the main house, or inside it.

I knew I was being paranoid, but I've always figured that it's better to be over-cautious than dead. I just didn't think O'Riordan was the type to change her mind and suddenly cooperate with two people who'd already been exposed as impostors in their unofficial investigation into her husband's murder, especially when by doing so she would almost certainly incriminate herself.

I should have pulled out, gone back with Tina

to Manila and followed up on the lead I'd got from Tomboy. But I didn't. Instead, curiosity got the better of me, and I motioned to Tina to follow as I crept along the inside of the wall, staying behind the tree line.

It took us a full five minutes to skirt the garden, passing round the back of the outbuildings until we reached a side door to the main house. During that time, no movement came from inside.

I tried the door. It was locked.

'Hold this,' I whispered, starting to hand Tina the gun. 'I need to get this open.'

'I can do it,' she whispered back, producing a set of picks from the back of her shorts. 'I've had plenty of practice. But if Mrs O'Riordan's really got genuine information, she's not going to be too happy with us breaking in like this.'

'She'll still give us it, though. Whereas if she doesn't have any genuine information, this way we stay alive.' I took a step back. 'I'll cover you.'

Tina was quick and professional, and had the door open in under a minute, which was a lot better than I'd have managed.

I told her I'd lead the way and pushed the door slowly open with the end of the suppressor, cocking the pistol at the same time. Before I went inside I looked at Tina, and saw that she had an uncertain expression in her eyes. I was just about to reiterate that I didn't mind going in alone when she produced the .22 pistol from where it had been nestling under her T-shirt, and released the safety catch.

'Go on,' she hissed.

I stepped into an empty, darkened storeroom with a washing machine in one corner. Another door opposite led through into the house proper, but this one was open, and as I went through it I came into a narrow hallway with a small washroom to the left, the toilet visible through the half-open door. The air con was pumping full throttle and I found myself shivering. The first glow of light appeared from round the corner and I stopped and listened.

I felt the tension rising in me. We should have been able to hear something if Mrs O'Riordan was here waiting for us. Movement; music; the TV; something. But this place was as silent as a morgue.

And then, as I came round the corner, gun outstretched, into a huge space-age kitchen, I saw them.

They were tied to separate chairs in the middle of the floor, side by side with their backs to us. Both had slumped forward, their blood having mingled on the black-and-white tiled floor to form a single dark pool.

I took a tentative step forward, then another, glancing down at the bodies. The brother, Jean-Paul, had had his throat cut, and the front of his overalls was stained heavily. Mrs O'Riordan had been shot in the back of the head, the golfball-shaped exit wound turning her left eye into a fleshy black pulp. Close up, I could smell the beginning

269

of their decay, even though the air con was disguising the worst of it. It was obvious they'd been dead for several hours, possibly just after Mrs O'Riordan had made the call.

It was, as I'd suspected all along, a trap.

But it was also an opportunity. Clearly, whoever had killed Mrs O'Riordan and her brother was still expecting us to approach the house from the front, which meant we might be able to take him or them from behind. I didn't like to involve Tina, but she'd made her choices. Just like I had.

My finger tightened on the trigger and I turned in her direction.

Which was when the huge figure in the balaclava loomed out of the darkness behind her.

'Down!' I yelled, my voice exploding in the silence.

Instinctively, she ducked. Just as instinctively I fired into the space she'd left behind as the man in the balaclava, a gun in his own hand, went to grab her. I hit him three times in the upper body, sending him crashing backwards, the gun clattering from his hand.

At the same time I swung round towards the far door as it flew open, and a second figure appeared, holding a revolver outstretched, already firing. I dived out of the way as a bullet whistled past my face and smashed into one of the kitchen units, sending a hail of splinters through the air. Landing on my side behind Jean-Paul's chair, I cracked off three shots in his direction, through the gap between the two chairs, as he continued firing at me.

A round took off the top of Jean-Paul's head, and a third ricocheted off the tiled floor between my legs, missing my groin by inches, before embedding itself in another kitchen unit. Splinters stung my face but I ignored the pain, and how close I'd come to being hit, and fired back through the gap in the chairs, even though I only had a partial view of my assailant, and was running low on bullets.

Three more shots rang out in quick succession, and though I was partly deafened by the noise, I could hear they were coming from Tina's smaller .22. I stole a glance at her. She was already up on her feet in a two-handed firing stance, a look of intense concentration on her face. The figure in the doorway had disappeared.

I ignored the hammering of my heart and stood up as well. By my calculations, I had three rounds left, and since Tina's .22 only held five, she had two. Which meant we couldn't afford to get involved in a protracted gunfight. I'd taken one of them out and that would have to do. Now we needed to get out.

I inched along the kitchen sideboard until I was directly opposite the door from where the second assailant had appeared. The guy had been a good shot. Trying to hit a moving target with a big gun in darkness, especially when you're moving yourself, is no easy task. He'd got very close, and I'd

271

been very lucky, which is the kind of combination you really don't want to rely on.

From my new position, I could see out into a grand hallway. It was lit by a tacky-looking chandelier hanging from the vaulted ceiling. There was no sign of the gunman.

I heard Tina's gasp through the ringing in my ears, and as I swung round I saw her silver .22 fly through the air before skidding across the kitchen floor, way out of reach of both of us. The first assailant, the big guy I'd shot three times, had Tina in a vice-like headlock and was pulling her back into his shoulder. The bastard must have been wearing a Kevlar vest, and he had a pistol with suppressor against her temple.

Twelve feet separated us. I raised my own gun.

'Drop it or she dies,' he said in a thick Russian accent.

Tina struggled beneath his grip, and he drove a knee into the small of her back. She winced in pain, and her breath came in tortured gasps. She stopped struggling, although her expression was defiant.

My eyes drifted back to the doorway. The second gunman was still nowhere to be seen.

'Now,' hissed the big man. As he spoke, he increased the pressure on Tina's throat, and her eyes widened. 'You have three seconds. One . . .'

So much of life comes down to snap decisions. 'Two . . .'

There was no way he was going to let us live.

'Th—'

I pulled the trigger, shooting him right between the eyes.

He stumbled backwards, and his gun went off. I blinked reflexively, and when my eyes opened again, Tina had fallen down. For a split second I thought she'd been hit with his final shot, but then she started choking and rubbing her throat. I felt a surge of relief, watching as the big man wobbled precariously, the hole in his head smoking, until finally he fell to the floor. Dead this time.

'Let's go,' I grunted, hauling Tina to her feet, knowing we were going to have to move fast.

Which was when I saw the silhouette appear in the back window. It was the other gunman.

He opened fire, and I threw Tina down as the glass exploded inwards, firing my last two bullets back at him.

I had no idea if I'd hit him or not, and there was no time to find out. 'Go! Go! Go!' I yelled, shielding Tina as we scrambled across the floor, making for the far door.

More shots rang out, ricocheting round the room, and I felt a bolt of shock tear through my left shoulder, spinning me round. As I rolled on the floor, I saw the .22, made a grab for it with my good hand – adrenalin driving me forward – and emptied out the last two rounds in the general direction of the window.

Again, I didn't know if I'd hit the guy, but it bought us a valuable couple of seconds, and I used it to bundle Tina out the door and into the hall. 'Out the front and keep running,' I said, overtaking her. 'He's going to try and cut us off.'

I sprinted past the staircase, ignoring the pain in my shoulder, and yanked open the front door. Then we were charging down the drive in the direction of the main gate, just as the gunman appeared round the side of the house. He crouched down in a firing stance, and I saw that he no longer had the big revolver. Instead, he had a pistol with a suppressor attached. However, he was a good twenty-five yards away and it was going to be hard for him to hit either one of us. Or so I was hoping, as I clenched my teeth and kept going, head forward like a champion sprinter, willing myself on.

But for some reason he didn't fire, and two seconds later we were through the gate and out on to the road.

And that's when I heard the sound of a car approaching rapidly. As I turned in its direction, I was blinded by head-lights. Instinctively, I flung Tina out of the way, then tried to dive clear myself. But I wasn't quite quick enough, and my legs were caught by the bumper, sending me sprawling into the dirt.

I lay there, unable to move, as the car screeched to a halt, and the two cops who'd stopped us earlier jumped out and pointed their weapons at me.

I looked up into the eyes of the nearest one – the fat little psychotic, Frogface – saw the way his finger was tensing on the trigger of the pump-action shotgun he was holding, and suddenly realized that these guys had no intention of bringing me in. There aren't that many people in this world who can pull a trigger and not give their actions a second thought, whatever we might like to think, but this guy was definitely one of them.

I was a dead man. It was as simple as that.

CHAPTER 38

Shocked and pumped up by the experience she'd just had, but otherwise unhurt, Tina sat back up on the tarmac and looked over to where Milne lay on his back. The two uniforms from earlier were approaching him. The squat, younger one was the closest of the two, and he was holding a large pump-action shotgun. As he drew closer he took a quick look up and down the road, and that was when Tina realized what he was about to do.

Milne opened his mouth to say something, but didn't move. She could see he was hurt, but how badly she wasn't sure.

Without hesitating, she leapt to her feet and yanked out her warrant card, speaking rapidly but with the utter confidence she knew she needed if they were both going to get out of this in one piece: 'I'm a British police officer! Do not shoot that man! He's not resisting arrest. If you shoot him, you'll have to shoot me, and there'll be a major inquiry. You'll lose your job, your liberty, everything.'

The older cop pointed his revolver at her, but

she could see a flash of doubt cross his face. The younger one, meanwhile, fixed her with the kind of blank stare that said he either didn't understand or, more likely, didn't care.

'You cannot kill a British police officer,' Tina continued, her eyes scanning the front of the house for any sign of the other gunman. 'If you do, you will have to answer for it. You want that? Do you?'

The older cop said something in Filipino to his colleague. The younger one looked displeased, and said something back, and they had a brief, barked discussion.

'Right, you are both under arrest,' said the older one finally, pulling a set of old-fashioned Western-style cuffs from his belt. 'You must come with us.'

The younger one barked an order for Milne to turn over and put his hands behind his back, kicking him at the same time.

For a moment, Tina thought Milne might try something, even though it would be suicidal given the look on the younger uniform's face, but he did as he was told and the cuffs were placed on him.

Their eyes met. Milne looked resigned to his fate, but it was clear he didn't want her to share it. 'Run, Tina!' he snapped as the older uniform approached her, cuffs in hand. 'Run!'

For a split second she was hit by indecision. If she made a break for it, it would be tantamount to admitting that she'd had a part in the murders in the house, and she'd be a fugitive in a foreign land. She might even end up with a bullet in the back. But if she stayed, there was no guarantee either that she'd be safe. She didn't like the way these two had suddenly turned up here in the middle of nowhere. It was too coincidental.

Which meant they were probably in league with the killers.

The older one took her arm. 'Turn round,' he demanded.

'Run, Tina, for God's sake!' she heard Milne cry, followed by the sound of him being struck hard.

She'd taken some kickboxing classes at the police gym the previous year – part of an obsession she'd developed for fitness that she knew bordered on the unhealthy. But it served her well now because she caught her captor with a ferocious uppercut that sent him reeling.

She turned and darted across the road, launching herself into the undergrowth, and running through it as fast as she could, no idea where she was going, ignoring the way the bushes and branches slashed at her face, just trying to put as much distance between herself and the house as possible.

She got about fifty yards before she ran into a ditch, lost her footing, and fell forward into a thick puddle of foul-smelling mud, unleashing a swarm of insects. Exhausted, she lay where she'd fallen, slowly getting her breathing back under control. She heard the police patrol car drive away, and wondered what would become of Milne. He'd saved her life tonight. At least once. Probably twice. When the big Russian bastard had grabbed her and pushed the gun against her head, she'd genuinely thought that was it. She remembered the way he'd violated her home three days earlier and half a world away, and now, at his mercy again, the hatred and rage had coursed through her. She'd wanted Milne to kill him.

And he had. He'd put a bullet between her tormentor's eyes. Without batting an eyelid. That took guts. Most men, virtually all men, would have dropped the weapon. He hadn't. It made her respect him. And now he was being taken away, either to prison or to his death, and she would never have the opportunity to thank him for what he'd done.

She found the mobile in her pocket, considered calling Mike Bolt back in England, and getting him to raise the alarm. But what could she say that could possibly help Milne? Nothing. He was finished either way. Perhaps death was even preferable. Calling Mike would only be a fast-track way of losing her career and ending up in a Filipino prison for aiding an offender.

But the fact that she'd left him at the mercy of those two cops hurt. 'There's nothing more you could have done,' she told herself. 'And anyway, remember, he deserves all that's coming to him.'

But she was no longer sure she believed it.

One of the many mosquitoes buzzing round landed on Tina's face, and she slapped it away angrily.

And then heard a twig crack behind her.

She froze, palm still held against her cheek.

There was the sound of movement in the under-growth – bushes being steadily pushed aside. Getting closer.

Tina pressed herself deeper into the mud, trying to work out whether it was best to break cover or stay where she was. She was partly concealed by a large fern, but her clothing – a white T-shirt and khaki shorts – would surely stand out in the darkness.

She held her breath, her whole body tense, and ever so slowly turned her head.

Two black work boots, scuffed at the tips, filled her vision, just a few feet from her elbow. The person they belonged to wasn't moving. For all she knew, he could be staring down at her right now, ready to pull the trigger, leaving her to die here in a lonely, dirty backwater thousands of miles from home. Tina had to use all her willpower not to make a grab for his legs, or jump up and run. Instead, she stayed exactly where she was, still not breathing, listening to the thump-thump-thump of her heart, wondering for how long she could stay like this.

The figure didn't move.

She counted to five in her head, wondering what the hell he was doing. Wondering, too, how long she could continue to hold her breath.

And then he took a step forward, brushing the fern aside, and his boot landed in the mud, inches from her face. She heard him curse quietly under his breath and slap away a mosquito, recognizing the voice as belonging to the other, smaller man who'd tried to kill her back in England, and who'd almost certainly been the one who'd murdered Nick.

Anger suddenly overcame fear, and before she could stop herself, Tina had grabbed one of his legs with both hands and launched herself upwards, completely upending him.

He fell on his side into the mud, clearly shocked by her sudden attack, but already bringing his gun round to fire at her. He was wearing a balaclava, but Tina recognized the blue eyes beneath. It was definitely the man who'd tried to drown her in her bath.

She was quick, jumping on top of him, knees first, as he rolled over on to his back, and winding him. She grabbed the gun arm with one hand, shoving it away, then snatched up a handful of mud and shoved it into his face, trying to rub it into his eyes.

But he was quick too. And strong. With a single grunt of exertion, he flipped his body up, knocking her off him. She kept hold of his gun hand, though, and lashed out with her legs, as they rolled in the mud, fighting savagely. But he still had the gun, and he was stronger than her. Her only advantage was the fact that he'd been temporarily blinded by the mud. But he'd already rolled on top of her, and was wrestling the gun free, using touch rather than sight to fight this battle.

Tina knew she'd made a mistake taking him on but she still had one free hand and she used it to deliver a single rapid uppercut to his jaw. It wasn't the best of shots but it knocked him off her, and she used the split second it afforded her to scramble away from him, roll through the undergrowth, and jump to her feet, keeping low.

A shot rang out, the sound partly muffled by the suppressor. It passed close, but Tina kept on running, relying on the fact that with mud in his eyes and darkness all around it was going to be hard for him to hit her. Another shot rang out, but this time it sounded further away.

Finally she reached the road. In the absence of any street or house lighting it was impossible to tell whether or not it was the one they'd parked on, but there wasn't any time to hang around trying to work it out. She tried to get her bearings, made a guess in which direction the car was, and started running along the road in that direction, conscious of the sound of her footfalls on the uneven tarmac as she scanned the trees on either side for any sign of her assailant or the car he'd driven here in.

And then, thank God, the track up which she and Milne had parked barely half an hour earlier appeared, and she saw the vague blue glint of the rental car's paintwork, partly obscured by the palm tree.

Pulling the keys from her pocket, she raced up to the driver's door and yanked it open. Having seen far too many scary films in her time, she had a quick look in the back, saw it was empty, then got inside. Panting heavily from her exertions, she started the engine and drove slowly on to the road, without turning on the lights. She looked both ways, saw no one, and accelerated away in the direction of Manila, putting her foot down and keeping her head low, knowing her assailant was still in the vicinity, and wanting to present as small a target as possible.

The side window exploded inwards, showering her with glass, and she screamed as the car momentarily veered out of control. She hit the verge and narrowly missed a tree before righting the wheel and stealing a look in her rear-view mirror.

He was out in the road now, a grim silhouette with gun out-stretched, and as she watched, a flame shot out of the barrel and glass shattered in the back window. The bullet ricocheted through the car, flying out of the top corner of the wind-screen, and Tina floored the accelerator, bent down so low in the seat now that she could barely see over the wheel.

The car veered off the road on to the scrub and hit branches and bushes, even an ancient road sign, before she managed to pull it back on to the tarmac, her speed hitting eighty km/h as she slammed into a pothole and negotiated a bend in the road.

And at that moment, as the man who'd tried

and failed to kill her twice now was swallowed up by the darkness behind, she felt a burst of elation which was better than any drug, even the booze. She might have been alone and hunted in a foreign land, but once again she'd made it.

Right then, nothing else mattered.

CHAPTER 39

Sitting in the back of the police car, it didn't take me long to work out what the plan had been. When we turned up at the house, I was supposed to get shot with the police-issue revolver that one of our assailants had been firing at me. That way it would look like the police had disturbed me, a murderous fugitive, in the midst of robbing the place, having first killed its occupants, and gunned me down. I guessed that they were supposed to get Tina out of there alive, or at least remove her body afterwards, since her presence in the house would have been harder to explain. It would be easy enough in a country like this to make her disappear, and that would have been that. Job done. And us out of Paul Wise's hair.

Thankfully, Tina had escaped – or at least I hoped she had. My situation, however, was far more precarious. The cops who'd cuffed and bundled me into the car had told me that I was under arrest, but I knew I wasn't. These guys were going to kill me, there was no doubt about that. In the Philippines, the hunt for justice simply isn't

285

carried out with the same enthusiasm you and I are used to in the west. Corners get cut. Cops get corrupted. People die.

The car moved slowly along pitch-black back roads, the older guy driving while Frogface watched me from behind the steel grille separating us, his eyes blank and cold, until eventually he got bored and started talking to his colleague in Tagalog.

I was exhausted from my earlier exertions, and now carrying an injured shoulder – though thankfully it was a flesh wound and nowhere near as bad as it could have been. But I knew I had to move fast. The doors were locked from the inside so my options were limited. At least the cuffs they'd placed on me were the old-fashioned metal ones with the hand-restraints linked by a short chain, which were the easiest to pick. The driver had also made a big mistake. By being in too much of a hurry to search me properly, he'd missed the small Swiss Army knife in my front left pocket that I was in the habit of carrying round with me.

The knife, I realized, was my one and only chance of getting out of here in one piece, and I experienced a sudden wave of panic – the first I'd had for a few years, since being held in that stuffy little room at Phnom Penh Airport – at the thought that this could finally be it. The kind of death I'd inflicted on too many others.

I fought the panic down hard. I hadn't survived all these years by folding in the face of danger.

Trying to move as slowly as possible, I manoeuvred myself round so I could reach into the pocket. As my fingers slipped inside, I held my breath. I was sitting at an odd angle. If either of the cops turned round, I was finished. But as my fingers found the knife, they continued to talk quietly in the front.

I slipped it out and hid it behind my back, turning back round in the seat just as the driver glanced at me in the rear-view mirror. He watched me suspiciously for a couple of seconds before saying something to Frogface, who nodded and said something back. I recognized one of the words he used. *Patayan*. It meant 'killing', and Frogface had turned my way when he said it, confirming what I already knew.

A few seconds later the car pulled off the road and headed down a narrow potholed track. Foliage brushed against the windows as it closed in on us, and I got the idea we were nearing our destination. Feeling round behind my back, I flicked open the knife's corkscrew and removed the tiny screwdriver that was wound through it. Now it was a matter of pushing the end between the notches on the swinging part of the cuff and the ratchet on the other, and shimmying them open. But because I'd been cuffed with my palms outwards, as was standard police practice, it was no easy task, particularly when bumping round in the back of a car.

My heart was beating like a hammer and my

wrists ached from the effort of trying to force them into a position they weren't used to, while I tried to keep my face as impassive as possible. The driver kept checking me in the rear-view mirror, and I could see the tension in his eyes as he psyched himself up for what he was about to do. Killing someone in cold blood's never easy, regardless of what it looks like in the movies. It's still the final taboo, and even if you're used to it, as I was, it takes a huge amount of willpower to pull the trigger. The driver, I was pretty sure, wasn't used to it.

The car slowed as we reached a break in the trees and I saw that we'd driven into a clearing. The sound of insects filled the air, and I could smell stagnant water.

I had to get this damn screwdriver into the hole. If I didn't, in the next minute I'd be dead.

Slowly. Slowly.

I shut out every thought, every sound, concentrating everything on picking the lock.

The car stopped and they both got out, Frogface clutching his shotgun. I felt the panic come again in an intense wave as Frogface opened the rear passenger door, looking round at the same time to check that there weren't any witnesses about. He smiled down at me. He was the man who was going to pull the trigger, and I knew by looking into those dead eyes that he'd be able to do it.

In desperation, I tried to manoeuvre the screwdriver into the hole between the notches and the ratchet one last time, contorting my wrists into a position they should never have been in.

I heard a single click as the screwdriver moved in a notch and immediately leaned back in the seat and pushed my arms against the cuffs, forcing them open.

I'd done it.

Just in time, because the next second Frogface leaned in and grabbed me by the collar, dragging me out. I didn't put up any resistance and kept my hands behind my back so that it looked like I was still cuffed. At the same time, I opened up the main blade on the knife.

We were close to the edge of a deep-looking swamp about twenty yards across, beyond which were more trees. Only the patrol car's headlights kept the place from falling into total darkness. As I stumbled in a pothole and steadied myself, I felt a drop of rain on my face.

Frogface pushed me in the ribs with the shotgun and motioned with his head towards the swamp. 'Walk,' he grunted.

The driver was coming round the front of the car, and he'd drawn his revolver, which he was keeping down by his side. The rain began to fall harder, great cool drops of it splattering on the dirt.

The fear of death surged through me then, at the thought that this might be the last rain I ever felt on my face, but so too did the adrenalin that comes with it. Fear's good. Let it get the better of you and it makes you slow and useless, but if you know how to harness it, it can be used to keep you alive.

And I did know.

In one sudden movement, I grabbed the barrel of the shotgun, aiming it away from me, and drove the knife up to the hilt into Frogface's gut, ignoring the sick feeling I got from the soft splitting noise it made. This was about survival, pure and simple.

Frogface looked temporarily startled and stumbled back. His grip on the shotgun weakened and I tried to yank it out of his hand, but he held on, even when I stabbed him again three times in quick succession. Sometimes it takes time for someone to know they've been stabbed, their own adrenalin temporarily masking the damage being done to them. Frogface was a case in point.

If anything, my attack seemed to galvanize him, and he propelled himself forward and drove his head up into my face. I managed to dodge the worst of the blow by turning my head but he still hit my cheek with a painful thud that wasn't that far away from breaking a bone. He was trying to shake me off, and I could see the driver standing only a few feet away, taking aim with his revolver, waiting for a clean shot, and I knew that if I let go of Frogface, I'd be dead. So I held on, keeping one hand fixed as firmly as possible on the shotgun barrel while I searched for an opening with the other.

Frogface slammed the side of his head into mine, bellowing in anger and frustration, and I lost my footing.

But as I slipped in the dirt, I rolled with the momentum, letting go of the shotgun in the process, then quickly launched myself back up at him, the two of us stumbling all the way back into the car. In the process he turned his head away from mine, exposing the dark flesh of his throat.

I was operating entirely on instinct as I jammed the knife into his neck. For a second there was no blood; then, as he staggered unsteadily, a narrow geyser of red shot out in a long spraying arc, his grip on me weakened dramatically, and the shotgun fell to the ground with a metallic clatter.

Frogface's colleague – clearly, as I'd guessed, no ice-cool killer himself – yelled something and came towards me, revolver outstretched, anger and shock in his eyes, the end of the barrel now only feet away from my head.

I yanked Frogface round, using him as a human shield, and ducked down as the driver pulled the trigger and the night exploded in noise. The bullet missed, and I thrust Frogface forward into him. For a moment the two of them became entangled, and as the driver pushed his colleague aside and turned back towards me, I jumped into him, grabbing his gun arm and butting him full in the face.

The gun flew out of his hand, but he still

managed to throw a quick left hook that sent me crashing to the ground. I raised my head and saw him lean down and pick up the shotgun.

Desperately I looked in the rain and darkness for where his gun had fallen. I spotted it lying beside a pile of dirt-encrusted bottles at the side of the road, and scrambled over on my hands and knees, hearing him pump the shotgun behind me. Grabbing the revolver in both hands, I rolled round on to my back so that we were facing each other through the rain, fifteen feet apart.

For a long, surreal moment, neither of us moved. Our whole lives had been distilled to this one piece of stinking swampland in the middle of nowhere.

And then I fired, half a second before he did, because he was already going down as the shotgun discharged, its payload going high and wide into the black night sky. He fell to one knee, clutching at his gut, and I pulled the trigger again, the bullet taking the top of his head off, and then kept pulling it until it was empty.

Finally the world fell silent and the only thing I could hear was the incessant ringing in my ears.

Slowly I got to my feet, the cuffs still dangling from one wrist, the revolver smoking in my hands, and walked over to where the two men lay. The driver was at an awkward angle, his head split open like a coconut by the second bullet, exposing a mass of brain matter, one arm down by his side, the other outstretched, fingers still clutching the shotgun. Frogface, though, was still alive. He lay on his front, face in the dirt, a steadily growing pool of sticky warm blood surrounding his upper half, his legs still kicking weakly like a clockwork toy reaching the end of its cycle.

I used my shirt to wipe the handle of the revolver I'd just used to shoot the driver and dropped it to the ground, before unholstering Frogface's revolver and taking two speedloaders, each containing six rounds, from his belt. I pushed them into the pocket of my jeans, clicked off the safety on Frogface's revolver, then leaned down, placed a foot on his neck, and shot him in the back of the head.

It was a mercy killing. I had no desire to leave him to bleed to death, and felt no satisfaction for what I'd just done. I'd killed two men. Men who doubtless had families and people who loved them.

I could smell death in the stagnant air, and I felt sick. I looked around at the silent woodland. The rain was torrential now, and I suddenly felt utterly alone. I had to find Tina.

But when I reached into my pocket to pull out my mobile phone, a terrible thought struck me. I might have got rid of the phone that Schagel had given me but it was possible, given the contacts he and Wise had within the Filipino police, that they could have got someone to triangulate the location of my phone throughout my current stay in Manila. They wouldn't be able to trace me any longer, but that didn't matter. The historical data would tell anyone interested where Tina and I had spent the previous night. Which meant that, if Tina had got away tonight, they could get to her there.

It was only then that I realized she'd never actually given me her phone number.

I cursed at such an elementary mistake and pulled the keys from the driver's pocket. I jumped inside the patrol car, turned it round, and drove back the way we'd come, knowing I had to get back to Manila as soon as possible.

CHAPTER 40

Tina was exhausted, wet, and in a state of shock when she unlocked the front door to the guesthouse, and went through the empty reception area in the direction of the stairs. Everything had gone wrong. First, Pat O'Riordan, the man who'd been her best hope of gathering evidence against Paul Wise, was dead. And now so were his wife and her brother, and Dennis Milne, the man who'd been her only ally left alive, had been caught. Either he was under arrest, in which case it was only a matter of hours before the authorities found out who he really was, or he was dead as well, having been dispatched by the two crooked uniforms.

She needed Milne now, because without him she was powerless to move forward. He'd had the address for the man called Heed, Wise's fixer in Manila. All she had were names: Heed, and Omar Salic and Cheeseman from the pages of O'Riordan's diary. Names that meant nothing on their own.

She was unarmed and alone in a hostile city, where people were trying to kill her, and with only the barest leads to work on. She thought about calling Mike Bolt again, to see if he'd managed to find out a location for Wise, but even if he had, what good would it do her? She could hardly turn up and demand he confess his crimes. In her heart, Tina knew she only had one alternative left: to return home, thwarted once again in her hunt for justice, but at least with her life and freedom intact. As soon as she woke the next morning, she was going to call the airline and get on the first flight back. The thought depressed her. Tina had never been one to accept defeat. She was a fighter. But she also wasn't stupid.

On her way up to her room, she inspected herself in the full-length mirror at the top of the stairs. She looked like crap. Her clothes were soaking, and her hair was matted and sticking to the side of a face that was streaked with dirt. She had a cut above her right eye, with a thick, soft scab, and another one on her right cheek, which was swollen. It was a good thing there'd been no one on the front desk.

She looked at her watch. It was almost midnight. The drive back on unfamiliar roads had taken her longer than expected, and she felt exhaustion taking hold. It had been an intense, draining few days, and she was still jetlagged from her flight halfway round the world.

She had the key in the lock and was just about to open the door when she stopped.

What if someone was in her room waiting for her? It wasn't as if Wise's people didn't have the resources to track her down. Tina had been ambushed three times in the past three days, and caught off-guard every time. It was fast becoming a habit. The first time, back at her cottage, hadn't been her fault. Neither, you could argue, was the second, when Milne had broken into her room. But tonight she and Milne had made a mistake by going back to the house in Ternate rather than following the lead they already had, and it had almost cost Tina her life. She couldn't afford another error. The law of averages was against her enough as it was.

She removed the key and turned away.

Which was the moment when the door was yanked open from the inside.

Tina turned and broke into a run, heading for the stairwell at the end of the corridor.

'Tina!'

Milne was standing in the open doorway. He looked as tired and rough as she felt.

'I've been waiting for you,' he said quietly.

She felt a lurch of relief so strong it almost knocked her over. 'Dennis.' She walked up and had to stop herself from hugging him. In the end, she settled for putting a hand on his arm. 'When did you get back here?'

'Ten minutes ago.' He motioned her to step inside, and shut the door behind them. 'I knocked on your door, and when you weren't there I thought I'd check that you didn't have any unwanted visitors.'

She smiled. 'Thanks. And thanks for earlier too. You saved my life.'

'You saved mine as well. If you hadn't intervened outside the house, those cops would have put a bullet in me. So I guess we're quits.'

'How did you get away?'

'I killed them,' he said simply, then saw the look on her face. 'I had to do it. They were going to kill me. You've got to understand that.'

They looked at each other for a few seconds without speaking, and once again Tina noticed the haunted look in his pale blue eyes, and the pain he was carrying with him. 'I understand,' she said at last. And she did. She'd killed before, when she'd believed it necessary, and she'd lost sleep over what she'd done. That didn't make her the same as him – and she was still sickened by some of the crimes he'd committed over the years – but there were definitely similarities between them.

'We've got one serious lead,' he said, sitting down on a rickety chair next to the bed. 'The man Tomboy delivered this mysterious briefcase to. Heed.'

'And Tomboy had no idea at all what was in the briefcase?'

'No. But because he worked for Paul Wise, and Wise is in the country, I assume it must be en route to him.'

'So we need to go and see Heed.'

Milne yawned. 'I'm too tired to go and see him now. It'll have to wait until tomorrow. And I'm going to go alone.'

Tina immediately opened her mouth to protest, but he held up a hand, and she let him continue.

'This is over for you, Tina,' he said gently. 'I don't care what you say. You can still walk away from all this. Go home, back to your life, and your job. I can't. The chances are Bertie Schagel's already betrayed me to the authorities in Manila, and I'm guessing I'm going to be getting the blame for the murders tonight, as well as Pat O'Riordan. I'm finished. I've been finished ever since the moment I made the decision not to shoot you.'

Tina looked at him, startled, as he continued to speak.

'Which was my choice. I don't expect you to thank me. But . . .' He sighed, looking up at Tina with a rueful smile. 'I'm glad I did it.'

She didn't know what to say. But she felt for him, then, the intensity of her emotions a surprise to her, even after all that had happened.

'When I go and see Heed, he's not going to want to talk,' he continued. 'But he's got the information we need. He knows about Lene Haagen, and I bet he knows what happened to her, and where she's buried. He also knows why O'Riordan died, who the person or people he was going to meet were. And I'm guessing he also knows what's in the briefcase. In other words, he's the man with all the answers. But I'm going to have to force them out of him, and it's not going to be pretty. And when I'm finished, I'm going to have to kill him. In cold blood. I don't want you there when I do that. Do you understand what I'm saying?'

'I do. But we don't have to kill him, do we? We can find out what evidence we need to put Wise behind bars, then tie him up, put in an anonymous call to the authorities, and get him arrested.'

Milne gave her an incredulous look. 'Be serious, Tina. What hard evidence do you really think we're going to turn up that stands even the remotest chance of convicting Paul Wise in a court of law? Especially in a country like this? You said it yourself: he's escaped justice for years. He's obviously good at it. I – and I mean I – need to track down Wise and kill him too. That's what you want, isn't it? When it comes down to it.'

And she had to admit that it was. A year or so ago it had been very different. She'd genuinely thought she'd see the day when she could face her nemesis across a British courtroom and see his face crumple as he was sentenced to the rest of his life in prison. But now she knew that would never happen. In the few days she'd spent in Manila, she'd been kidding herself that she could indeed uncover 'the smoking gun' that would bring Wise down. Milne was right. He was going to have to die.

He sighed. 'If I kill him, you'll get the justice you want. So will I. And you'll still be alive and free at the end of it.'

Tina sat down on the end of the bed. Once again, she didn't know what to say. Instead, she took out her cigarettes, and offered him one for the first time.

'No thanks. I quit a few years back. For health reasons.' He leaned back in the chair and gave a hollow laugh. 'I guess it seems a bit pointless, given my current situation.'

'Is there really no way out for you?' she asked, lighting her cigarette. 'Couldn't you get hold of a false passport and disappear until everything dies down? You're good at that sort of thing. You've got to be. You've survived the best part of a decade on the run.'

He shook his head. 'Not this time. Schagel knows what I look like, as well as the name I've been travelling under. He even controls my bank account. I'm trapped here in the Philippines, and he's going to make sure I don't get out.'

'I still don't understand what Schagel's part in all this is.'

'Neither do I. I think he and Wise must be in business together, but what their business is, I've no idea.'

'Children?'

'I suppose it could be. But this briefcase that they're so interested in isn't a child.' He shrugged. 'Heed knows the answers. I'll get them out of him.'

They both fell silent, lost in their own thoughts. Finally, Tina stubbed out her cigarette in the room's cheap glass ashtray. 'I need to turn in,' she said, getting to her feet. 'I'm shattered.'

'Me too.' Milne got to his feet.

'Do you think we're safe here?' she asked.

'I think so. But I can't say for sure. Schagel's got the number of the phone I was carrying when we booked in here, so it's possible if he's got the right contacts he could triangulate our location to this address, but it wouldn't be easy.'

'Do you think we should stay together tonight?'

He looked taken aback by the suggestion, and was clearly trying hard not to show it. 'Possibly. To be on the safe side. But I guess that's up to you.'

Tina wasn't sure if she was being over-cautious or if it was something more than that, but she said that it would probably be a good idea.

'I'll sleep in the chair.'

'It's OK,' she told him. 'We can share. But I'm warning you,' she added, with a smile, 'don't try anything.'

He smiled back. 'I wouldn't dare.'

Later, as they lay side by side in the darkness under the single sheet, both still partly dressed, she felt an urge for some human warmth. It had been weeks since she'd shared a bed with a man. That man had been Nick Penny, and she was immediately reminded of what had happened to him, and how desperate she was to make Paul Wise pay.

Milne wasn't moving, but she could tell he was awake. 'Thanks again for today,' she whispered.

'And thank you,' he whispered back.

Instinctively, she put an arm round his chest and pulled him close, and then he turned round and their lips met, and for a few moments all her fear and stress and anger disappeared, and she surrendered to more primal urges.

Their lovemaking was natural and intense, and afterwards they clung to each other for a long time, each afraid to let go, because they both knew in their hearts that this could well be the first and last time they were ever together. That tomorrow they might be parted for ever. Neither spoke. They didn't need to. Somehow, it made their fragile intimacy even stronger.

At last Milne pulled away from her and turned over, and a few minutes later, as she lay there staring at the ceiling, wondering what kind of person she'd become to be sleeping with a murderer, she heard him cry out in his sleep. 'I'm sorry,' he said, the words full of pain. 'I'm so sorry.' And she wondered if he was talking about her, or Emma, the woman he'd left behind.

She reached across and pulled him close, burying her face in his shoulder, her eyes wet with tears, until finally sleep overwhelmed her too.

CHAPTER 41

Nargen was in a foul mood as he walked into the club. It was noisy and full of scantily clad teenage Filipina girls and middleaged western men, the former outnumbering the latter by at least five to one.

As soon as they spotted him, a dozen of the girls surrounded him like locusts. They screeched their hellos above the heavy beat of the music, asking if he'd like a drink or some fun, but he pushed his way through them as if they didn't exist. Oriental women did nothing for him. Especially uneducated whores.

He walked past the long stage in the middle of the room, on which more girls in knee-length boots and leather bikinis danced and pouted, trying and failing to look sexy and sophisticated.

He let out an audible growl as he thought back to the evening's events. Once again, his attempt to kill the woman, Boyd, had failed, and in the process he'd lost his right-hand man. Tumanov could be replaced easily enough, of course – there were plenty of ex-special forces men looking for work – but that wasn't the point. No, the point was that his professional pride had been hurt. For a man who'd always been so successful in executing his orders, it was embarrassing to have been thwarted not once, but twice – and by a woman. He'd wanted to continue the hunt for her, to prove that he was capable of putting her in the ground, but he'd been overruled by Schagel. Which was why he was here now, being pestered by worthless little whores.

At the furthest end of the club from the main entrance there was an unmarked door painted the same black as the walls. It had no handle, only a small keypad, also painted black, and it took Nargen a few seconds to find it. He typed in the four-digit code he'd been given, and listened as it set off a buzzer on the other side of the door.

A few seconds later, the raspy voice of Mr Heed, the strange man who'd picked him and Tumanov up from the airport, came over the intercom, demanding identification.

Looking up so he could be seen by the camera that pointed down from the ceiling, Nargen introduced himself, and a second later the door clicked open. He went inside and found himself in a narrow, dimly lit corridor, with a flight of stone steps to his left. The door closed and locked behind him, immediately shutting out the noise of the club. Trying to ignore the vague unease he felt, Nargen descended the steps, aware of a dank smell, similar to an old wet raincoat, filling his nostrils.

Heed was waiting for him at the bottom of the steps, clad in a long black dressing gown, a hand in one of the pockets. His nicotine-coloured hair was slicked back, thin and wet against the scalp, and he wore a smug, satisfied expression. His feet were bare, and Nargen, who always prided himself on his appearance, was vaguely disgusted to see that the toenails jutted out like gnarled, yellowing talons.

'I'm here for the package,' he said.

'I know you are,' said Heed with a smile that never quite reached his eyes. He took a couple of steps backwards to allow Nargen into the cellar-like hallway. 'It's in there,' he added, motioning towards an open door.

Nargen looked at him carefully, wondering if this was some kind of trick. He didn't like turning his back on men he didn't know, especially when they looked as cunning as this one.

Heed met his gaze with the same mocking smile. 'It's all right. Go, go.'

Nargen went through the door and into a small, airless kitchen, lit only by a single bulb hanging from the ceiling. He wondered if Heed actually lived down here, without any natural light, and thought that if he did, then there must be something terribly wrong with him.

The package, a large black briefcase, was on a small table in the middle of the room.

Nargen stopped and took a deep breath. His mouth was dry. It was so innocuous-looking. But he knew what was inside it. Schagel had told him. It was too valuable for him not to, and it was why he was being paid so much money to deliver it.

Slowly, carefully, he picked it up from the table, tensing his muscles to take the weight, but when he turned round he saw that Heed had a pistol in his hand.

He put the case back down on the table, contemplating going for the Sig Sauer in his jacket pocket, before deciding against it. He was quick, but not that quick.

'Why are you pointing that at me?' he demanded.

'Insurance,' said Heed. 'I want you to let the people you're working for know that there is no point trying to kill me.'

'I wasn't aware they did want to kill you.'

'I have a strange feeling about that case,' Heed said quietly, his narrow little fish eyes moving towards it like magnets. 'I think that whatever is in it spells great trouble. And knowing its recipient, Mr Wise, as I do, I'm concerned that he might decide to eliminate anyone who's come into contact with it, a list that as you know includes me. So I'm telling you this. I have no idea what's in it, nor do I want to know. If anyone should ask me about it, I will deny all knowledge of ever being in possession of it. In other words, the people you work for have nothing to fear from me. But' – and here he raised a liver-spotted hand, and fixed Nargen with a malignant glare – 'if anything should happen to me – were I to meet an unpleasant end – then things that I know about Mr Wise, and also Mr Schagel, the man who sent you – very bad things, I might add – will become public. And that will be unfortunate for both of them.'

'I'm here to collect the case, that's all,' said Nargen, thinking that Heed was wise to be so wary. Earlier that evening. Nargen had been given instructions to kill him when he collected the package. Unfortunately, this no longer looked a possibility. It was another black mark against Nargen's name, but there was nothing he could do about that. He would have to carry out the task some other time when Heed's guard had slipped sufficiently; although for the first time he felt a slither of concern that he too might be expendable. He would have to watch his own back over the next twenty-four hours.

Apparently satisfied with Nargen's answer, Heed took a step backwards so that he was no longer blocking the doorway while Nargen picked up the case for a second time and walked out into the hallway. A corridor snaked off into the darkness to his left, and he thought he could hear the sound of a child's whimpering coming from somewhere down there. It was, he decided, time to get out of this claustrophobic, tomb-like place.

He took a last look at Heed, searching for an opportunity to take him quickly, but the other man had settled back against the far wall, his gun still trained on Nargen, and the look on his jaundiced, parchment-dry face told him that Heed knew exactly what he was thinking.

With the child's whimpering growing louder in his ears, Nargen turned and walked back up the steps, feeling Heed's eyes burning into him.

The briefcase weighed heavily in his hand, as if its terrible contents were trying to drag him down.

The sooner he was rid of it, the happier he would be.

PART III

THE AXE FALLS

CHAPTER 42

The bed was empty when I woke up. Daylight streamed in through the open window, beyond which came the steady sound of traffic. It was hot in the room and I threw off the single sheet, remembering what had happened between Tina and me the previous night. It had been a long time since I'd made such frantic, desperate love. The last time had been with Emma.

I'd dreamed of her in the night. It was the same dream I often had. In it, I would hear knocking on the front door of my house in Laos, and when I opened it, I would see Emma standing there. A two-year-old child would be by her side, clutching her hand tightly. Almost always the child was a boy, only on rare occasions a girl, but the child never looked at me. He or she always stood there, head down. Emma would have a look of utter sadness on her face as she asked me why I'd abandoned them both. And I was always so desperate to tell her that it was because of all the bad things I'd done – things that I now felt truly sorry for. But I knew that I couldn't, because she'd be too

313

sickened by what she heard ever to want to see me again. So in the dream I never spoke. I would stand at the door in silence, my eyes wet with tears, until finally she turned and led our child away. Sometimes I would follow them a little way, trying desperately to think of words that would make her understand. Other times I would stand rooted to the spot, watching them go, until finally they faded from view altogether. And then the words would come in a great, painful flurry, and I would shout how much I loved her, how much I loved both of them, and how sorry I was that it had come to this, before, mercifully, the dream ended and the blackness of deep sleep took hold.

Sitting up in bed, I took a deep breath, allowing the wave of sadness to wash over me, before forcing myself back to the present. I looked at my watch, and saw that it was almost ten o'clock. Ironically, given everything that had happened, I'd slept a hell of a lot better than I'd done in a long time.

Tina was nowhere to be seen and I wondered if she regretted what we'd done. I hoped not. Although I'd felt guilty about sleeping with her afterwards, as I did when I slept with anyone other than Emma, it had still been an intense and emotional experience, and it struck me that in other circumstances, Tina was the kind of woman who could have dragged me out of the darkness, allowing me to put the past where it belonged – in the past.

But that wasn't going to happen. I was going to have to abandon her, just as I'd abandoned Emma. She was the one with the future, which meant she had to go home to England. It was up to me to finish things here.

I drank some water and showered in the tiny windowless bathroom, and was just getting dressed when the door to the room opened and Tina came back in. She had a newspaper under her arm and her expression was grim.

I started to ask her if everything was OK, but she threw the paper on the bed, with the head-line facing upwards, and I knew straight away that whatever it was going to say was bad. 'Murdered Reporter's Wife Gunned Down with Brother' it screamed. I picked up the paper and unfolded it, which was when I saw the sub-heading beneath, 'International Fugitive Sought', and the three-inch-by-three-inch colour photo of me next to it. From the shirt I was wearing I could tell that it had been taken three days earlier on Bertie Schagel's yacht in Hong Kong.

So the bastard had sold me out.

It was to be expected, of course, but even so, the fact that I was front-page news still came as a shock.

I read the rest of the article. Not surprisingly, given O'Riordan's position on the paper, it was their lead story, continuing on pages two and three. No motive was given for either of the killings, but then there was no immediate need for one. The police already had their suspect. There was a short background piece on me, concentrating on the fact that I'd fled the UK at the end of 2001, after allegedly committing a series of murders, and hadn't been seen since. I was described by Manila police chief Ricardo Gutierrez as armed and extremely dangerous, and he was quoted as having warned his officers to shoot me on sight unless I surrendered immediately. Which basically meant they were going to shoot me on sight regardless, something that would suit Bertie Schagel perfectly. There was nothing about the deaths of the two police officers the previous night, but it had probably happened too late to make the early editions. Thankfully, there was also no mention anywhere of Tina.

'What are you going to do?' she asked me.

I sighed. There were enough ex-pats in Manila that I wouldn't stand out like a sore thumb, but it was no Bangkok or Hong Kong, and I reckoned I had a maximum of twenty-four hours before the law caught up with me.

I could have run, I suppose. Made for the coast and one of the Philippines' seven thousand islands, disappearing from view until all the furore had died down. After all, I'd done it before. Except this time I had no money, and my crimes had been committed here, not in a country six thousand miles away. In reality, I'd reached the end of a long and bloody road. There'd be no retirement in the hills of Laos, no reunion with Emma and our child. But no prison either. I wouldn't – couldn't – let them take me alive. The idea of spending the rest of my life behind bars was simply too much. All I could do now was try to redeem myself in the short time I had left.

'I'm going to do what I said I'd do,' I told her. 'I'm going to find Heed, and Paul Wise, and everyone else involved in this, and I'm going to kill them.'

'They're going to get you eventually, Dennis. You know that, don't you?' She looked genuinely upset as she said this. Which was something, I suppose.

'I know,' I said, thinking how slight she looked, standing at the end of the bed like a blonde Audrey Hepburn, the sunlight from the window making her pale skin glow. I really didn't want to leave her here, but I knew I had to. 'That's why you can't come with me. At the moment, the police aren't looking for you. You can go to the airport, change your flight, and get the hell out of this place. Stay with me and at best you end up behind bars in some shitty Filipino prison for aiding and abetting a fugitive. And at worst you die. I can't let that happen to you.'

But my plea was already falling on deaf ears, because Tina wasn't listening. At least not to me. Instead, she had her ear pressed against the door.

'There are people coming,' she whispered.

And then I heard it. The sound of heavy foot-falls coming up the stairs.

Tina opened the door a crack, before shutting it immediately and putting the chain across. 'It's the police. They're here.'

I cursed. 'OK, they're going to come in shooting, so get under the bed. Then, when it's all stopped, reach out with your warrant card in your hand and identify yourself as a police officer. I've got to go.'

Grabbing the gun and speedloaders from the bedside table, I vaulted over the bed and made for the open window. We were on the second floor and it was a good twenty-foot drop to an alleyway below. The alleyway was empty but there were some overflowing sacks of rubbish piled up on the other side which would break my fall if I could reach them.

Behind me, I could hear movement outside the door. Hoping that Tina would take my advice, I clambered up on to the ledge, shoved the gun into the back of my jeans, and leapt into the open air, legs flailing, heart flying up into my chest.

I landed feet first in a sack of rubbish, bounced back out of it, and threw out my hands to lessen the impact as I was propelled into the wall. After rolling over through a load of foul-smelling detritus and old food, which was now spilling out on to the ground, I got to my feet, feeling a dull pain in my ankles but otherwise largely unhurt.

A split second later there was a crash, and I turned round to see Tina land in exactly the same pile of rubbish, except she managed it with a hell of a lot more grace, and did this kind of parachutist's roll before jumping back up again.

'What the hell are you doing?' I demanded as I set off up the alleyway at a run. 'I thought I said stay behind.'

'Sorry, Dennis, I don't take orders from anybody,' she said, appearing at my side. 'We're in this together, remember?'

And, call me selfish, but I couldn't help it. I was pleased.

CHAPTER 43

The Juicy Peach, the club where Tomboy told me he'd delivered the briefcase, was on a quiet dead-end backstreet just off United Nations Avenue. The frontage was narrow and painted black, with a small unlit neon sign above the locked front door, next to a video camera covering the entrance, and it was sandwiched between a dress shop and a motorcycle repair garage, both of which looked closed.

We'd made the journey over on foot, both of us having decided that driving round in a bullet-ridden rental car would probably attract the wrong sort of attention. It had taken over an hour, with me wearing a baseball cap and sunglasses that Tina had bought for me at a street stall, and we were both hot and sweaty by the time we stopped outside the door, grateful to be in the shade at last. A sign said that the club opened at four p.m. It was now 11.30, but I was keeping my fingers crossed that the man Tomboy had delivered the briefcase to, Heed, was in residence.

There were two new-looking locks on the door,

and I turned to Tina. 'Think you can get through these?'

'Easily,' she said, taking the set of picks from the pocket of her shorts.

True to her word, she had the door open in the space of two minutes. During that time the street remained empty, and I was even confident enough to slip the gun out of the waistband of my jeans as we stepped inside. Tina shut the door behind us, re-locking it.

We were in a small, deserted foyer with an empty coat and gun check-in counter to our left, and a flight of steps straight ahead that corkscrewed down into the silent darkness below.

'I'll lead the way,' I whispered. 'I want you to stay back.'

She shot me an annoyed look. 'I'm perfectly capable of looking after myself, thanks.'

I put a hand on her arm. 'Listen, Tina, I know you're no pushover, but right now there's no point you taking unnecessary risks. I've got the gun, and Heed may be armed.'

I started down the steps, gun outstretched in front of me, thinking that if I had to go to work on Heed to find the answers I needed, I really didn't want her to see it.

As we reached the bottom, the staircase opened out into a large, cavernous room with a bar directly in front of us, and beyond that a central stage with a dancing pole on either end. The bar was lit up, bathing the room in a dim glow, but all the chairs were stacked on tables and nothing moved.

Tomboy had said Heed lived in the basement, so we crept carefully across the floor of the club until I spotted a door at the end, behind one of the tables, marked Staff Only. There was no handle on the door, just a keypad. A camera pointed down from the ceiling.

I listened at the door, then turned to Tina. 'Do you think you can get in?' I whispered, conscious that I was right in the path of the camera.

She ran a finger up and down the doorframe and shook her head. 'There's nothing to pick. This door's brand new and the system looks high-tech. We're only getting in there if he wants us in.'

I stepped back out of range of the camera, gesturing for Tina to do the same. 'Then we're just going to have to wait for him to come out. The place opens at four so he's going to have to appear before then.'

We crouched down behind the table facing the door, using the chairs on top of it as a screen, and waited in silence. As a cop and an ex-cop, we were used to hanging around, having to be patient. On the static surveillance ops that I'd done as a detective in Islington CID, I used to go into an almost trance-like state – the kind I guess people who practise yoga go into – and I did that now, ridding my mind of all the many problems assailing it, and slowing down my breathing so I was in a state of near-relaxation.

Half an hour passed, then an hour, and I was on the verge of dozing off when I heard the sound of footsteps coming down the stairs behind us. Nudging Tina, I moved round the table so we couldn't be seen, and watched as a slightly built middle-aged Filipino dressed in a shirt and tie came into view. He lifted a flap and went behind the bar, lighting a cigarette as he opened the till, before crouching down out of sight.

Indicating for Tina to stay where she was, I crept between the tables, getting closer and closer as the barman stood back up and began filling the till.

When I was about ten yards away, I came out from behind one of the tables and strode towards him, holding the gun out in front of me. 'Hands in the air now. Shout out and you're dead.'

He did exactly as he was told, but eyed me carefully as I approached. 'You're messing with the wrong people if you're planning on robbing this place,' he said.

I stopped in front of him. 'I want to speak to your boss, but I've got a feeling he doesn't want to talk to me, so you're going to buzz down to him and tell him that there's a problem with the till. Then you're going to ask him to come up here. Because if you don't, I will kill you. Do you understand? If you don't believe me, have a look at the front of that.' I motioned towards the paper on the bar in front of him. 'That's me.'

He looked down. 'Yes,' he said. 'It is.'

'So, you know I mean what I say.'

'How do I know you won't kill me anyway?'

'Because I'm not that kind of man.' I ushered him out with the gun. 'Now, move. And make sure you speak loudly enough so I can hear what you're saying. If I think for one moment you're trying to warn Heed about me, you're dead. And I promise you he's not worth dying for.'

I pushed him with the gun barrel and followed five yards behind as the barman walked the length of the club, hoping that Heed wasn't watching through any of the security cameras that lined the walls. Tomboy had said he was a dangerous man, which meant the element of surprise was essential.

Joining Tina behind the table, I pointed the gun through the chair legs in the direction of the door. The barman glanced back in my direction as he stopped in front of it, saw that I was training my weapon on him, and punched a set of numbers into the keypad.

A few moments later, a muffled voice came over the intercom, and the barman introduced himself and spun the yarn I'd given him about the broken till. He sounded convincing enough, and when he was done, he turned my way. 'He's coming up,' he said quietly.

'Step away from the door,' I hissed back, and again he did as instructed.

I took a deep breath, and my finger tensed on the trigger a few seconds later as the door was pulled open and an unpleasant-looking western man walked slowly out, wearing the kind of look that makes children cry.

Even from five yards away I experienced a welling up of revulsion. There was something about him, an aura, that hinted at sickness and death. His parched, flabby skin was an unhealthy shade of yellow, and looked as if it would disintegrate if it were ever exposed to the light of the sun. He was wearing an ancient purple lounge suit and an old discoloured white shirt, and he looked like a walking corpse. He could have been fifty. He could have been eighty. It was very difficult to tell.

'So, what's the problem?' he demanded in a low yet strangely musical voice that bore only a hint of its Australian roots.

'Me,' I said, coming out from behind the table, conscious of Tina standing up too.

He turned my way with a leering smile that showed off stained, uneven teeth. 'Ah, Mr Milne. I wasn't expecting to see you here. Or you, Miss Boyd. To what do I owe the pleasure?'

I was a little disconcerted by his lack of nerves, and by the fact that he knew Tina by sight, but knew better than to show it. 'We need some answers,' I told him, pointing the gun at his chest. 'Now, step away from your friend and put your hands in the air.'

His speed was incredible. In one lightning-fast movement he looped a hand round the barman's neck and swung him round in front of him so that he was using him as a shield, while at the same time pulling a gun from under his jacket. Before the barman could react, his body juddered wildly as Heed shot him twice, the bullets passing straight through him and narrowly missing me as I dived for cover. Heed kept firing as he retreated towards the door, using the barman's body as a shield, his bullets ricocheting wildly off the floor.

I glanced at Tina, who was lying on her front with her head in her hands, then I rolled on to my side and, using the table as partial cover, opened fire, aiming for the lower part of Heed's legs, knowing that I couldn't kill him. Trying to keep my arms as steady as possible, I cracked off three shots, their noise explosive in the confines of the room. One bullet took off the barman's kneecap, but Heed kept moving towards the door.

Then he stopped, and although I could only see his lower half I could tell he was punching a combination into the keypad. I leapt to my feet, holding the gun two-handed, prepared to shoot him in the belly if it would stop him. But the door was already swinging open, and before I could get a shot in, Heed fired back. I ducked, and when I straightened up again, Heed had dropped the barman's body in the doorway and jumped back into the darkness, disappearing down the steps just as I pulled the trigger for a fourth time, aiming low.

The bullet missed but, unfortunately for Heed, the barman's body was propping open the door.

'Stay there,' I hissed at Tina, who was already getting to her feet, and made for the open door.

I stopped just outside in case it was a trap, but through the ringing in my ears I could just make out footfalls coming from the bottom of the flight of stone steps inside the entrance. Motioning once again for Tina to remain where she was, I started down them, moving ever so slowly, knowing that one wrong move and this bastard would take me out all too easily.

The steps curved round 180 degrees, and I poked my head round inch by inch, wishing I could hear and see better. But there was no one there. Before long I found myself looking into a darkened stone hallway that looked more like a cellar than anyone's living quarters. A light burned from somewhere inside, giving the place a dim glow, and a smell of damp filled the still, cold air.

The silence was loud in my ears as I crept down the last of the steps and came out into the hallway proper. A narrow corridor ran off into the darkness to my right, while to the left it opened out a little with doors on either side, before narrowing again into more darkness. One of the doors was partially open, revealing what looked like a kitchen behind it, and it was from here that the only light in the place came.

Narrowing my eyes in an effort to accustom them to the gloom, I made my way over to the kitchen door and pushed it further open with the barrel of the gun. There was no one inside.

I looked right, then left, trying to work out which way he'd gone, knowing that if I made a mistake, I'd be dead.

Then I heard it. A muffled cry, coming from behind one of the doors, only ten feet away.

I tensed, raising the gun. Although the air was cold, I could feel a sheen of sweat forming on my forehead. I was getting a terrible claustrophobic feeling, and it took all my willpower to remain where I was. Listening. Waiting.

I risked a quick glance over my shoulder, but there was nothing behind me, and I could no longer hear anything.

The muffled cry came again. From just behind the same door. I took a step forward, the gun feeling heavy in my hands.

And that was when the door opened and I was confronted by a sight that no man should ever see.

CHAPTER 44

They emerged from the room as if fused together.

The girl was naked and thin and dirty, with the hardened, yet still strangely naive, face of the street urchin, and she was twelve years old at most. Her round brown eyes were wide with terror as Heed held her up in front of him, her head forced into the crook of his shoulder. His gun was pressed hard into her cheek, and his watery fish-grey eyes glinted with a malignant cunning. He had the look of a man who knows he's found his enemy's weakness.

'Drop the gun or she dies,' he said, an unmistakable excitement in his voice. 'And you know I'll do it, don't you? I'll kill this child, and it will be your fault.'

I kept my gun trained on him, knowing that, of course, he meant it. I could almost see the evil that seemed to come off him in intense, rancid waves.

But I also knew that if I did drop my gun, he'd kill me anyway. And then the girl.

Behind me, I thought I could hear movement

on the steps, and hoped it wasn't Tina descending into this gloomy hell. Unarmed, she could do nothing. In fact, she could only make things worse.

'Drop the gun, Milne. You may be a killer, but surely even you don't want the death of a child on your conscience.' He winked at me and nuzzled the girl's neck in a sickeningly intimate gesture. 'Her name's Layla, by the way.'

Layla's eyes burned into me, and I felt a rivulet of sweat run down my forehead and on to my cheek.

'Don't do this, Heed,' I said, conscious of the weakness in my voice. 'This is between you and me.'

'If you drop your gun, I will let you walk out of here, and Layla will live to see adulthood. I'm going to count to three and if your gun's not on the floor then I'm going to pull the trigger. One . . .'

I knew he wasn't going to let her live. Or me. Yet for the first time in my life my gun hand began shaking, because I also knew that after all the terrible sins I'd committed over the years, to sentence a child to death by my own inaction seemed at that moment to be the worst of all.

'Two . . .'

The world stopped. I faced Heed down. He smiled at me. He knew my weakness.

His finger tensed on the trigger and Layla began to whimper beneath the yellow, liver-spotted hand covering her face.

'Three.'

I lowered the gun forty-five degrees.

Then fired.

I was aiming for his kneecap, but because I was trying to look as if I was cooperating, I had barely a quarter of a second to make my shot, and with my hands still shaking, I missed.

Another shot rang out, and suddenly Layla was flying towards me. I caught her in mid-flight but the momentum drove me backwards, and I landed hard on the ground as a bullet ricocheted off the ground very close by.

Heed fired again as I pushed Layla to one side, trying to get her out of the firing line. But this time he was pulling the trigger on an empty gun.

As I lifted myself up to fire my last shot at him, having to pull my arm out from under Layla and aiming now for Heed's abdomen, he threw the gun, hitting me squarely in the forehead with a painful thud at just the moment I pulled the trigger for the sixth and final time.

Then, in another surprisingly deft movement, he turned and ran up the corridor, the blackness quickly swallowing him up.

That was when I saw that Layla was dead – her face almost lost under a growing curtain of blood seeping from the coin-shaped hole where the bullet had exited.

I howled with frustration and rage, my voice echoing through the corridor, and I leapt to my feet as the adrenalin surged through me, determined to capture this monster if it was the last thing I ever did.

'Jesus! What's happened?' cried Tina from the bottom of the steps. Then she saw Layla's small naked body. 'What's he done?' She hurried over and crouched down beside the little girl, hunting for a pulse.

Pulling the second speedloader from the front pocket of my jeans, I reloaded the .45 and ran off after Heed, ignoring the blood running down from the cut on my forehead where the gun had hit me.

The corridor veered left sharply and plunged into darkness as I moved along it, no longer trying to be careful. I forced myself to slow as I almost tripped over a box on the floor. Then, through the gloom, I could just make out an aluminium extension ladder at the end of the corridor, leading up through a specially cut hole in the masonry towards ground level. This would definitely be his escape route, and I was walking towards it when a silhouette lurched out of an adjacent alcove, and a flash of metal slashed through the air.

As I swung round to face him, trying to dodge the blade, I felt it slice through my jacket, only just failing to break skin. Instinctively, I pulled the trigger on the .45, but Heed had already grabbed my wrist and yanked it skywards, and the bullet flew uselessly away. Adrenalin and anger surged through me and I managed to grab the hand holding the knife and force it away from me.

'Time to die, Mr Milne,' whispered Heed in a relaxed sing-song voice, his sour, hot breath scouring my face.

He drove me hard against the opposite wall, driving the wind from my gut. His strength was incredible for such an unhealthy-looking individual and I could feel the knife getting closer and closer to me as I struggled and fought against his grip.

And then I heard rapid footsteps and a second later Tina was on him, her clenched fist careering into the side of his head with such force that I felt it.

'He's got a knife!' I yelled as Heed let go of me and fell back against the extension ladder.

But Tina was quick, and Heed had been caught by surprise. She let him have it with two stunning left hooks that connected perfectly, before grabbing his knife arm and twisting it up behind his back. 'You bastard,' she hissed through clenched teeth, grabbing a handful of his hair and slamming him headfirst into the wall with an audible crack.

The knife clattered to the floor, and Heed looked dazed.

But Tina wasn't finished yet, and she slammed his head into the wall again.

I grabbed her arm. 'No more, Tina, we need him alive. He's got to talk.'

She flashed me a look of such naked hatred that I automatically let her go. I wasn't sure who it was directed at, me or Heed. But after a second, she released her grip on him and he fell to the floor.

'Was he the one who killed her?' she demanded.

I nodded. 'He shot her when I was starting to lower the gun. Then he tried to shoot me.' It was a lie, but I knew I couldn't tell her the truth. That I'd risked Layla's life to save my own, and that in doing so I had effectively killed her. That was something else for me to live with.

Tina didn't say anything, just took a deep breath, as if steeling herself for the task ahead, before leaning down and pulling Heed up by his hair. 'So let's make this murdering bastard talk.'

CHAPTER 45

Tina found some masking tape in one of the kitchen drawers and we tied Heed to a chair in the kitchen. He was still only semi-conscious, but we were taking no chances and I kept the gun trained on him until she was done. Next I filled up a cup with cold water from the tap and threw it in his face. When he didn't move, I repeated the procedure, and the third time I did it he finally shook his head and opened his eyes, focusing on us both.

After a few seconds, he smiled, showing brown, uneven teeth. His eyes were now flinty and alert.

I turned to Tina. 'You might want to wait outside.'

She shot Heed a look of pure contempt. 'No thank you. I'm not squeamish. Do what you have to do.'

There was an old electric kettle on the kitchen worktop and I filled it with water and turned it on. As the water boiled, I approached Heed and stood in front of him. 'I told you why we're here. For answers. You're going to give them to me. It just depends how easy or hard you want to make it.'

Heed kept smiling up at me, his eyes scanning like probes, hunting for weaknesses. There was an aura of fearlessness about him that unnerved me. He should have been a lot more scared, given his position. Instinctively, I wanted to turn away from his gaze, but I forced myself to hold it, remembering that the creature in front of me had just murdered a young child.

Bastard.

A thin plume of steam poured out of the kettle. I picked it up and poured half the contents into his lap, watching with grim satisfaction as he bucked and writhed in the chair, his face turning a strange brass-like colour as he fought against the pain, refusing to cry out. I waited a few seconds for the pain to die down, then repeated the procedure with the remainder of the boiling water. This time he let out a rasping wail, and began to cough.

'You might think you're the devil incarnate, Mr Heed,' I told him, 'but you're not. You're flesh and blood, just like anyone else. And I can hurt you very, very badly.'

'Fuck you!' he snarled, his eyes blazing.

'We know all about you,' I continued. 'We know you work for Paul Wise. We know you were involved in the abduction of thirteen-year-old Lene Haagen from a Manila hotel two and a half years ago. We also know that a briefcase containing something valuable was delivered to you on Friday night.'

'Seems like you know everything then, doesn't it?'

'No. We don't. We need to know what's in the briefcase, where it is now, and the whereabouts of Paul Wise. You can answer all those questions.'

'Why should I help you? You're going to kill me anyway.'

'I won't lie. You're going to die. But I'm no sadist, and if you answer my questions, I can make it quick.' I took the Swiss Army knife from my pocket and opened it to reveal the main blade.

Heed looked at Tina. 'Are you going to let this mass murderer torture me, Miss Boyd? Do you, as a serving police officer, really want to be involved in that?'

'Yes,' she said firmly, 'I do.'

As she spoke these words I thought I saw the first flash of doubt ripple across Heed's jaundiced features.

'Why don't you just talk, Mr Heed?' I said quietly, placing the blade against the corner of his left eye, moving across his field of vision so that Tina couldn't see what I was doing. I really didn't like the idea of torturing the information out of him, however terrible his crimes might have been, but I'd extracted answers this way before, and sometimes it's the only way to get them.

I put pressure on the blade, wondering if I had the mental strength to take out one of his eyes.

Heed flinched. He tried not to, but he couldn't help it, and I could see his Adam's apple rising like a growth as he swallowed.

'Why are you protecting Paul Wise?' asked Tina,

coming closer, so that she could see where I was holding the knife. I didn't move it. 'Do you really think he gives a shit about you? He's got a history of getting rid of his friends when they're no longer any use to him. Particularly ones that know about the skeletons in his closet, like you. Your days are numbered anyway. Now you've got the chance to make sure his are too.'

I sensed a flicker of interest as Heed weighed up the possibilities.

'Tell Mr Milne to remove the knife,' he said as calmly as he could, 'and perhaps we can talk.'

She looked at me, and I took the blade away, but kept it down by my side.

'I want you to promise that you won't kill me,' he said, still clearly suffering from the effects of the boiling water. 'You can leave me here and call the police if that's what you want. You can even tell them what happened. That way justice will be served, and I will suffer the consequences of what I've done in a court of law. But I want your word, Miss Boyd. That you will not kill me.'

She looked at me and I gave her a small nod in return.

'OK,' she said reluctantly. 'You have my word.'

'What do you want to know?'

'The truth. You work for Paul Wise, don't you?'

'I *do* work for him, yes.'

'Is he in the country at the moment?'

'Yes.'

'Where?'

'He owns a house south of here. On a place called Verde Island.'

Tina looked at me. 'Isn't that the place we passed yesterday on the way to your friend's place?'

I nodded, surprised that Wise had property so close to where I used to live. 'It is. But it's also a fair-sized island.' I turned to Heed. 'What's the address?'

'The house is called Treetops,' he said without hesitation. 'It's a big white place on the south-east tip.'

At one time, I'd regularly taken dive boats out to the southern tip of Verde, which was one of the best dive sites in the northern Philippines. 'I don't remember any houses there.'

'I'm not lying. I have a navigation device with the exact co-ordinates pre-programmed into it. It's in the bottom drawer over there.'

While I waited, Tina rummaged through the drawer until she found a small Tom Tom-style device. 'Is this it?' she asked him.

He nodded. 'It's under reference seven-five-two-three.'

Tina punched in some numbers. 'I think I've found it,' she said, coming over to me.

I looked down at the screen. There was a slightly blurred aerial Google Earth photo of the bottom section of an island that could have been Verde. Three houses were visible, set some distance apart amid the thick vegetation that ran up from the secluded rocky coastline. The one nearest the tip was big and white, and looked to be on a larger plot than the others.

Tina showed the screen to Heed, and he confirmed that it was Wise's place.

'Now, as I said, we know about the briefcase,' I told him, 'and we know it was delivered here by Tom Darke on Friday night. What's in it?'

The big question.

'I don't know,' said Heed.

My face darkened, and I immediately brought the knife back up so that it was only millimetres from his left eyeball. 'Don't lie.'

'I'm not,' he said, his voice calm. 'It's a large briefcase, and all I know is that whatever's inside is valuable. It was sent here from overseas – I believe by your employer, Mr Schagel. I had to arrange its pick-up from the docks, and have it brought here. I was curious as to what was inside, but the case was very securely locked, and I was paid a great deal of money not to let my curiosity get the better of me.'

I looked around. 'So where is it?'

'It's been delivered to Wise's house on Verde. It was picked up here last night.'

'By whom?'

'One of Schagel's people. A Russian. I don't know his name. Now, will you please move that blade away from my eye?'

I did as he'd requested and exchanged looks with Tina. I was pretty sure that Heed wasn't lying about not knowing what was in the case, just by the way he was answering all my other questions without hesitation.

'Why was Nick Penny murdered?' Tina asked him.

He looked confused. 'I don't know any Nick Penny.'

'He was a journalist in England murdered last week on Paul Wise's orders. He'd been in touch with Patrick O'Riordan very recently.'

Heed shook his head. 'I don't know anything about that. I do know about O'Riordan. He was executed by Mr Milne here on the orders of Paul Wise. I don't know the reason why he had to die. All I know is that the logistics had to be dealt with very quickly. Mrs O'Riordan supplied me with the keys to the house that you used when you executed him. She was very upset when she found out about her husband's male lover. She also informed me when the two of you came to visit her.'

I could see that Heed was trying to drive a wedge between Tina and me. His whole demeanour had changed, as he tried to appear reasonable and cooperative, while at the same time he was trying to make me look like just another ruthless hitman. From the cold expression on Tina's face, it didn't look like he was succeeding.

'O'Riordan knew about the young girls, didn't he?' said Tina. 'The girls you've been sourcing for Paul Wise over the years. Including Lene Haagen. And don't bother lying about it, because we know.'

Heed was silent for a long moment before answering. 'Yes,' he said at last, 'I've supplied girls to Wise. O'Riordan did find something out about it, but he was warned off. Lene was a mistake. Wise wanted a western girl. He preferred them. He'd had one before in England, and one in Cambodia too.'

'Letitia McDonald,' Tina cut in, her expression darkening.

'If you say so,' Heed said.

'She was just twelve years old.'

'Yes, well, I tried to persuade him that it was a foolish move—'

'But you did it all the same.'

'Yes. I did it all the same.'

'And where are the girls now?'

He sighed, no trace of his earlier arrogance now. 'They went to Wise's home on Verde Island and they never came back.'

The room fell silent as we digested this information. But, tragic though it was, it still left unanswered questions. And one in particular was bothering me.

'You said O'Riordan was warned off from writing about the disappearance of the girls, and I know from the archives that he did stop writing about it. So, why did he have to die now, two and a half years later?'

'As I said, I don't know.'

I raised the knife again. 'Take a wild guess.'

Heed's eyes focused on the blade, and for the

first time I could see fear in them. 'I can only assume he found out something about the package,' he said quietly. 'But what it was I honestly don't know.'

'Do the names Cheeseman and Omar Salic mean anything to you? O'Riordan had a meeting planned with them on the day he died.'

Heed shook his head. 'The names are unfamiliar.'

I felt my frustration growing, and wondered if he was deliberately holding back information, purely out of malice. I looked at him for any sign that he was playing with us, but could see nothing in his expression to suggest he was.

'Think,' I told him. 'It may save your eye.'

'I don't know those names. I promise you.'

'Then I don't have any more questions.'

I looked at Tina. I could tell that she was frustrated as well.

'I don't have any either,' she said.

Heed fidgeted beneath his bonds, the dry skin of his face stretched into an expression of uncertainty. 'I've kept my side of the bargain,' he said, opening and closing his hands, the long fingernails scratching the material of his ancient suit. 'It's time for you to keep yours.'

I turned to Tina. 'You might want to wait outside.'

'But you promised me, Miss Boyd,' said Heed, his voice rising as the first signs of panic began to set in. 'You gave your word that you wouldn't let him do this. It's murder. Pure and simple. Call the police if you have to, but this is wrong.'

'If we let him live, he'll escape justice,' I told her. 'Remember what he's just done. He killed that little girl.'

'You killed her, Milne. It was you who shot her, not me. It was him, Miss Boyd. He did it, I promise you that.'

Tina took a deep breath, and looked at us both in turn.

'Stop him,' pleaded Heed. 'Don't let him kill me. Please. You're a police officer.'

She stood there for two, maybe three seconds, and then, without a word, she turned and walked out of the room.

I raised the gun, fighting down the nausea I was feeling. 'It's time to go to hell, Mr Heed.'

'Don't do it,' he said through gritted teeth, the sweat running down his face in streams as he writhed in the seat, his fish-grey eyes wide with a terrible mix of fear and pleading as all his cruel bravado evaporated in the face of his impending death.

But I did do it.

CHAPTER 46

Paul Wise paced the front veranda of his villa, ignoring the intense heat of the mid-afternoon sun that was barely tempered by the breeze coming up from the sea. For the first time that he could remember, he was genuinely worried.

Thanks to the incompetence of Bertie Schagel's men, Tina Boyd was still alive and at large in Manila. By all accounts she was even teamed up with the man Schagel had sent to kill her, whom Wise had now found out was the former police officer Dennis Milne. If he'd had a clue that Schagel was using someone like Milne, he'd have forbidden his involvement. Milne was a vigilante, the kind of man who liked to think he was above everyone else. A judge, jury and executioner righting supposed wrongs, and who was probably looking for him even now. There was a certain grim irony in that. A hitman turning on the client who was paying his wages for reasons of morality.

But at that moment, Wise had bigger fish to fry. In a few hours' time he had a meeting that could be life-changing. A group of men were coming to buy a highly valuable and very illegal briefcase from him. If the sale was successful, he would end up a very rich man. However, if anything went wrong, and the sale didn't happen, then he was as good as finished. The stakes were that high, and the problem was, he didn't trust the men who were buying it. They were also coming here to his beloved island retreat. Ordinarily, this wouldn't have been a problem, but Wise no longer had what he felt was the necessary level of security to deter his visitors from trying to take the case without paying for it.

He'd been promised two of Schagel's men to provide protection, but one had been killed in the previous night's botched operation against Boyd and Milne, and the one who had turned up was less than impressive. Balding and middle-aged, with cheap spectacles and even cheaper clothes, he looked more like a down-at-heel accountant than a professional assassin. Schagel had even had the temerity to describe him as one of the best in his field – a veteran of Spetsnaz, the Russian special forces – but so far he'd failed to kill Tina Boyd on two separate occasions and had also been unable to take out Heed when they'd been alone the previous night. Nor did Wise have anyone else who could protect him. He didn't trust the bodyguard who'd travelled to the Philippines with him, and had lately become paranoid that the man might be working for the British government, so he'd sent him home to northern Cyprus. He did have a couple of trusted locals who acted as security at the villa, and who carried legally held guns, but he doubted they'd be much use if things turned nasty.

In truth, Wise was beginning to get a bad feeling, not only about the meeting, but about his current situation in general. The contents of the briefcase terrified him, and the fact that it was here in his home only quickened his constant, nervous pacing. It had even crossed his mind several times in the past twelve hours to call the meeting off and fly straight back to northern Cyprus.

There was, however, a simple reason why he didn't.

Money.

At one time, Wise had been an extremely rich man whose net worth had been in the high tens of millions, but thanks to the credit crunch, followed by the controversy engendered by the stories that had come out about him the previous year, he'd been forced to dispose of a large number of his business assets, many at a loss, in an effort to keep a lower profile, and his income had plummeted as a result. The controversy had also cost him his wife. She'd left him within weeks of Nick Penny's libellous allegations, and was now threatening to drag him through the divorce courts unless he handed over some extortionate sum of money. As a wife, she was no great loss. He'd never been much interested in her, preferring much younger company, but the threats she was making were a huge inconvenience, and a drain on resources that could possibly get far, far worse.

The huge amount of money he'd make tonight would offset much of these earlier losses, and put him back on the path to the serious wealth he'd once enjoyed, and which he had always so desperately craved.

Not a bad return for one meeting.

But there were so many things that could still go wrong. Even if the sale went through, the buyers still had to keep their end of the bargain. And if they didn't, then he could end up bankrupt and destitute. It was that serious.

It angered him that he'd ended up in this position. It was another thing to blame that bitch, Tina Boyd, for. She truly was a thorn in his side, and now he'd lost the chance to make her suffer. One day, though . . . One day he would have her at his mercy and then she'd die screaming like the annoying little whore she was.

The thought made him shiver with an intensity that was part frustration, part excitement, and he felt himself go hard at the prospect of all the savage things he would do to her if she ever fell into his grasp.

For now, though, her death would have to wait.

He looked at his watch. 3.30 p.m. Four and a half hours until his guests arrived with their money.

CHAPTER 47

The traffic was appalling all the way out of Manila. They were in a Toyota stolen from a back road not far from the Juicy Peach, with Milne behind the wheel.

They rode in silence, both still shocked by the events at the nightclub and the death of the young girl, Layla. They'd had to leave her body where it had fallen, something Tina had found particularly hard. Milne had wanted to set fire to the place to destroy any evidence of their presence there, but Tina had refused point blank. She wanted to make sure the girl was found, so that at least she could be buried properly. They'd compromised by wiping all surfaces clean of fingerprints, which wasn't exactly foolproof, but would hopefully suffice in a city like Manila, where crime-scene investigations were generally less sophisticated than those back in the UK.

Now, at long last, they were free of the gridlocked city and on their way to Verde Island to confront Paul Wise. Tina could feel the revolver that Heed had used to kill the barman and Layla rubbing against the small of her back where it was wedged into her shorts. Before they'd left Heed's hellish basement living quarters, she'd found a box of bullets in an office drawer. It disgusted her to be in possession of a weapon used in two such brutal murders, but she knew she needed it for the task ahead.

There'd been a thousand times in the past six years when she'd fantasized about having Wise at her mercy, putting a gun to his head and pulling the trigger, but now that it could soon be a reality her emotions were far more conflicted. She actually felt physically sick.

Over the last hour or so she'd experienced several desperate urges for a drink to steady the nerves. She'd found a quarter-full bottle of whiskey in the Toyota's glove compartment (which didn't say much about the owner), and more than once she'd come close to taking a slug, telling herself that just the one wouldn't hurt, not after all the terrible things she'd witnessed since she'd arrived in this god-forsaken country. But she'd stopped herself. Every time. This was not the moment for weakness.

Instead, she lit a cigarette and examined the contents of the laptop on her knee. It was Heed's. As was the mobile broadband dongle sticking out of one of the USB ports. Unsurprisingly, she hadn't found any smoking gun on its hard drive. In fact she'd found very little of note, but then she'd suspected that someone like Heed would be careful not to put anything that might incriminate him on a computer.

'What did you bring that for?' Milne had asked her. 'We're only going to have to get rid of it later. I told you: you're never going to find the evidence to convict Paul Wise.'

'I want to know what's in that briefcase,' she'd told him.

'We can ask Wise when we see him.'

'We may not get the chance, Dennis. To be honest, we have no idea what we're getting into here. Wise may have security up to the eyeballs. I don't think we should rely on being able to question him.'

He'd shrugged. 'Either way, Heed's laptop won't help you. He didn't know what was in the brief-case either, remember?'

'I don't like unanswered questions,' she'd countered. 'It's the copper in me. The solution's out there somewhere, and right now I've got nothing better to do, so I'm going to try to find it.'

After that exchange, they'd slipped into silence again.

Tina clicked on the Internet Explorer icon on the desktop screen and waited. The connection provided by the dongle was slow, but eventually she got online, and immediately Googled the name Omar Salic. Even though she'd already Googled it two nights earlier and got no joy, she thought it might be worth trying again, since if he was supposed to have been meeting Patrick O'Riordan, something might also have happened to him.

And it had. After a quick trawl through the usual Facebook and Linkedin hits, she spotted an article from a local newspaper called the *Manila Bulletin*. It was from the previous day's edition and concerned a double murder in the Tondo area of the city. The bodies of a man identified as Omar Salic and his wife Soraya had been discovered in their apartment. They'd been stabbed to death, and initial autopsy reports suggested that the murders had occurred some time over the weekend. The bodies had exhibited evidence of torture and police were appealing for witnesses. No mention was made of possible motive.

Tina took a last drag on the cigarette and threw it out of the half-open window as she re-read the article. This had to be the Omar Salic O'Riordan had been planning to meet the previous Saturday. The timing was too coincidental for it to be otherwise, and Omar Salic was hardly a common name. Even so, his murder didn't provide Tina with any further clues.

She continued trawling through the Google lists for any further references to the murders but there was nothing else about them.

She Googled the name Cheeseman for a second time. Once again, though, there was nothing remotely relevant. She added the word Manila to the search, and got no hits at all. Rather than leave it, she went back to the original search, and methodically went through every hit for Cheeseman listed (and they were many and varied), trying to work out how each one could possibly be connected to their case.

'Getting anywhere?' asked Milne, interrupting her thoughts.

'I'll tell you when I do,' she replied testily, trying hard to concentrate. Annoyed, but as yet un-defeated. She didn't like to give up on things. She never had. It was one of the reasons she was such a good detective.

'Think,' she told herself. 'Think.' There must be a way of finding out what she needed to know. There always was.

She stared out of the window in silence, hardly seeing the buildings as they drifted past, becoming fewer and fewer as they headed south, every part of her focusing on the hunt for clues, anything that could possibly help.

And then, from somewhere in her dim and distant past, she remembered something. At primary school there'd been a kid in her class whose last name was Cheeseman. Except, if she recalled it correctly – and after all these years she wasn't at all sure that she did – he'd actually spelled it Cheesman. She thought about it for a moment. Was it possible that O'Riordan had spelled the name wrongly in his diary?

Tina took a drink from the bottle of water by her side and Googled Cheesman.

Again, a jumble of names came up, nothing standing out. So again she added the word Manila to the search.

And saw it straight away.

A newspaper article, this time from that day's *Manila Post*, the same paper that had featured the photo of Milne on its front cover. Next to the headline, in bold, was the name Alan Cheesman. Tina read and re-read the article, feeling irritated that the search engine hadn't suggested the alternative spelling in the first place. Then, typing quickly, she ran a new Google search.

'Did Tomboy tell you anything else about the briefcase?' she asked after a few minutes, without looking up.

'Like what?'

'Like, was it heavy?'

Milne thought for a moment. 'Yeah. He said that it was heavy and valuable and illegal.'

Tina leaned back in her seat and ran her fingers through her hair. Then she slowly exhaled.

'Jesus, Dennis. This whole thing. It was never about the missing girls.'

He frowned. 'What? What is it about, then?'

She looked at him, her face drawn tight with tension. 'I think I know what's in the briefcase. And if I'm right, then we're in real trouble.'

CHAPTER 48

'**I**t's a bomb.'
They'd come to a halt on the highway in more heavy traffic.

Milne turned round in the driver's seat. 'How the hell did you work that out?'

'The Cheesman Pat O'Riordan was going to meet is a senior member of staff at the US Defense Attaché Office here. He's quoted in the *Manila Post* today. It's actually on the front page but neither of us noticed it because we were too busy looking at the photo of you. Anyway, he's saying in the article that there's been an upsurge of terrorist chatter, suggesting that a major attack on US interests in the Philippines by Islamic fundamentalists linked to al-Qaeda is imminent. Apparently an informant from within one of the fundamentalist groups had come forward in recent days backing up evidence of a plot, and was going to supply more information, but he was murdered at the weekend.'

'Did they give a name for the informant?'

'No, but a man called Omar Salic was murdered along with his wife in Manila this weekend, which is far too much of a coincidence.'

Tina lit another cigarette with shaking hands, adrenalin-fuelled excitement surging through her.

'God almighty.' Milne's features creased with concern. 'So Cheesman must have known O'Riordan had information on the plot if they were due to meet, which means that, as the man who killed him, I'm also now a terrorist suspect.'

Tina put a hand on his arm. 'Right now, I don't think that's going to make any difference. You can't be any more wanted than you are already.'

He snorted. 'No, you're probably right. What I can't understand, though, is why Paul Wise, or Bertie Schagel for that matter, would be involved in something like this.'

'I can,' said Tina. 'Money.'

'But there can't be that much money in selling terrorists a bomb, if that's what you're thinking Wise is up to. And anyway, surely terrorists can make their own bombs?'

'It depends what kind of bomb it is. If it's something particularly lethal – chemical, biological, something like that – then it's highly unlikely they'd be able to. I've just done a Google search and from what I can gather there's plenty of extremely dangerous material in the old Soviet Union that, put into a briefcase, could create something truly nasty. And by the sound of things, it's not very secure. Someone like a businessman with extremely good contacts could probably get hold of some.'

Milne nodded slowly. 'Someone like Bertie Schagel.'

'Exactly. Say he sourced such a bomb, and either he or Wise set up a deal to sell it to terrorists, then suddenly it all makes sense. Pat O'Riordan found out about the plan – maybe Omar Salic contacted him – and O'Riordan probably then contacted the US Embassy and talked to Cheesman, and they agreed to meet. I imagine Cheesman had only been given the barest of details of the plot, which is why O'Riordan and Salic both had to die before they gave him any more.'

'It's still only a theory though, isn't it?'

'But you have to admit, it's one that makes sense. Wise was never worried about being found out for the abductions of those girls. But he was terrified of anyone getting wind of a plot like this. That's why everyone, including Nick Penny, had to die. So that it could be kept absolutely secret. It would also explain why Wise is in the Philippines now. To oversee the sale of the bomb.'

Tina took a drag on the cigarette, and blew out the smoke angrily.

'You know, Wise has got form doing something like this. Three years ago, just before the financial crisis flared up, he tried to have a bomb set off in London that would have caused havoc and massive loss of life. He was betting that the reaction would be a stock market crash, which would have netted him millions. Maybe he's betting on the same thing happening again now. A spectacular attack against US interests, wherever it was in the world, would scare the crap out of the markets.'

She stopped speaking, shocked in spite of herself. She'd always known that there was no limit to Paul Wise's depravity, but to have another example of it rubbed in her face yet again was still hard to take.

'If what you're saying is true,' Milne said after a few moments' silence, 'then Wise is going to want to get rid of that bomb fast. It was picked up by one of Schagel's goons last night, which means it would have been with him within a matter of hours. We haven't got much time.'

'That's what I was thinking,' said Tina, experiencing a renewed sense of urgency. She looked at her watch. It was 4.50, and they were stuck in heavy traffic. 'We can't sit like this. Not with what's at stake. You're good at breaking the law. How about a bit of dangerous driving?'

He gave her a sardonic smile, which made him look surprisingly handsome, and for a fleeting moment Tina could see what he must have been like when he was a young man, before the corruption set in, with his life and career stretching ahead of him.

'You shouldn't encourage me,' he said, and pulled the Toyota out on to the hard shoulder, flooring the accelerator.

CHAPTER 49

They killed the boat's driver almost as soon as they were out of Puerto Galera harbour. It was dark in the bay, and there were no other boats in the vicinity, making their task easy, even though the driver seemed suspicious of the four southerners he'd taken on board. While Mohammed distracted him by talking about the basketball results, Anil had stolen up behind him and yanked his head back like a goat's, cutting his throat with a single deep slash. The driver – a gnarled old fool, but a strong one – had fought back hard, but Mohammed had grabbed one wrist and Khalil had come forward and grabbed the other, and together they'd forced him to his knees, waiting while he'd bled out until his struggles finally ceased.

After that Anil had taken the wheel, taking them out of the bay, round the Sabang headland, and out into the open sea of the Verde Island Strait, while the others had cleaned up the blood on the deck. Then they'd tied the driver's corpse to the boat's anchor, before flinging him overboard. The water, Anil knew, was hundreds of metres deep and it was

359

unlikely anyone would ever find a trace of him. Even if they did, it wouldn't matter. No one knew them in Puerto Galera, and no one had seen them board his vessel.

Anil felt a rush of pleasure as the wind blew through his long hair. In an hour's time, they would, God willing, be in possession of a device that would wreak havoc among the Yankee kafir and their northern allies. It had taken months to raise the money to buy it, a large portion of which had come from contacts overseas. Now, thanks to the treachery of their former brother, Omar Salic, their target, the US Embassy, was on alert.

But it would do the Yankees no good. They could double their security. They could triple it. It didn't matter. Such was the power in the bomb, and such was its lethal payload, that it could be detonated a hundred metres from the front gate and would still cause death and destruction, not only in the embassy itself, but also in the wealthy bay area, and the hotels to which the western kafir were drawn like leeches.

Anil had been given the honour of driving the car containing the bomb. Mohammed would be next to him with his finger pressed against the detonation button. If Mohammed was shot, his finger would automatically release from the button, setting it off. So the plan could not fail. Anil's group, the Sword of Islam, would be known and feared the whole world over. His name would be spoken of with awe – a just reward for his service to Allah and the cause.

One more hour. That was all it would take. And then he would have the bomb in his hand.

And by nightfall tomorrow, he would be a hero of the Islamic world.

CHAPTER 50

And so it had come to this. The final act of a violent life that had started with such promise. But now I had the opportunity to put things right, by killing Paul Wise and – if Tina's theory was correct, and the more I thought about it, the more I was sure it was – by intercepting a bomb that was destined to kill potentially thousands of innocent people.

I had to succeed. Only then could I go to my grave in peace, knowing that I'd atoned for the many sins I'd committed over the past fifteen years.

Fear pulsed through me. Not fear of failure. Fear of death. I didn't want to die, to slip into a darkness from which I could never return. Not without seeing my child. Not without one last sight of Emma, the only woman I'd ever loved. Not without breathing the fresh forest air of Luang Prabang. But all of those things were gone now, and I had no one to blame but myself. I'd sentenced too many men to the darkness, including some who'd done nothing to deserve it. Now, finally, it seemed it was my turn.

It was coming up to seven when I turned the Toyota on to a narrow track that wound down a steep hill towards the sea, and a private dock where at one time Tomboy and I had run boat transfers direct to our resort on Big La Laguna Beach. Our plan was a simple one: steal a boat and head straight out to Verde Island. In the far distance, through the trees, I could just make out its vague, hulking shape, barely illuminated by a handful of lights that twinkled in the night sky.

The journey down here had been long and hard going, and had involved me breaking pretty much every traffic law in the Philippines, but we'd made it, and Tina had even managed to fall asleep for the last half-hour. It crossed my mind not to wake her. She looked so peaceful with her head rested against the window, her mouth ever so slightly open. But as I drove into a small car park cut into the trees about halfway down the track and killed the engine, she opened her eyes and yawned.

'I can't believe I fell asleep,' she said, looking round.

I saw the almost imperceptible change in her expression as she remembered what we were here to do, and how dangerous it was. 'You don't have to come with me, you know. You've done enough.'

'No,' she said firmly, looking me right in the eye. 'We're in this together. And don't flatter yourself. You need me.'

I smiled. 'Come on then.'

We got out of the Toyota, and I stretched, trying

to take the stiffness out of my back, while Tina lit a cigarette. At the other end of the car park was an old abandoned jeepney, which now looked like it was being used as a makeshift home. Two local women, one young, one old, were crouched over a small fire next to it cooking a meal while half a dozen grimy-looking kids, none above the age of ten, ran backwards and forwards playing a game of tag, their laughter drifting over to us.

I stood there watching them for a few moments, suddenly remembering my own childhood, when I was part of a loving family. Playing out in the garden with my mates from down the road. And my sister, Mary, too, who was three years younger than me and always wanted to join in our games. If we didn't let her, she'd burst into tears, and then I'd feel sorry for her and tell her it was OK, she could play. Jesus, my sister. We'd grown apart as we'd reached adulthood, after Mum and Dad died, and I hadn't seen or spoken to her in more than ten years. I didn't even know if she was still alive.

I felt a huge longing for her then. A need to call and speak to her. To let her know that I wasn't all bad, no matter what she'd read and heard.

'You know,' said Tina, coming up beside me, 'the thing I've noticed most about the Philippines is that everywhere you look there are young kids and babies, and all the young women seem to be pregnant. Yet they all live in such poverty.'

'That's the Catholic Church for you,' I said, still

watching the kids as they charged round in the dirt. 'This country's got the fastest growing population in the world, yet they still preach against contraception. And they're supposed to be the good guys.'

'There's no hope for these kids, is there? They're going to grow up poor, produce more children, and die poor.'

'I guess so,' I said, not wanting to think about that. Thinking instead about happier times.

'It makes you wonder what the hell the point of it all is.' She took a long, angry pull on her cigarette, her eyes darkening. 'I hate this world sometimes. The fact that it's so full of wicked, greedy, selfish people, and even when you lock them up, more keep appearing to take their place, in this never-ending, pointless cycle.'

'We see the worst of it,' I said, 'because of the paths we've chosen. But you know what? For all the shit and pointlessness, for every Heed and for every Wise, it's still a beautiful world.' I thought about Laos. Home. 'I live in this small, friendly old town a long way from here, where the people are poor but also happy. Life's simple. It goes on day to day. People don't get murdered, or very rarely anyway. There's not much TV, no cases of child abuse. No scandals involving philandering politicians making underhand deals for nothing. The town's surrounded by lush green forest, and rivers you can kayak down. There's a huge waterfall about half an hour away by car, and sometimes I climb up to the top where there's a view right across the valley below, and I swim in one of the ice-cold pools carved out of the rocks. And whenever I'm there, I forget about all the bad things I've done; all the losses I've had; everything . . . And I'm happy.'

I let the words trail off, wondering whether I'd ever see it again.

Tina put a hand on my arm, and gave it a gentle squeeze. 'Thanks,' she said quietly. 'I'll bear that in mind.'

I wanted to take her in my arms and kiss her then, to hold her for a few minutes before we set off, but I stopped myself. There was no time. Instead, I turned and continued down the track, with Tina following.

A high chain-link fence lined the area round the small stone pier, with a guardhouse in the middle. There were lights on inside and I could make out the silhouette of a man in a cap behind the glass. Beyond the guardhouse, a dozen or so outriggers bobbed up and down in the darkness of the ocean. But it wasn't them I was looking at. It was the brand-new speedboat at the end.

I took the gun from my waistband. I had five more bullets. It wasn't a lot, but it was going to have to do.

'I need to deal with the security guard. Wait here.'

Tina took a quick breath in.

'I'm not going to hurt him,' I answered, knowing

what she was going to say, before turning away and walking over to the guardhouse.

I opened the door and strode inside. The guard – middle-aged, bespectacled, harmless – looked up from the tiny portable TV he was watching, and I pointed the gun at his head as if greeting him like this was the most natural thing in the world.

'Stand up, take your gun slowly out of your pocket, put it on the desk, then stick your hands in the air.'

It all went smoothly. He wasn't going to argue. I told him I wouldn't hurt him, but he must have seen something in my demeanour that made him doubt me, and twice he begged me not to kill him as I bound him with his own handcuffs, before locking him in an adjacent storage room with a bottle of water, having relieved him of his mobile phone and the keys to the speedboat.

Five minutes later we were roaring away from the jetty in the speedboat, and twenty minutes after that we were travelling along the west coast of Verde – a rocky, tree-covered outcrop about three miles long, which looked largely deserted. Tina sat on the edge of the boat, looking down at the deck, an expression of intense concentration on her face, the familiar cigarette in her hand.

I slowed the boat as we rounded Verde's southern tip. 'This is the place I used to take the divers,' I told her, pointing through the gloom to a couple of rocks standing a few feet above the narrow, rolling waves, feeling a tightness in my chest as once again I remembered happier times when, for a while at least, life had been so much less complicated. 'It doesn't look much, but underneath those rocks is some of the best fish life and coral anywhere in the Philippines. Have you ever dived?'

She managed a weak smile. 'A long time back. When I was backpacking. Before I went and wrecked it all by joining the police, and ending up in situations like this.' She threw the cigarette overboard and pulled Heed's revolver from the back of her shorts, checking the chamber before clicking it back into place. Our eyes met. 'I'm ready for this, you know.'

'I know,' I said. 'So am I.'

And I was too. I felt much calmer now. Almost at peace with myself. Knowing I was doing the right thing.

'When we land, we make for the house, OK? I don't know who's going to be there. It might even be that Wise isn't in residence, but if he is, he'll have security. We've got to try to get right up close to them, then try and take them out as quietly as possible. That means using a knife.' I patted my pocket, where my Swiss Army knife was concealed. I had no desire to use it again as I'd done the previous night. Stabbing's a method of killing that's always sickened me by its very intimacy, but sometimes you just haven't got a choice, and this looked like it was going to be one of those times. 'It's going to be messy, and people are going to die. There's no way round that.'

She nodded.

'The essential thing is we keep Wise alive until we've located the bomb, if there is one, and found out where and to whom it's gone. After that . . .'

I let my words trail off. We both knew what would happen after that.

Payback.

I steered the boat past the rocks, giving them a wide berth, and a few minutes later we came round on to the eastern side of the island. There were even fewer lights on here but I could make out the shapes of houses, spaced far apart, up on the top of a long winding ridge, beneath which was thick forest. I recognized Wise's place from the Google Earth photo earlier. 'That's it,' I said, pointing to the first house, a grand-looking stucco villa with a well-lit access road leading up to the front from a secluded palm-fringed beach a little way down the coast.

I slowed the boat to a crawl and turned off the lights, moving quietly towards the adjacent beach, remembering it as a place we used to bring divers in the surface interval between dives on the southern rocks. There were no houses here then, but that had been a long time back now.

When we were fifty yards short of the shore, I cut the engine altogether and let the boat drift in on the waves, before dropping anchor in clear shallow water next to some rocks.

The night was quiet and peaceful, and above us a crescent moon shone down from a starry sky.

It was the kind of night for relaxing with a beer in good company, not for killing.

I looked across at Tina. 'Ready?'

She nodded, the determination set hard on her lean, angular face. 'Ready.'

Without another word, we slipped out of the boat and waded to shore, guns drawn.

CHAPTER 51

Paul Wise looked at his watch. 7.35 p.m.

He was standing on the veranda at the front of the villa looking down the hill towards the sea. Beside him stood Schagel's man, Nargen, while one of his local people, Rico, stood guard by the steps down to the driveway, a pump-action shotgun in his hands. A single access road, lined on both sides by thick, natural foliage running for more than a hundred yards on either side, connected the villa to Wise's private beach and dock where the men he was meeting would be landing. Wise felt a little better with Nargen there. The Russian had a natural calm about him that was reassuring under the circumstances. Even so, he was still extremely keen to get this whole thing over with. Having outsiders on his land, men he didn't know, felt like a violation.

A few minutes earlier, he'd seen a speedboat come round the tip of the island, but it had pulled in before reaching his beach. He wondered whether it was the men he was waiting for. If so, he couldn't understand why they would have stopped short of the rendezvous point. And the

371

fact that the lights had clearly been turned off before the boat reached the shore set off his nerves again.

'Do you have cameras covering the route up here?' asked Nargen, interrupting his thoughts. He had a soft, cultivated Russian accent that was nothing like Wise's idea of how a Russian special forces soldier should sound.

Wise nodded. 'There are cameras covering all the approaches, including through the woods. They're linked to a control room inside. I have a member of staff watching them full-time.'

'How many are you expecting?'

'I don't know,' he said. Liaising with them had been Schagel's job – and now, typically, Schagel was nowhere to be seen.

'It doesn't matter. If we can see them coming, we can take precautions.'

Wise nodded, and glanced over at Rico, who was clutching his weapon tightly as if he feared he might drop it. He was trying to look calm and professional, but was fooling nobody.

The phone in the pocket of Wise's cream suit rang. He pulled it out and checked the number. It was Delon, his camera operator.

'Boss,' said Delon breathlessly, 'I've picked up intruders on camera 7.'

Camera 7 was housed in thick woodland on the south-eastern approach to the villa, some two hundred metres distant. Anyone coming that way didn't want to be spotted.

'How many?'

'Two. A man and a woman.'

'Describe them.'

'They're westerners. The man's tall with dark hair. The woman's blonde.'

'Keep them covered,' snapped Wise, and hung up.

So, somehow Milne and Boyd had found him. His first reaction was anger that they'd managed to locate his precious hideaway, but that anger only lasted a few seconds. Then a more familiar emotion took over. Pleasure. This was an opportunity, and one not to be missed.

'What's happening?' demanded Nargen.

Wise told him. 'I want them intercepted.'

Nargen smiled. 'It will be a pleasure. I owe both of them for what they did to my colleague.' He removed a long black pistol from a holster beneath his jacket, and screwed on a large silencer.

'And I want the woman, Boyd, alive.'

Nargen coolly met his eye. 'I'm only here because I'm being paid to protect you until you've exchanged the package for the money. If I can get the girl alive, I will, but I'm not risking my life over it.'

Wise wasn't used to being talked back to, but he was also pragmatic enough to know that he had to tread carefully here. 'I will pay you one hundred thousand dollars in cash, money I will have as soon as the exchange is made, if you bring her to me conscious and in one piece.'

'I'll do what I can,' said Nargen with an infuriating shrug, cocking the pistol and turning away.

'A hundred thousand dollars,' repeated Wise, thoughts of all the terrible things he could do to Tina Boyd flooding his brain. He'd waited years for this moment. It would be his reward for successfully making the exchange.

And for that bitch, it would be the beginning of a nightmare that would last until he'd squeezed every drop of pain from her, leaving her begging for death.

CHAPTER 52

Tina crept through the trees in silence with Milne ten feet in front of her. The foliage was less thick than it looked from a distance and was mainly made up of palm and acacia trees that hissed gently in the sea breeze. They moved slowly and carefully, both of them keeping a tight hold of their guns as they looked left and right, checking for any sign of ambush.

Tina felt a terrible heaviness in her heart. The quest for justice she'd first set out on more than six years ago with the murder of her partner DCI Simon Barron, and then of the only man she'd ever really loved, John Gallan, was finally coming to an end, and once again she found herself wondering whether she had the strength to do what had to be done. If Paul Wise was unarmed and begging for mercy, would she be able to kill him, or would she instead rely on the man in front of her to do her dirty work?

Up ahead, Milne stopped and listened. They'd been going for at least five minutes now and she could see the first light from Wise's villa glinting through the undergrowth, as well as the lights from the access road leading up from the beach.

'What is it?' she whispered, stopping behind him.

'I heard something,' he whispered back.

And then it happened. Just like that. A figure appeared from behind a fern bush ten yards to their right, a gun outstretched in front of him, already pulling the trigger.

As she turned to face the gunman, she heard two loud pops, and Milne went down on his knees with a loud grunt, dropping his gun.

Tina opened fire, the revolver recoiling in her hands as she let off three shots in rapid succession. But she was aiming too high and the gunman had darted back down out of sight. She risked a rapid glance at Milne. He lay on his side in the dirt, one hand resting on a growing dark patch on his side. He wasn't moving. But Tina knew that there was no time to dwell on that now. Right now the priority was her own survival. She needed to find cover, and fast.

Squinting against the darkness, and keeping her weapon trained on the spot where the gunman had been, she retreated into the undergrowth, wondering whether in fact her bullets hadn't been high at all and had actually hit him. She didn't think so, and she wasn't going to risk approaching his position to find out. Instead, she slipped into the shadow of an acacia tree, using its hanging branches as cover, occasionally peering round the trunk in the direction of the road. She could no longer see Milne but thought it likely he was out of action, perhaps even dying. But she couldn't afford to think about that prospect now.

After she'd maintained her position for several minutes and her ears had stopped ringing, she risked reloading the revolver with the spare rounds she'd brought with her, and began moving again in the direction of the house, but in a much wider arc than before, using the lights for guidance, knowing that she was hugely vulnerable to ambush. Every sense was tuned into her surroundings. This was life and death. She'd been in such positions before, but this was different. Now she was alone on an isolated island. Worse still, the people she was after knew she was here, and had just taken out her one ally.

The edge of the villa loomed up behind the foliage. A flight of steps led to a veranda that looked like it stretched the width of the villa's frontage. She took a few careful steps closer, her movements slow and exaggerated, and stopped and listened. Amid the swaying of the trees in the breeze she could hear the sound of feet moving on the steps.

Taking refuge behind the trunk of a palm, she watched as a wiry-looking Filipino emerged through the bushes. He was holding a shotgun and looking round, as if he'd heard something.

Ten feet separated them. Tina held the gun by her side and moved her head back so it was out of sight, her heart beating hard.

And then he walked right into her field of vision. He was barely a yard away now. If he inclined his head just a few inches, he'd see her.

Instead, he turned his back and unzipped his trousers, the shotgun dangling casually from the crook of one arm, as if he were out on a pheasant shoot.

She adopted a firing stance, the revolver's barrel pointed directly at the base of his skull.

But there was no way she could pull the trigger. She told herself it was because the noise would alert Wise and his people, but it wouldn't have mattered if she'd had the best silencer in the world on her gun. The fact remained that, unlike Milne, she simply couldn't kill in cold blood.

She could stun him, though. Make him lie down, then use the stock of his shotgun to knock him out while she went into the house. It wasn't exactly foolproof – particularly as she was sure that this guy was far too careless to have killed Milne, which meant that someone else was still out there – but it would have to do.

The gunman was in full flow now.

Tina took a step forward. 'Drop your gun,' she said firmly.

'No,' said a voice behind her. One she recognized all too well. 'You drop yours.'

CHAPTER 53

Nargen was thinking about the extra hundred thousand dollars he was going to earn as he told Tina Boyd to drop her weapon. In front of her, Rico, who was supposed to be helping him with security, was desperately zipping himself up.

'It's just as easy for me to kill you,' he told her evenly. 'Like I killed your friend. Now, if you haven't dropped it by the time I count to three . . .'

She dropped it, and Nargen kicked her hard in the calf, sending her down to her knees. In one swift movement he picked up her weapon and stuffed it into his waistband before using his boot to force her down into the dirt.

'Cover her,' he snapped at Rico as he holstered his own weapon and pulled out a pair of restraints. He didn't add the instruction to shoot her if she made a move, believing it all too likely that this idiot might hit him instead. She was a difficult one, this bleached-blonde policewoman, so he had to be careful. Under other circumstances he might even have found her attractive, but right now she simply represented money to him. And plenty of it.

Having bound Tina Boyd's hands behind her back, he hauled her to her feet and pushed his gun into the base of her skull. He gave Rico a contemptuous look. 'Get back to your post, and keep watch for our arrivals. Make sure you keep them outside until I get back. And don't get caught out again. Do you understand?'

Rico nodded, and raced back to his position on the veranda, looking far too nervous for Nargen's liking.

'Now, don't give me any more trouble, woman,' he hissed in Tina's ear, yanking her bound wrists up behind her back until she cried out. 'Come on.' He shoved her forward and, keeping the gun pushed hard against the base of her skull, guided her up the steps. When they reached the front door, he knocked hard on it. 'Here you are,' he said as Wise opened it. 'You owe me a hundred thousand dollars.'

'Get her inside,' demanded Wise, moving aside to let them in before slamming the door shut.

He stood there, almost bouncing up and down, hands pressed tightly together, a look of childlike excitement on his pudgy face. He was, thought Nargen, an unpleasant little man with cunning, rat-like eyes, the type you wouldn't trust under any circumstances. But Nargen had met a lot of people like that – you tended to in his job – and as long as they paid for his services, he didn't much care.

'Where's the other one?'

'Dead.'

'Good. Good, good, good.'

Wise stepped forward and grabbed Tina by her hair, holding her face up to his. She struggled in Nargen's grip, and he had to drive a knee into the small of her back and yank up her wrists to quieten her. 'You dirty, dirty little whore,' hissed Wise, his lips curled back in a malicious smile, like that on a child pulling wings from a fly. Then he cleared his throat and spat full in her face. 'You're mine now. All fucking mine.'

'Fuck you,' Tina hissed back, trying to butt him with her head.

Wise's eyes blazed with anger. 'Get her down on her knees!' he snapped at Nargen. 'Now!'

Nargen didn't like being talked to like that, client or not, but he swallowed his pride for the hundred thousand dollars on offer and kicked Tina's legs from under her, using a gloved hand to push her head down.

'That's it, that's it,' muttered Wise, and kicked her in the face. There wasn't a huge amount of force in the blow, but his polished black shoe connected well. 'Keep holding on to her,' he instructed, taking a step back and kicking her again.

This time he caught her under the chin and her head snapped back painfully. She tried to fall to the side but Nargen held her firmly in place. It looked to Wise like her nose had been broken. Blood ran out of it in twin rivulets and dripped on to the marble floor. Her resistance appeared to have ebbed away.

Wise grimaced as he saw the blood. 'Messy bitch. Quick, bring her this way.'

Nargen hauled her to her feet and Wise led him down a brightly lit hall, stopping about halfway down, next to an ornate china vase as high as his waist, with long palm fronds jutting from its top. Carefully, he moved the vase to one side, then pressed the palm of his hand against a spot on the wall at face height. A low door concealed by the paintwork opened, and Wise bent down to step through it.

Nargen followed, only just managing to squeeze himself and Tina through it. He then had to negotiate a flight of steep steps down into a concealed, windowless but very brightly lit basement with a single steel bed in the middle. The cold, heavily conditioned air smelled strongly of disinfectant, and all the surfaces had been scrubbed so clean that they shone. There were powerful halogen lamps suspended from the ceiling directly above the bed, as well as a case of surgical tools open on the table next to it, and it would have reminded Nargen of an operating theatre if it hadn't been for the leather head, wrist and ankle restraints attached to chains that were strategically placed at various points on the bed.

'Put her down here,' said Wise, patting the hard mattress that, as he got closer, Nargen saw was dotted in places with old and faded but unmistakable flecks of blood.

As he threw her down on the bed, he noticed that, though her face was twisted in pain and covered in blood, her eyes were still alert. Wise's thick lump of mucus and spittle still hung from her cheek, making Nargen feel vaguely nauseous. He held her in place, keeping his gun trained on her, while Wise placed the leather head restraint round her neck, buckling it more tightly than he needed to. He didn't bother with the wrist restraints as her hands were already bound behind her back, but instead yanked her legs wide apart and fitted the ankle restraints. All the time this was going on, Tina Boyd stared up at him contemptuously, showing a bravery that he admired. She was wise enough to know that there would be no mercy, and made no attempt to search for any.

'All right,' said Wise, when he'd finished. 'You can leave us now, and shut the door behind you. Call me on my mobile when our guests arrive.'

Nargen turned and mounted the steps without looking back, pleased to get away from the smell of disinfectant and someone as clearly deranged as Wise. He could never understand men like him, men who had no control of their emotions and got too carried away with killing. It was a task that always had to be carried out carefully and methodically. That way you made fewer mistakes.

He shut the false door, noticing that it had been soundproofed, but didn't bother replacing the vase, and walked back down the hallway, looking at his watch. Five to eight. The visitors would soon be here, and he would soon be gone. He thought about the one hundred thousand dollars he'd just earned. Added to the rest of the money Schagel owed him, his overall payment would be more than double that figure. So it had been well worth it, even if things hadn't gone entirely smoothly, and had resulted in the loss of his right-hand man. Still, he thought as he walked out the front door, Tumanov could be replaced easily enough. There were always plenty of ex-Special Forces looking for work.

It took him a second to spot the hunched figure propped up against the balustrade facing the door, holding the gun unsteadily out in front of him with both hands. A few feet away from him, lying sprawled out on the veranda's deck in a pool of blood, was the body of the Filipino, Rico.

Nargen was a man of swift reactions. He brought his own gun up in one fluid movement.

But he was too late. Dennis Milne had already pulled the trigger, the force of the .45 round from the police revolver lifting Nargen completely off his feet and sending him flying back into the house.

He just had time to curse himself for not finishing Milne off with a headshot when he'd had the chance, and then everything went black.

CHAPTER 54

As soon as I pulled the trigger, I knew I'd got him with a good shot, but I didn't have the strength to hold up either the gun or myself after that and I slid down the balustrade on to my behind.

He'd got me with a couple of good shots earlier, and now my shirt was completely drenched in blood and my vision was blurring. The bullets had smashed several of my ribs and done God knows what to my internal organs. I'd never been shot before, which I guess in my line of business is something of a bonus. There was no pain, just a spreading, numb shock, and the feeling of my strength steadily sapping away.

The stagger up to the house was the hardest walk I'd ever done. When I'd first gone down, I'd wanted just to lie there and let death do its work, but the need to see this through had forced me first to my knees, then finally to my feet. Each and every step had made me wince, but I've always been determined when I've put my mind to it. And the need for vengeance was driving me on.

There was a guy with a shotgun on the veranda,

but he'd had his back to me, and I'd managed to crawl up the steps without him hearing me. I'd had no choice but to put a bullet in him, knowing that it would alert everyone else to my presence, although incredibly, the man I'd just shot had stepped out of the villa as if he hadn't heard anything, which was the kind of stroke of luck I desperately needed right now.

I felt something gurgling up in my throat, and I choked on a mouthful of blood, before spitting it out. I could make out the man I'd just shot lying on his back, just inside the door. He wasn't moving. The interior of the house was silent and I wondered what had happened to Tina. Through the trees, I'd watched her being brought up here a few minutes earlier, so she had to be in the house somewhere. I knew I had to help her. I owed Tina Boyd. I'd come very close to killing her on behalf of Schagel, and even though I'd saved her life the previous night, I still didn't feel the debt was repaid. And I wanted her to live. Desperately. She was fundamentally a decent person, on the side of the good guys. Even if it was the last thing I did – and I was beginning to realize that it probably would be – I had to make sure she got out of this place.

But my strength was ebbing away fast now, and my breath was coming in painful gasps.

I rolled over on to my side, fingers finding the handle of the revolver. Three rounds left. More than enough. With a huge effort, I clambered to my feet and half stumbled, half staggered across the veranda and through the open front door.

It felt like walking into a fridge, and I swayed, almost losing my balance. I grabbed the wall for support, momentarily overcome by a fit of shivering, which I knew was the onset of shock.

I took a couple of deep, rasping breaths and forced myself to rise above the pain.

Slowly, I looked round the grand hallway. It was very bright, and very white, and very clean. And totally impersonal. Aside from a large canvas of something abstract – a series of jagged lines in various shades of what I think was blue, although it was difficult to tell in my current condition – there was nothing to give even a hint about the sort of person who lived here. No photographs. No nothing. It was bland and cold – which, though I'd never met him, probably described Paul Wise perfectly.

And still there was no sound coming from anywhere.

Trying as hard as possible both to ignore the growing pain in my chest and to keep my wits about me in case of an ambush, I took a few careful steps forward. And that's when I saw the heavy drops of blood on the floor. They were fresh, but there weren't enough of them to suggest that whoever had spilled them was badly hurt.

I moved on and poked my head round a half-open door, looking into an immense living room the size of an apartment. It was empty, so I retreated and began a slow, unsteady stagger down a long white corridor with doors on one side and windows on the other. I used the wall for support, the gun heavy in my free hand, knowing that I had to keep going until I found Tina.

But then a terrible wave of nausea hit me, and even though I leaned into the wall with my shoulder, trying desperately to keep my balance, I wasn't able to stop myself falling to the floor.

I lay where I'd landed, the gun still in my hand, my head resting against the wall. A four-foot-high china vase, the only ornament I'd seen in here, stood nearby and I tried to focus on it to stop myself from losing consciousness. I had no strength left. Nothing. I was finished.

I shut my eyes, feeling an overwhelming fatigue that seemed to envelop all other thoughts, and I knew it was over. The end of a bloody, wasted life.

And then I heard it. Coming from somewhere behind the wall. Faint yet unmistakable.

A woman's scream.

CHAPTER 55

The fear kept coming in intense, gut-churning waves as Tina lay bound and helpless on the bed, knowing that she was at the mercy of the one person who wanted her dead more than anyone else.

Wise was grinning at her, his hairless, almost childlike face full of a terrible sadistic glee. 'Do you know something?' he said, slapping her face hard. 'I've waited years for this moment, and by God, I'm going to savour it.' He slapped her face again. 'I'm going to hurt you so, so badly, you're going to be begging for me to finish you off.' Slap. 'Do you understand that, you little bitch? Do you?'

Tina worked hard not to rise to the bait. The fear was debilitating, but now there was a new emotion: pure hatred for this abomination who'd done so much harm in the world, and who deserved so much to die.

For a few precious seconds, it gave her strength.

And then, out of the corner of her eye, she saw him reach down and produce a thin, sharp scalpel that shone in the bright lights of the overhead lamp, and the raw fear returned with a vengeance.

He saw her reaction to the scalpel and smiled. 'I'm going to cut you nice and slowly with this. Just because I can. Then I'm going to fuck you. Even though you're not my type. Far too old, I'm afraid,' he said with a wink. 'I like them nice and fresh. But I want to violate you. Humiliate you. And then, when I finally grow bored, and your *famous* spirit finally breaks, you're going to disappear, just like all the others.'

She met his eye, knowing that whatever happened, there was no point begging for mercy because that would only give him satisfaction. The bastard was turned on enough as it was. She wasn't going to play along for him.

'You cowardly bastard,' she said, before she could stop herself, a pitying look on her face. 'Is this how you killed those little girls? When they were helpless? I bet that makes you feel a real big man, doesn't it.'

'Slut!' he hissed, his face contorting with rage as he lashed out with the scalpel.

She felt a hot, sharp pain on her cheek and let out an involuntary scream.

Wise came closer so her view was completely dominated by his face, and she could smell his breath. 'I'm going to cut you to pieces, you whore. You had your chance to walk away. To live. Instead you try to take me on. You've been an annoying little fly for a long time now, and now it's time to make you pay.'

She ignored the warm sensation of the blood

flowing down her face, the rage returning to her as she struggled in her bonds.

'Sorry, my dear, but I don't think you're going anywhere. Are you?' He reached down and grabbed her roughly between the legs, pinching her through the material of the shorts. Grinning at her.

'You cowardly little runt,' she snarled back at him. 'You can't do anything unless your victims can't fight back. You're absolutely pathetic.'

He slapped her hard round the face. 'How dare you talk to me like that? I'm a fighter, do you understand that? A fighter. That's how I got to where I am today. To all this. I've got more money than you'll ever have.' He released his grip and gave her a dismissive sneer. 'You're nothing. Nothing at all. And soon you're going to be buried in my garden along with the others, in a place where no one can ever mourn you. Where you'll be mine for ever, and where I can piss on your bones every single bloody night.'

She looked at him with utter loathing. 'Fuck you.'

'Brave words,' he said, calmer now, looking at his watch. 'I've got a business meeting I need to attend, but first I think I'll just make you suffer a little for being so offensive.' He eyed her carefully, much as an artist might view a half-finished canvas. 'I think I'll have one of your nipples.'

She struggled against her bonds as he pulled away her shirt and bra and squeezed her right nipple between his thumb and forefinger, then twisted and writhed on the gurney with a furious desperation, making it impossible for him to make a decent cut.

He stepped away, looking irritated, and dropped the scalpel on the gurney. 'Right. It seems I need to get those hands of yours in proper restraints. That way you won't be able to put off what's coming to you.' He turned away and rummaged in an overhead cupboard before coming back with a half-full bottle of clear liquid and a filthy-looking rag. He poured some of the liquid on to the rag and loomed over her. 'Time to say nighty-night.'

In one last fit of desperation, Tina let loose an ear-piercing scream, her voice reverberating around the room.

And then, a second later, there was a huge crash and the door flew open.

CHAPTER 56

From her restricted viewpoint, Tina just had time to see Dennis Milne tumble painfully down the steps, and the clatter of something bouncing across the floor. Then there was a shocked, uneasy silence.

Unable to believe he was still alive, Tina twisted her head as far as she could, but Wise was standing in the way with his back to her. It didn't sound like Milne was moving.

'What the hell are you doing here?' demanded Wise, more anger in his voice than fear. 'And where's my security?' He bent down then stood back up, gingerly holding Milne's gun. 'Answer me, you arsehole.'

He stepped away from the gurney, which was when Tina saw Milne properly. He was sat up against the opposite wall. His shirt was almost completely covered in blood and his face was grey. She wanted to call his name, to tell him it would be OK, but her heart was already sinking. He couldn't help her. He was dying.

And then, as Wise stood over Milne, pointing the gun down at him, Tina noticed something.

The scalpel Wise had cut her with was still sitting on the gurney, no more than a few inches from her right hip. If she could just get hold of it, she could cut the restraints binding her wrists behind her back.

She twisted her body so she was almost on her side, reaching out with her fingers, unable to see what she was doing any more as she tried to locate it.

'Answer me!' shouted Wise, and she heard the muffled sound of a kick to the body. Milne made no sound himself. 'Where's my security? What's happened to them?'

The tip of Tina's middle finger touched the handle of the scalpel. Straining with every sinew, ignoring the terrible pain in her arms and the blood dripping down her face, knowing that Wise could spot her at any time, she managed to use her fingernail to pull the scalpel towards her, until finally she was able to grip it properly between her fingers.

She relaxed on to her back, positioning the blade so it was resting against the restraints, and began carving as fast as she could.

Wise was staring up at the open doorway while Milne sat unmoving beneath him, his head hanging to one side. 'If you can't answer my questions, then you're not much use to me, are you?' said Wise, turning back to Milne and raising the gun in both hands. 'Want to watch this, Tina?'

He glanced across at her, and she stopped cutting, hoping he didn't notice that her back was raised several inches from the gurney.

He didn't. Instead, he squinted down the gun's barrel and squeezed the trigger.

Nothing happened. It wouldn't move. He hadn't cocked the gun.

Tina kept cutting desperately, her teeth clenched with the effort, ignoring the blood that was still running down her face on to the mattress, hatred driving her on.

She felt the scalpel cut flesh, winced against the pain, kept going.

Wise seemed to realize his error, and gingerly pulled back the hammer, releasing much of the tension in the trigger, and making it far easier to pull.

The restraint fell away from Tina's hands, but as she went to unstrap the one holding her neck in place, Wise turned and saw her. His expression darkened and he pointed the gun at her. 'Don't move, bitch!' he yelled, but there was real panic in his voice and Tina ignored him, grabbing desperately for the neck restraint.

Wise squeezed the trigger again, this time putting real effort into it, and the gun fired, filling the room with smoke and noise.

But he'd made the amateur's mistake of aiming too high, and the bullet missed her.

She pulled the strap free, released her ankles and rolled off the gurney as he made to fire a second time, grabbing the open box full of surgical tools on the table and flinging it at him.

As he ducked out of the way, she charged him down, screaming at the top of her voice.

He swung the gun back in her direction, his eyes widening as he realized it was too late to pull the trigger, and then she was on him, driving the scalpel deep into his cheek, and sending them both crashing into the wall, only just missing Milne.

Wise cried out and fell to his knees, dropping the gun. She pushed him down so she was sitting astride him, the rage tearing through her. Seeing the gun on the floor, she snatched it up and pushed the barrel into the centre of Wise's fore-head, cocking the weapon. Wanting so desperately to fire. But stopping herself. A drop of her blood landed on his cheek.

'We know about the bomb,' hissed Tina, forget-ting the fact that it was still just a theory. 'Where is it? Tell me now or die.'

'Just inside the lounge,' he answered shakily as blood pumped from the deep cut on his cheek, all the arrogance gone from him now. He looked like a fat, frightened child, his eyes scanning hers for mercy. 'Please don't hurt me. I know I've done wrong—'

'Shut up.' She climbed off him and dragged him to his feet by the lapels of his suit, using the barrel of the gun to push him against the wall, taking no satisfaction in the fact that her theory had been proved correct. It would have been a lot easier if it hadn't been. 'Dennis, are you OK?' she asked, without looking round. 'Can you walk?'

'I don't think so,' he said weakly. 'Leave me here. Get the bomb and get out.'

She risked a look over her shoulder. He was leaning on one elbow, and though he still looked awful and his shirt was red with blood, and her chances of saving him were minuscule . . . even after all that, she knew she couldn't leave him here.

She stepped back from Wise, and helped Milne up. 'Come on, you can make it.' Somehow she got him up and let him rest against her shoulder. 'What did happen to his security?'

'I killed them. Both.'

'Well, if you can do that, you can get out of here. Come on.' She helped him forward and told Wise to start up the steps. 'And don't try a thing, otherwise I'll put a bullet in your spine, you little shit.'

Wise looked absolutely petrified, and did exactly as he was told, moving slowly enough so he wouldn't give Tina any cause to carry out her threat, while Tina herself hauled Milne over to the steps, and began dragging him up after Wise.

'I can manage,' he grunted. 'Make sure you don't lose that bastard.'

Knowing he was right, she let go of him and kept close to Wise until they were back in the hallway. She stood behind him, pushed the gun into his back and waited for Milne to crawl out of the doorway and slowly get to his feet.

'What type of bomb is it?' she snapped at Wise, pointing the gun at his head, her hand absolutely steady.

'I think it's one with radioactive materials,' he answered nervously, taking an instinctive step backwards. 'But I'm not sure.'

'Who are you selling it to?'

'I don't know. The deal was set up by his boss,' he said, nodding towards Milne.

'Bertie Schagel?'

'That's him.'

'But the people buying it are coming here, aren't they? That's why you had the security?'

Wise sighed. 'Yes.'

'When?'

'Any moment. If you leave here now, you might still miss them.'

'We need the bomb first.'

'It's dangerous to handle. If it goes off, this whole island will disappear, and us with it.'

But it was a risk Tina knew she was going to have to take. She needed to get it off the island so they could either dump it at sea or alert the authorities.

She glanced at her watch. It was seven minutes past eight. 'Take us to it.' She gave him a shove.

With Milne following slowly, Wise led them the length of the hallway, past the open front door where the Russian who'd tried so hard to kill her these past few days lay dead on his back, before turning into a huge, sumptuous-looking living room with floor-to-ceiling windows on three sides.

'There,' said Wise, as Tina followed him in.

An innocuous black box-style attaché briefcase sat in the space behind the door. But two things set it apart from one any office worker would carry. Firstly, it was bigger than usual; and secondly, there was a button with a small red light next to it just below the locking mechanism on the case's hinged frame. The light was off.

For a few seconds, Tina stared at it – still keeping the gun trained on Wise – thinking about the people, like Nick Penny, who'd died because of this ordinary-looking case, and the many others who would suffer the same fate if it fell into the wrong hands.

Milne came in behind her, and slowly shut the double doors. His face was deathly pale, and he was leaning against the handle. 'There are people here,' he said quietly. 'They're just outside.'

Tina cursed, and glared at Wise. 'How many of them are there?'

'I don't know,' he said nervously, sweat running down his brow. 'I've never dealt with them before.'

She could hear them now, talking quietly in a foreign language, sounding like they were just inside the front door.

'Is there a back way out of here?'

Wise nodded, and pointed to a pair of closed French windows at the far end of the room.

Milne stepped forward uneasily, and picked up the case. He looked at Wise. 'What's the code for arming this thing?' he whispered.

Wise didn't answer.

Milne turned to Tina. 'Make him tell me.'

She could hear the whispered voices coming closer, only just the other side of the lounge doors now. Once again she raised the gun and pointed it at Wise's head.

'Nine-one-one,' he whispered quickly. 'To arm and disarm.'

Milne flicked the wheels on the case's combination lock and the red light immediately came on.

Which was the moment when the double doors opened and a group of hard-faced Filipino men in cheap suits appeared in the doorway, the front two holding guns.

Tina grabbed Wise and used him as a shield as she retreated towards the French windows, pointing the revolver at the newcomers.

The men began to shout in Filipino, clearly confused by the situation, looking like they were about to fire at any second.

'No one move or this goes off!' shouted Milne with surprising force in his voice as he stumbled away from the wall, his thumb hovering over the bomb's external detonation button.

He stood between Tina and Wise and the gunmen.

Again, there was more agitated shouting in

Filipino. Tina had been in enough volatile situations to know that these guys could start shooting at any moment. Her grip round Wise's neck tightened, but she could detect a change in him. He too was looking for an escape route.

'Tina, get the hell out of here, OK?' said Milne, without looking round. 'And make sure you kill that little runt you're holding. Then run as fast as you can.' As he spoke he retreated as well, so that all three of them were moving together in the direction of the French windows and freedom.

And then he stumbled and fell to one knee, and his finger momentarily moved away from the button.

One of the Filipinos yelled something – it sounded like an order – and both gunmen aimed their weapons at Milne's head.

Tina fired first, aiming as low as possible, the recoil from the round sending her arm jerking up into the air. But she hit her target, the gunman on the left, and he lurched backwards, prompting the rest of them to exit the room and pull the doors to for cover, one of them poking a gun round the woodwork and cracking off a couple of wild shots.

Tina fired again, aiming through the door, and the .45 round left a golfball-sized hole in it. Someone shouted out from the other side – whether in fear, anger or pain, she couldn't tell – and for a moment there was silence.

Milne was trying to get to his feet, but as Tina

leaned forward to help him up, Wise scrambled free of her grip and bolted for the French windows, yanking them open. She didn't even have time to curse. Instead, using a strength born of pure adrenalin, she pulled Milne and the bomb back towards her, ignoring the fact that it might go off at any time as she concentrated all her resources on simply staying alive.

One of the gunmen behind the doors opened up again with a couple of wild shots. This time they passed too close for comfort, and Tina pulled the trigger on the .45 for a third time.

Except nothing happened. She was out of bullets. And Wise was escaping.

'Shit!' she yelled, realizing they were sitting ducks.

And then, with an almost superhuman effort, Milne tightened his grip on the case, regained his feet, and he and Tina lurched through the French windows and on to another veranda.

'Get out of here, now!' grunted Milne, his bone-white face contorted, as he stumbled over to the far balustrade.

Tina could see Wise running along a grass verge at the bottom of a flight of steps that ran down from the end of the veranda. She had to get him.

At that moment, the doors to the lounge were flung open and three Filipinos came charging into the room, all of them holding guns. Seeing Tina, the first one fired, his bullet shattering glass.

Tina took one last look at Milne, saw him topple

over the edge of the balustrade, still clutching the briefcase, and then, keeping her body as low as possible, she darted across the veranda in pursuit of Wise.

CHAPTER 57

Wise had a head start of twenty yards, but he was middle-aged and out of shape, and Tina was fitter now than she'd been in years, a legacy of all that time in the gym. A year and a half ago she'd been walking with a slight limp, courtesy of the bullet in the foot she'd received from a man who was working for Paul Wise, but now her only reminder of the injury was a raised misshapen scar. Now she ran ten K three times a week.

Now she was running for her life.

And for payback.

She took the steps three at a time, jumped the last four, and sprinted along the narrow verge, with the wall of the villa on one side and a steep drop down to the tree line on the other. There was more shouting in Filipino from up on the veranda, and a shot cracked past her head. Holding her nerve, and trusting that hand-guns fired at moving targets in darkness were rarely accurate, she kept running, bursting through the tree line just as three more shots rang out in quick succession, ricocheting through the undergrowth.

The trees ended, to reveal a rectangular swimming pool sitting in the midst of a newly mown lawn, with views down to the sea cut out of the greenery. Wise was ten yards ahead of her, making for more trees on the other side. As her feet hit the flagstones by the pool's edge, he looked over his shoulder, saw her, and tried to increase his pace.

But as he passed a summer house and ran through some palms into a secluded little copse with a love seat at one end, Tina caught up with him. Hearing her approach, Wise let out a desperate howl of terror, but it was too late. She leapt on his back, bringing him to the ground like a lion taking down a wildebeest.

He hit the grass hard and she flipped him over, raining punches down on his face as he begged for mercy, making no effort to resist, his eyes filling with tears.

'I'm sorry!' he wailed through the blood as she hit him again and again until finally her fists ached and all she could hear were his weak, tortured sobs and her laboured breathing.

She sat up straight then, keeping his arms pinned at his sides with her knees, looking down at him. His face was a bloody mess, his eyes already beginning to swell up. She knew she had to kill him. This was the moment she'd fantasized about a thousand times.

Yet something stopped her. The realization that she was a serving police officer, paid to uphold the law. That she couldn't commit cold-blooded murder, whatever the provocation.

'Please don't do this,' whispered Wise, his voice cracking. 'I know I've done wrong, but even I don't deserve this.'

She felt herself wavering. She couldn't do it. Not with her bare hands. Not with anything.

And then she saw it. Two yards away, in the shadow of an acacia tree. A little mound of polished stones.

And then another, just the same, next to it.

'Oh Jesus.'

This secluded copse with the love seat in one corner was a graveyard. It was the burial ground for Wise's child victims, a place where he could sit and relive his experiences with those he'd murdered. Lene Haagen lay here. Other girls too. Tina would have ended up here if Wise had had his way.

He knew she knew. She could see it in his eyes.

'Please . . .' he begged.

But it was too late, because suddenly the rage came flooding back in a great avenging wave, and everything that Paul Wise had ever done – not just to her and to those close to her, but also to every poor child who would never go home because of his savage, twisted lusts – tore across her vision, and her hands clamped round his neck in a grip so tight that in that moment nothing could have broken it.

Wise kicked and bucked beneath her, but it did

him no good. It was as if a madness had consumed Tina, and even as she watched his face go blue and his eyes widen as the last breaths were dragged from his body, she kept squeezing. Harder and harder, until the pain in her hands was almost unbearable. And even when he lay there unmoving, his tongue lolling obscenely from his mouth, she maintained her iron grip, repeatedly lifting his head from the ground and smacking it back down again, as if trying to expel all the evil that had festered within him.

It was only when she heard footfalls on the pool's flagstones and turned to see one of the gunmen approaching that Tina realized she had to move. He hadn't seen her yet, but he would in a few seconds. And suddenly she was reminded that Milne had armed the bomb and told her to run. It was possible that he was going to detonate it, in which case she had to get out. And fast.

The moment she got to her feet, the gunman saw her and raised the gun.

But Tina was faster. As he opened fire, she sprinted past the love seat and into the warm embrace of the forest, her legs going faster and faster as a strange euphoria overcame her. She'd done it. Paul Wise was dead, and she was going to make it out of here alive. She felt like laughing out loud.

She'd won.

CHAPTER 58

And so now here I am, leaning back against a tree, the stars just about visible through the forest canopy. When I fell over the balustrade – five, ten, however many minutes ago – I toppled down a steep bank, rolling over and over, somehow remaining conscious and keeping hold of the case, until finally I stopped here. I'm hugging the briefcase to my chest, my thumb resting on the detonation button, and I'm amazed that I've lasted this long.

A steadily building coldness is enveloping me, and I can barely see. I know the gunmen who came here to buy the bomb are looking for me. I can hear them moving about in the bushes, shouting to each other in angry, panicked voices as they hunt for their prize.

They're getting closer. I heard one a little while back fumbling about somewhere not far to my right. I kept quiet, wanting to give Tina as long as possible to get out. I hope she made it. And that she killed Wise. I have faith that she did. She was some woman. Probably the toughest I've ever met – and I've met a few in my time. It was a pleasure to know her, even if it was for barely forty-eight hours. So much has happened in that time. My life has gone from thoughts of a long and contented retirement to thoughts of my imminent death.

And yet I feel strangely peaceful.

I take a deep breath and try to readjust my position against the tree so I'm more comfortable, but in the end, I just don't have the strength.

I'm not sure if I've imagined it, but I'm pretty sure I just heard the sound of a boat's engine in the distance, and I'm thinking that this means Tina's got out. Immediately, I feel myself relax.

And I think back over my life. My childhood; my long, infuriating, but sometimes happy career as a copper. And then the descent into corruption that led me ultimately to this place, where I will die a lonely death.

And then I push such negative thoughts from my mind, and I think of Emma. But not what might have been if we'd stayed together. Instead I go back in time. To when I was eighteen years old. And I dream.

I dream of a different life. One in which after my A levels I didn't become a copper but went to university. I dream that I got a degree and went travelling round the world. That I met Emma as a young woman somewhere beautiful, like here in the Philippines. Or maybe Thailand, where we did genuinely spend so much time together. I dream that we travelled together. Saw magnificent sights;

shared incredible experiences; stood hand in hand at the top of mountains; kayaked down mighty rivers. Together. Always together. Until finally we settled down in the beautiful verdant hills of Laos where we ran our own business. I dream that we had children – two, a boy and a girl. Jack and Rosie. The names we'd always had in mind.

I dream that I'm walking up to our house in Luang Prabang, having been away for a few days, and Emma's on the doorstep, her auburn hair falling round her shoulders, wearing the white dress I used to love so much. And standing with her are our children, and they come running to greet me. And I dream that I take them in my arms and squeeze them tight, because they are so, so precious to me. And then, still carrying them, I walk over to Emma, and we kiss and stare into each other's eyes. And I can see the love radiating out at me, and I know that I'm radiating it in return, because she really is the most beautiful woman in the world, and I really am the luckiest man . . .

And then a dark shadow falls across my vision, and the shadow's holding a gun, and I press the button with the last of my strength.

And dream of nothing.

CHAPTER 59

When Tina heard the blast, she was on the boat and already several hundred yards out to sea, having hotwired the engine in the absence of any keys.

As she turned towards the noise, she caught a bright flash illuminating the night sky, followed by a second loud boom as the shock waves carried across the sea towards her. A moment later, a huge fire erupted where Paul Wise's villa had been, and thick black smoke poured upwards into the sky.

Tina's first thought was practical. There were other people on the island, and they were going to have to be evacuated. She still had her mobile on her and she pulled it from her shorts pocket. There was a decent reception, and she racked her brains, trying to work out who to phone. Then it came to her. Scrolling down the list of her outgoing calls, she found the number for the *Manila Post*, and dialled it.

As soon as the call was answered at the other end, Tina explained that there'd been a bomb with a radioactive leak, gave the location, and told the person to contact Alan Cheesman in the Defense

Attaché Office at the US Embassy and repeat what he'd just been told. Then she hung up, switched off the phone and threw it into the sea. It was a pay-as-you-go model, not registered in her name, so there'd be no way of tracing it, or the call, back to her. Tina had long ago learned to cover her tracks.

She steered the boat round the headland, careful to dodge the rocks Milne had shown her earlier, before accelerating again when she rounded the southern point of the island, wanting to put as much distance between her and the bomb site as possible. She tried not to think about the man who'd just detonated it, saving her own life as well as those of God knows how many others, because she knew that if she did, she'd break down. When it had come to it, Milne had been there for her. There were few people in her life whom Tina could say that about.

And now he was gone.

So was the euphoria at finally killing Wise. Now she just felt drained, shocked, and vaguely depressed.

Taking a deep breath and steeling herself against the emotions threatening to overwhelm her, she set a course for the bright lights of the mainland, and thought about home.

MANILA

One Week Later

'Are you ready?' asked Mike Bolt, poking his head round the door of the interview room.

'They're letting me go, are they?'

'Believe it or not, yes. And it took a hell of a lot of string pulling, I can promise you.'

Tina got to her feet, picking up the bag containing the few possessions she had left from her journey to Manila. 'Thanks, Mike. I really appreciate it.'

'Christ, Tina,' he said, moving aside to let her through. 'You really are incapable of doing anything by the book, aren't you? The way you get into these scrapes doesn't help anyone. Least of all you.'

'All I've ever wanted was justice,' said Tina obstinately, following him down the empty corridor, unable to stomach the idea of a lecture from Mike about all her faults, even though she knew he had a pretty sizeable point.

Mike gave her a sidewards glance. 'I'm sure that's what Dennis Milne used to say.'

413

Tina sighed but didn't say anything. She wasn't going to rise to the bait. Not after close to a week of resisting it.

After she'd fled the island that night, she'd managed to get back to the mainland and the port city of Batangas without getting intercepted by any of the police boats coming out of the city in the direction of where the bomb had exploded. She'd docked the boat on a deserted stretch of waterfront east of the city. Unable to locate the Toyota she and Milne had travelled down in, she'd managed to get a cab to take her back to Manila, and found a private hospital where they'd cleaned her up and stitched the deep scalpel cut on her cheek. Finally, she'd holed up in a small hotel where she spent the rest of the night watching live news reports covering the explosion on Verde Island.

The following morning, she'd picked up the car she'd hired two days earlier and driven it back to the airport, hoping to get a flight back to the UK. However, when she dropped it off at the Hertz office, the fact that it was peppered with bullet holes and she was still battered and bruised had, unsurprisingly, aroused the suspicions of the staff there, even though she'd come up with a story about how she'd been attacked and then shot at in an attempted robbery. She'd still been filling in a damage claims form when four uniformed police officers had entered the building, guns drawn, and arrested her on the spot.

Tina had known things were bad when they took her to the headquarters of the Philippine National Police in Quezon City, on the outskirts of Manila. For the next two days they'd questioned her day and night about her role in aiding and abetting the supposedly-still-at-large fugitive Dennis Milne. Tina was experienced enough to know they didn't have much on her, so she denied everything, claiming she was simply on holiday. The main evidence against her, though – the belongings they'd found of hers in the hotel room where she and Milne had stayed on their last night together, and the fact that she'd jumped out of a window rather than wait to answer questions when the police had arrived to arrest him – was pretty damning.

Tina had claimed not to know Milne's real identity, and said she'd jumped because she didn't know the men outside the door were police. No one believed her. But the fact was, there was nothing linking her to any of the killings Milne had been suspected of committing, and because Tina stuck rigidly to her story, there was little the police could do, particularly when it became clear to them that Tina was a decorated British police officer with no criminal record, and no known prior contact with Dennis Milne.

Finally, two days later, after several visits from the British consul, during which he too had urged her to cooperate with the authorities, she'd finally seen a welcome face, in the shape of Mike Bolt.

He was, he told her, there in an official Soca capacity as part of a new inter-agency anti-drugs partnership, and couldn't promise to get her out, but would do what he could.

And now it seemed he'd been successful.

When Tina had been signed out of Filipino police custody and she and Bolt were inside his hire car and en route to the airport, he turned to her, a cold expression on his face. 'So, what really happened, Tina?'

'Haven't the Filipino police briefed you?' she asked, gently rubbing the fresh two-inch scalpel scar on her right cheek, a habit she'd developed over the past few days.

'They have. And they don't believe you, and neither do I. You owe me. I want the truth.'

'Is this off the record?'

'It depends how far you've gone.'

She'd gone a long way, further than she'd ever been before. But Mike was right. She owed him the truth. And, in the end, she trusted him.

So she told her story. All of it. Including how she'd killed Wise. She thought it might make her feel better to get it off her chest, but it didn't. It made it worse.

When she'd finished, Mike took a deep breath and shook his head. 'Jesus, Tina.'

'You wanted the truth. There it is. What are you going to do? Turn me in?'

'No,' he said, just as she knew he would. 'But I'm going to have to speak to the US Embassy about the bomb, and who was involved in the plot. And tell them that Dennis Milne's probably somewhere among the rubble. Although I won't involve you.'

'Was anyone else killed?' she asked. 'And how bad's the radio-active damage?'

'It's been contained to a small section of the island, and it's a lot less than initially feared. They haven't been able to recover any human remains yet, and I'm not entirely sure there's going to be anything left to recover.'

She thought of Milne then. She wondered what he'd been thinking when he pressed the button, and how lonely he must have felt. 'I did what I thought was right, Mike,' she said wearily.

'And do you think you can just go back to being a police officer upholding the law after everything that's happened?'

'I hope so,' she said, but she wasn't sure if she believed it. Or whether she wanted to or not. Her life had changed for ever these past few days and it was difficult to imagine anything ever being normal again.

'Did you find out anything about Bertie Schagel?' she asked after a few moments' silence. She'd mentioned the name to Mike when he'd visited her two days earlier, as the man who'd supplied Wise with the bomb.

Mike shook his head. 'The name doesn't appear on any of the databases. Have you got any other information we could use to ID him?'

'No. All I've got is the name.' She felt deflated. Wise was dead, but Schagel – or whatever his name was – was still out there. It felt as if she still had unfinished business. 'Do you mind if I smoke?'

'Do you have to?'

'Yes. I think I do.'

'Go on, then. I suppose in the greater scheme of things, it's one of your lesser sins.'

Which Tina had to admit, as she lit the first cigarette she'd had in close to a week, was probably true.

'You also asked me about someone called Emma Pettit who was living in Bangkok. Who's she in all this?'

'She was Milne's girlfriend for a while, and the mother of his child. He had to leave her, and he never got to see his child. It hurt him a great deal. I wanted to . . .' She let the sentence trail off. 'I don't know what I wanted to do, maybe get a message to her or something. Let her know that he still cared about her and the child.'

Mike turned his head from the road ahead, and for the first time there was sympathy in his expression. 'Emma Pettit never had her baby. She was killed in a car crash two and a half years ago near her parents' house in Worcestershire. She was eight months pregnant.'

The words hit Tina hard, and for a few seconds she couldn't speak.

'I'm sorry,' said Mike. 'At least he'll never know.'

'No,' she said quietly, fighting back the tears. 'I guess not.'

She was reminded of a saying her mother always used: what goes around comes around. Milne had set himself on his path to destruction as soon as he carried out his first killing. There'd never really been any way back for him, and he'd died as he'd lived, and in reality as he'd deserved. That didn't mean the world was fair of course. Sometimes bad things happened to good people. Like Emma Pettit and her unborn baby. But there was also justice. Those who sin always end up paying. Like Wise. Like Heed. Like Tomboy Darke. And like Dennis Milne.

And Tina had sinned as well. She'd taken the law into her own hands and killed in cold blood.

One day, it would be her turn to pay.

It was, she thought as she looked out the window and into the traffic, just one more thing she'd have to learn to live with.

EPILOGUE

Bangkok, August

Thunder rumbled across the dirty grey sky as Erik Theunissen walked down the steps of his house in Bangkok's upmarket Thong Lo area and across the gravel driveway to where his car was waiting to take him to Suvarnabhumi Airport. From there a Thai Airways flight would take him to another of his homes in Phnom Penh where, he'd been reliably informed, a particularly attractive young girl was waiting. The girl's handler had told him that she could be treated roughly and wouldn't make a fuss as long as the money was right. Theunissen was paying three thousand dollars for the privilege, so the money was definitely right, and as a man who gained huge sexual satisfaction from inflicting pain, he was already getting excited about the night ahead.

In fact, everything was going well for Erik Theunissen. He'd just secured a deal to supply a hugely valuable stolen Georges Braque painting to a Chinese businessman for eight million dollars, five of which was pure profit. He was also close to success on an even more lucrative deal to supply engines for use in unmanned military drones to the Iranian government, which would net him more than twice as much if it went through. Theunissen was a fixer, a man who could source anything if you had the money to pay for it, and he was very good at what he did.

It was, however, an inherently risky business. Six months earlier he'd done a deal to supply a dirty bomb to a group of Islamic terrorists based in the Philippines, and it had gone spectacularly wrong. The bomb had exploded at the home of his business partner before the deal could be made, and both his partner and the customers had been killed. Without them there'd been no money, and Theunissen had been left more than a million and a half dollars out of pocket. He'd also spent a lot of sleepless nights in the weeks following, wondering if any of the heat from what had happened would get back to him. He knew the Americans were particularly keen to find the man who'd sourced the bomb originally, since they'd been the intended targets, but Theunissen was good at covering his tracks.

His driver, a young, dark-skinned man from the north, was out of the car in a second and opening the back door for Theunissen with a respectful bow, taking his bag and putting it in the boot as Theunissen squeezed his considerable bulk into the back.

His bodyguard, Hans, a huge lump of a man,

...which was typical of him. And now that he was gone, and now that Theunissen paid him, he expected to be treated with respect.

'What time is our flight booked for?' he demanded.

Hans didn't answer.

Nor did he move.

'Hans, I asked you a question,' snapped Theunissen, exasperated.

Still he didn't answer. Had the damn fool fallen asleep?

Leaning forward in his seat, Theunissen slapped him on the side of the head. 'I asked you a question.'

But his words died in his throat when Hans's immense body teetered to one side and Theunissen saw blood running down from the coin-shaped wound to the side of his head.

At that moment, the driver – a man barely a month into his new job – opened the back door and pointed a gun at Theunissen, a weird little smile on his face. 'Allahu Akbar,' he intoned. 'This is for my brothers.'

And then Theunissen realized that he'd made a fatal mistake by underestimating the reach of the fundamentalists he'd sold the dirty bomb to.

He raised his hands in a desperate gesture of mercy, but he was already too late.